I0679105

Hidden Creek

After reading the first two books in the series, I was anxious to see how everything would work out in the life of Susan Penleigh. "Hidden Creek" is the best yet! I have always enjoyed stories with a bit of suspense. This one has that, plus it speaks to how we, as Christians, should handle the joys and sorrows of life. I am looking forward to your next book, Lynn.

BOBBIE RUSSELL, *a great grandmother who still enjoys reading good fiction*

A modern, fast-paced story, full of the events that have to be faced and overcome in daily life. Showing the strength of friendship, and what can be achieved with a loving relationship. Set in familiar surroundings of Northeast Texas, Hidden Creek is a really good read, and part of an enjoyable series.

ANN GALLANT, *author,* The Beauty Specialist, The Beauty Therapist, *and* The Beauty Electrogist

In the final book of the Running Forward Series, Lynn Hobbs has completed her story of Susan Penleigh, keeping one's interest throughout each book. There is a surprising development that really catches one's attention in Hidden Creek. It just wasn't expected. Christian values are refreshingly noticed in the entire series. We enjoyed following Susan's journey, and found it both suspenseful, and inspiring.

AMY & BOB BELL, *retired B&B owners*

This is a book that is uplifting to read. The main characters are devout Christians, who are not ashamed to share their beliefs and the Gospel with others. Again, it is heartening to read a book about ordinary people, even though they

sometimes have a lot of drama going on in their lives; of course, this keeps us from wanting to put the book down!
JAN BRAMLETT, retired, Texas Public Schools

Having read all three books in the Running Forward Series by Lynn Hobbs, I can say that "Hidden Creek" is Lynn's best work yet. The characters portray Christian individuals, who approach life as we all should, sharing their faith, reaching out to others and always ready to lend a hand. This last book in the series holds some unexpected developments. I only thought I knew how it was going to end. Thanks, Lynn, for a great read!
NANCY SUMMERS, avid reader of Christian literature

About the Author:

Lynn is a member of American Christian Fiction Writers, Pens: Crosswords Christian Writers, North East Texas Writers Organization, past treasurer (2011-2012) of East Texas Writers Association, Texas Association of Authors, GWFC- Texas Federation of Women's Clubs- Marshall Chapter, and a lifetime member of World Wide Who's Who. Lynn Hobbs book, Sin, Secrets, and Salvation, won 1st place in Religious Fiction for 2013 by the Texas Association of Authors. World Wide Who's Who awarded Lynn Hobbs Professional of The Year 2012-2013, in Authorship. The Author Show.com named Mrs. Hobbs as a finalist in their nationwide contest, "Fifty Great Writers You Should Be Reading" in 2012, and as a winner in 2013.

Married; two sons, three grandchildren, and one dog round out her family. Active in church, Lynn loves to read, enjoys houseplants, scrapbooking, canning, and quilting.

Retired from the Texas public school system, Lynn is a native of Houston, having moved to East Texas in 1962. Available for speaking engagements, Lynn has enjoyed speaking at Christian Ladies Retreats, Lions Clubs, and other events. A publisher songwriter, and published poet, Lynn has also won awards for her poems and short stories. Lynn is currently working on her fourth novel.

Follow her uplifting Christian blog, and check out her website at: www.LynnHobbsAuthor.com

Other works by Lynn Hobbs:
Running Forward Series
Sin, Secrets, and Salvation
River Town

Hidden Creek

Lynn Hobbs

Desert Coyote Productions
Longview, Texas

Text other than quoted material © 2013 Lynn Hobbs.
Cover design © 2013 Stacey Martinez.
Characters and situations depicted within © 2013 Lynn Hobbs.
Running Forward Publishing Rights © 2013 Lynn Hobbs, all rights
reserved.

No part of this publication may be reproduced, stored in a retrieval system,
or transmitted in any form or by any means, electronic, mechanical,
photocopying, recording, or otherwise without the express written consent
of the author.

The following is a work of fiction. Any resemblance to real persons, living
or deceased, is coincidental.

Library of Congress Control Number: 2013955085
EAN-13: 978-0-9859379-5-9
ISBN-10: 0-9859379-5-5

Typeset in 11pt Book Antiqua
Printed in the U.S.A.
First edition 2013

This book is dedicated to the Dragonfly Ladies of Caddo Lake in Northeast Texas. We are a group of about thirty. Once a month we meet at a local restaurant in the area and enjoy eating, visiting and helping those in need in our community.

Qualifications: you must be a Christian woman in our small area, and over fifty years old. Sometimes we are dragging and sometimes we are flying…hence Dragonflies!

Thanks to all of you for the encouragement in my completion of the Running Forward Series. I'll never forget how much you enjoyed reading each book, and the excitement of having the next one available. I look forward to our next monthly meeting, and I am proud to be part of the Dragonfly Ladies.

Acknowledgments

I give God the glory for the completion of my Running Forward Series: *Sin, Secrets, and Salvation*; *River Town*; and *Hidden Creek*...and thank Him for His guidance on my hand as I wrote each book.

My goal to give readers a clear understanding of a Christian viewpoint by the actions of my main character, Susan Penleigh, I believe, has been reached. Modern family issues desperately need prayer, and as a Christian, I hope I have adequately addressed some of those issues.

Special thanks to my mother, Lillie Clark, for all the hours of reading and editing as I wrote; and to all the rest of my family, church family, and friends—I couldn't have made it without you.

To my readers, thank you for such a favorable response to my series. Typing in the book titles at Amazon.com and leaving your review is so treasured. Your words of encouragement are greatly appreciated. I enjoy hearing from you, please visit my website: www.LynnHobbsAuthor.com

To my friends of over twenty years, who went above and beyond critiquing my book, Bob and Amy Bell, and Jan Bramlett; thank you very much for your help, your sincerity, and your expertise. I'm so pleased with the results!

To each person who took time out from their busy schedule to read my manuscript and endorse my work: I heartily thank and appreciate you. Words cannot express my gratitude.

To Don A. Martinez, Editor and Publisher of Desert Coyote Publications, I thank you for your insight and kindness through the entire series.

Contents

Two women, two men
Fight the wages of sin.
Who heals?
Who follows God's will?
Four journeys, four friends …
Turn the page, let the story begin …

Hidden Creek

Chapter One

Susan Penleigh tilted her head back and stared toward the horizon before focusing on the land. Dry greyish-green leaves scattered from massive oak trees—clearly a direct result of the devastating drought. A few tall pines had rare green pine needles. Speckled with brown blotches they appeared as velvet fur surrounding its branches. Numerous birds' light, merry songs rang out across the parking lot while a dusty smell lay heavy in the air.

Not your typical fall afternoon.

She heard the harsh sound of an eighteen wheeler braking from nearby Interstate Twenty and tightened her grip on the open car door.

Dear Lord, I can't endure another disappointment. If I'm not to be with Rick, then I pray for wisdom, Father, for I want to do Your will. In Jesus name, Amen.

A single tear slipped down her cheek and broke her strong resolve. Angry at herself for being so sensitive, she quickly entered her friend's car.

"Let's get out of here, Izabella. Please. I can't deal with this. Not now."

"You knew you might run into him here. His daughter has been at the rehab center for a long time."

"I know, but I can't explain this rush of emotion. It's incredible, and his encounter left me with so many questions. *That's* what I wasn't expecting."

Izabella refrained from speaking further, drove through the parking lot, and turned to exit. Without warning, a large, skinny dog with protruding ribs darted from behind a parked car and raced straight into their path. She swerved and missed hitting it.

Izabella yelled. She stopped the car and honked the horn, repeatedly. The frightened, long-legged animal loped away never looking back.

Breathless, Susan managed to speak, shoving tousled hair from her face with both hands. "Wow...are you okay?"

"I am." Izabella huffed and started the car again. "Wonder if someone dumped that dog?"

"Must have... there's nothing but county roads, and the highway around here. No neighborhoods. Poor dog."

"If you ask me, their owners should be dumped and see how it feels to survive. Some people have no business with animals."

"Izabella, some people *are* dumped. Haven't you noticed the increase of homeless people across the nation?"

"They should go to work and quit panhandling."

"We can't lump all of them into one category. With the awful economy, many *can't find a job*. I'm glad shelters are opening up."

"So am I." Izabella cautiously eased her car away from the rehab center and flashed a quick smile. "How'd we get off on that, anyway?"

"We do ramble."

Izabella groaned. "Ohh...am I seeing things?"

An assortment of cars and trucks were at a standstill trying to enter the highway.

"What is going on?" She groaned again.

Susan leaned her neck forward and frowned. "I think it's a stalled car. We may be here a while."

Izebella inched her vehicle into the line and laid her arms across the steering wheel. "Well, I must be getting used to the drought. It's still a pretty day." She shrugged.

"Not a cloud in the sky." Susan ranted. "Why hasn't anything changed? My world is falling apart and everything still looks the same; same big Texas sky, same Rick..." Her voice broke in mid-sentence betraying her calm appearance. "I can't bear to turn around. Is he still... standing there?" She glanced at Izabella.

A sudden peek at the rear view mirror and Izabella shook her head. "Yes. Listen, if this is painful, I can turn around when we get on the highway. We can go back."

"No. I'm not ready for more drama. Can you believe him? What a surprise...he wanted to pick up where we left off... after all this time apart. It's my gut feeling that's bothering me. Rick Yeager is a wonderful person. Maybe he really *was* too busy with his wayward daughter, and I *wasn't* put on the back burner. Keep driving. I'll try to sort this out."

◆

Rick squinted against the harsh glare of blazing sun on Isabella's car. Heart pounding in his ears, he gazed at the passenger's window while the vehicle departed the drug rehab center.

Susan appears distraught. I've got to concentrate...got to figure this out...can't believe she wouldn't talk to me.

Izabella had honked her horn sporadically and stopped the car. The near miss with the dog did not register with Rick though. He watched the car suddenly head for the line of traffic stopped on the

3

highway's on-ramp. Immobile, he stood with his legs spread apart as if concreted to the pavement. Rick's mind raced.

What in the world caused this? Have I said something wrong? I sure can't remember. Maybe I stayed away too long...

"Mr. Yeager? Mr. Yeager?"

He shook off the trance-like state and cleared Susan from his mind. The female attendant rushed down the sidewalk, a severe frown troubled her face. He watched her catch her breath. Alarm slammed his brain.

Now what?

"I saw you in the parking lot and ran out to tell you. Your... daughter escaped...the police have been alerted. She *is* dangerous." Words tumbled from the woman. Her chest expanded a rapid rise and fall.

Rick struggled to speak. "Wha ...what?"

"A drug addict will do anything to buy drugs. Tessa was *not* rehabilitated, Mr. Yeager."

His remark was gruff. "I am aware of the lack of progress, but my regular visits seemed to comfort her. This just happened? " Rick glared at the attendant and stark reality swept over his body. Fragments of disbelief concerning Tessa, disappeared. Each beat of his heart sounded louder than a jack hammer sending anguish throughout his body. Shaky, muscles and veins strained against his skin.

"Yes sir. Tessa failed to report for a scheduled psychological testing appointment thirty minutes ago. We discovered she was last seen outside feeding the birds but that was three hours before the appointment. Does she have friends here in Tyler?"

"Not to my knowledge. I can't imagine where she went." He glanced at his watch. "Ma'am, I'm sorry I snapped at you. I know you are only doing your job."

"It's okay, Mr. Yeager. We'll contact you if we have news of Tessa. Please do the same."

"Of course."

The roaring of a car engine brought their conversation to a halt.

"What on earth?" The woman sputtered and covered her ears.

"No telling but it's getting closer." He scowled at the parking lot entrance. With tires squealing, a police car made the curve and slid in.

A police car.

Rick took a deep breath and said half aloud, "It's about Tessa. I know it is."

The officer parked and flew from the vehicle. Rick heard the attendant gasp.

They gaped at the officer while he dashed past them and entered the main office. The attendant lunged forward and charged in behind him. Rick remained frozen in the same spot.

The police.

The significance hit him hard creating a deep ache in his heart. His breathing quickened and tension painfully knotted his insides.

Oh Tessa, what have you done this time?

He squared his shoulders and stood at attention. Ready for whatever may come, he waited for the police officer to return.

Rick looked on while the officer emerged from the rehab center and walked in a long, steady stride towards him. The attendant did not follow.

Only you and me, I knew it would be like this.

"Mr. Yeager, I'm Lieutenant Dotson with the Tyler Police Department. Your daughter, Tessa, has been apprehended during a bank robbery here in Smith County."

"A bank robbery?" Rick groaned. "That can't be my daughter."

"Yes, it is your daughter. Anyone entering a bank or simply standing in line is recorded on the bank's cameras. She is on their surveillance tape. There are many witnesses."

He sprinted to the officer. "Was she by herself? Were others involved?" Rick yelled, and felt his face flush.

"We don't know if this was spur-of-the moment, or if she schemed with friends. The investigation is ongoing. I will tell you this. The elderly teller Tessa demanded money from died."

Shocked, Rick opened his mouth, but nothing came out. For a split second his breathing was suspended. His raspy voice broke when he finally spoke. "Died? From fright?"

"It's on tape, Mr. Yeager. The judge will decide."

"She needs an attorney."

"By law she will be appointed one." The officer sighed, and stared at Rick, compassion etched on his face. "Your daughter escaped twice from a court-ordered drug rehab program. From one father to another, Mr. Yeager; I can assure you the judge will *now* send Tessa to the Gatesville Women's Prison."

"Can I see her?"

"No sir, you may not. She is held in restraint."

"Thank you for the information." He nodded.

The officer reached out and shook hands with Rick. "I'm sorry I had to bring such bad news."

"Thanks." Rick moved toward his truck, opened the door, and entered the cab. Slouching in the seat, he swallowed as bile rose from his throat. Ransacking the glove compartment, he grasped the bottle of Extra-Strength Tums. Popping two in his mouth, pent- up tears slid down his face in a rapid flow.

It's shocking to grasp how quick Tessa has deteriorated as a moral person. I'm disappointed I couldn't help her more, but I am not her Savior. Dear Lord, only You can help her now. She is in Your hands.

He spotted the cell phone on the front seat and after a moment's hesitation seized it. Bolting upright, he poked each key roughly attacking the phone while his determination grew. He entered Susan's number in a matter of seconds and placed the call on speaker-phone. She answered on the first ring.

"Hello?"

"Susan, it is imperative we talk. I wasn't expecting to see you earlier."

"Rick, I hadn't heard from you in a long time. I was overwhelmed. I didn't know what to say. We came to visit Lisa. I had met her at the refugee shelter, and she agreed for help with her drug addiction. I brought her to rehab a few weeks ago."

"So… *that's* why you were here. I wondered about some other things, too. Susan, will you have dinner with me tonight?"

"Uh, yes, and I am living in River Town with Izabella. Do you know her address?"

"I know where she lives. How about six o'clock?"

"Okay…wait…where are you?"

"Still at the rehab center."

"I'll be right there."

Rick heard a brief click followed by a dial tone. He blinked and drummed his fingers against the steering wheel. Surprised by a new-found calmness, he sensed a new turn of events.

And for the better, I won't mess this up. I won't let her down.

Lost in thought, Rick sat in the truck until a loud tapping on the window startled him. He twisted to one side and saw Susan standing rigid, concern shadowing her face. She held her mouth together in a tight line.

Izabella's car idled nearby.

Rick fumbled with the door handle, gave a powerful shove, and leaped out. Immediate eye contact held while both stood still. Rick held his arms out, and Susan ran to embrace him.

Thank you, Lord, she has returned.

Rick rubbed her back in circular motions. He savored the sweet, clean smell of her hair, and they stepped apart. Rick bent and planted a kiss on her forehead.

"I've missed you," Susan whispered.

"I've missed us."

"I didn't know there was an us."

"That explains my other question...why you were so distant with me earlier." He sighed. "Susan, we must work on this together, and I do want us together."

"Rick, I understand why you moved, but we live two hours apart. How...?"

"Let me interrupt." He embraced her and stroked her hair. "I apologize for not including you in my attempt to help my daughter improve."

Susan tilted her head and scowled. "Your *attempt*? Do I detect something is wrong?"

"Yes. Reality hit me square in the face… again. Tessa can be so deceptive. She will require more treatment than a rehab center can offer." Shaking his head, he quit talking and pressed his lips tightly together.

"Rick, go on, what happened?"

Overcome with shame, his checks suddenly flushed and a ruddy complexion appeared. He spoke in a subdued tone. "I came for my regular visit. I thought she was improving. They said she escaped this facility and robbed a bank in the past three hours." His voice cracked. He stiffened and held in a sob.

"Oh, Rick…I am so sorry. I know what a struggle this must be; an emotional roller-coaster. You look exhausted. Have you had lunch?"

"No. I can't eat, not now."

"We need a place to talk."

"Where?"

"Just drive."

"Okay."

Susan waved at Izabella. "Rick will bring me back to your home, later."

"It's a long way to River Town. Are you sure?" Izabella yelled out from her car and frowned.

"Yes."

Susan watched Izabella wheel the vehicle around and leave.

Rick started the truck, buckled his seat belt, and Susan hurried to fasten hers. Within minutes they were on Highway 69.

"I remember a park off of this highway. I think it's called Love's Lookout Scenic Park."

"Any idea when we'll arrive there?" Rick shifted his weight in the seat.

"Well, technically, we are still in Tyler. So, it's about forty minutes from us, before we get to Jacksonville. We drive past it on our way to Izabella's home in River Town." She paused. "How are the boys doing?"

"M and M? That's their nickname in case you didn't know. Doing great, couldn't ask for better young men. Take pride in their work... a lot of help. You should see the old farmhouse we are remodeling."

"Making progress then?"

"Oh, yes, and they are a lot of company. Hard to believe they ended up victims of the wildfires. How long did they stay in Marshall at the refugee shelter?"

"I'm not sure. I know their home burnt to the ground. While at the shelter, they assisted volunteer firemen each day."

"They talk very little concerning their past, and I don't pry. Strange, though, neither Matt nor Mead ever mention their parents."

"From what I heard, the parents were in and out of jail; the boys had no other family."

Rick's thoughts drifted to an earlier conversation when the boys first moved in with him.

"Susan, I guess you know Matt was incarcerated when he was younger. He was upfront, explained how his bad choice to burglarize a car hurt him. Never

10

could graduate with his class, and didn't get a GED either. He tells everyone about it."

"I knew, and I also knew he only needed a chance to start over. I'm glad you took the brothers in when you did. You were their way to a new beginning."

"Well, *I'm* glad you phoned and asked if they could work for me. I wanted to mentor them, and did, and now they are part of my family."

He turned his attention to driving, glanced at his speedometer, and set the cruise control. Susan sat relaxed.

What is she thinking about?

He considered Susan and M and M living through the historic Texas drought and wildfires of 2011, and the effect it had on them.

I can't imagine what they experienced at the shelter...

"Must have been an ordeal living at the refugee shelter," he pondered aloud.

Susan shook her head. "It had its high and low moments. I'll never forget the many faces and raw emotions. It was like your whole life was held open for public display. No secrets, nothing private. Friendships grew and prayers were said. We moved forward with our lives. We had to."

And during that time I left River Town, moving to Tyler with one main objective...helping my daughter make it in rehab.

"Susan, I can't avoid talking about Tessa any longer. I won't dump this mess on you, but she is part of me."

"I'll stand beside you Rick, and God will lead us. You can't carry the whole world on your shoulders."

She turned to look at him, and they shared a brief smile.

A comfortable silence engulfed them for the remainder of the ride.

Susan gasped when they arrived at the park. "Look at the rolling hills...how beautiful. Even with the drought the forest is breathtaking." Hues of red, yellow, orange, and brown welcomed them, mixed with light, beige patches of dead grass.

Rick zipped into the parking lot, killed the engine, and both climbed out of the truck.

"Sure is." His gaze roamed the area, and he grabbed her hand. They strolled, taking in the view, and found a bench. Neither spoke while basking in the warm sunshine. Minutes passed when Rick abruptly stood.

"It's almost magical here. Splendid hills and valleys, and I can see for miles and miles." He looked down at Susan, lifted her chin, and gazed into her face. "I don't want miles between us."

"Rick, I don't want anything between us."

"Where do you want us to live?" The words rushed out, and Rick's heartbeat sped.

Her face beamed. "River Town, of course, and..." She paused.

"And?" Rick flinched.

"And we are a we?" She bit her bottom lip.

"Yes, we will be married, if you'll have me." He swallowed hard.

"Counseling with the pastor first?" She gave a half smile, eyes dancing with mischief.

Rick lifted her from the bench, and their laughter rippled through the air until he stood her on the ground.

Susan brushed her fingers across the side of his face.

He covered her hand with his, and his pulse elevated as his senses heightened.

"Lady, I wouldn't have it any other way. This is our time."

His cell phone jarred the pleasant conversation. He withdrew it from his pocket.

"Hello?" Rick listened a moment. His mouth flew open, and he yanked the phone from his ear as if it hurt him.

Chapter Two

Izabella hummed the familiar wedding march to herself and glanced at Susan and Rick in the rear view mirror.

Yes, I think they'll end up married and married soon.

Traffic in Tyler was sporadic, and she zipped onto Interstate Twenty toward River Town.

Maybe Ben Wakefield will call.

Izabella gasped as her fingers trembled on the steering wheel.

Even thinking of Ben overwhelms me. What a startling fact...and the idea of being in his company leaves me weak. What has happened to me? This attraction is most unusual. Hard to ignore yet hard to deal with.

She exhaled loudly and focused on the increasing traffic.

No time for nonsense.

Dismissing all thoughts of Ben, she relaxed and drove the two hour trip back to River Town. Pulling into her driveway was another matter. Shocked, she stared at Ben leaning against his truck parked near the front of her house.

Izabella stopped the car, mesmerized.

What is he doing here?

Giddy, she ran to him and lost control of her proper manner.

"Ben, what a pleasant surprise. Hope you haven't waited too long."

"No ma'am." He tipped his hat and continued his slow, southern drawl. "I must admit it is a worthwhile endeavor."

Izabella's heart rate increased and heat sped to her face.

Grow up, girl, quit acting foolish.

She eyed him, suspiciously. "Well, Ben, it's good to see you, too."

"I may be intruding on your plans, but I speak with honorable intent. May I enjoy your company for dinner this evening? Izabella, I *cannot* get you off my mind. Please overlook my boldness but an evening together will be most memorable to me." Ben gazed wide-eyed at Izabella.

"I'd love it."

"Well, come on."

"Oh no, I have to freshen up. Give me a few minutes."

Ben nodded. She dashed inside the enormous house.

◆

He scanned the two story home and the immaculate, landscaped grounds.

She must be loaded.

Fall was in the air and a gust of wind sailed by him. He involuntarily shivered and chuckled.

Mine for the taking...and her girlfriend Susan won't interfere. I'll wrap them both around my little finger... razzle dazzle...

Ben meandered across the lawn and kicked at the ground when he spotted a cat sneaking behind a bush. Leaping into the air, it darted off and vanished. He snickered and returned to the main entrance of the home.

He remembered when he first met Izabella. His brother had been in the hospital, and Susan brought

Izabella with her when she came to visit Logan. Static electricity crackled from their hands during their handshake. It was so startling that they both flinched and were immediately attracted to each other.

And I hadn't been in town but a few hours. Talk about looking a gift horse in the mouth... what great timing...and who cares that Logan and Susan have since broken up? No sweat off my back...

◆

Izabella soon emerged and locked the front door.

"Ben, am I dressed appropriately?" She raised her arms to display the navy and white pantsuit adorned with a single strand of pearls.

He advanced closer. "You look fine, Izabella. Shall we?"

"Yes." She accepted his arm. He accompanied her to the car. In all appearance, a perfect gentleman. Ben helped her into the vehicle, buckled her in, and swiftly shut the door. He pranced to the driver's side and slipped in the car whistling a happy tune.

Completely at ease, Izabella let her guard down.

A thick mop of hair, eyes narrowed at just the right moment of conversation, muscular arms and legs...how handsome can one man be?

She sighed and tried not to picture his silhouette leaning earlier against his truck. So sure of himself and so masculine...

I'm glad he chose my car to drive instead of his truck. More room, and I do have a full tank of gas after filling up in Marshall.

Izabella eased back into the padded cushion and stretched her legs.

How special to have a man in charge...

She wiggled, sinking deeper into the passenger's seat.

Ben started the ignition and in one swift motion, nuzzled her ear.

"Enjoy the evening. Dinner will be soon, followed by an optional lifetime, if you agree."

"How mysterious, Ben. Please continue. " For a long moment, Izabella couldn't breathe, and her mind whirled at his possibilities.

Ben shifted into gear, exhibiting utmost care, and drove her powerful vehicle onto Interstate Twenty. "In this case, I promise an exceptional evening of fine dining on delicious seafood." He sat tall in the driver's seat and obviously relished his new role.

Izabella inhaled noisily.

Arriving within the hour at Ralph and Kacoo's in Bossier City, Louisiana; Ben left Old Minden Road and parked near the restaurant. Chest thrust out, he sprinted to her side of the car. Izabella noticed his strong body posture while they headed into the famous eatery.

He is most impressive.

Seated, selections were made from the menu, and Izebella soon savored the soft texture of fried oysters. She chewed a delicate morsel and eyed Ben's profile.

"Thank you for an exceptional meal, Ben. I can't hold another bite."

"You are welcome." He devoured the remaining shrimp and snatched at his extra-large napkin. "Ready to leave?"

"Yes."

Tossing several dollar bills on the table, the napkin fell to the floor and Ben slipped on it as he stood. "Ooph," he mumbled and caught his balance.

"Ben, are you…"

"I'm fine."

He quickly paid for the meal, escorted Izabella out of the restaurant and to the car. Reaching for the passenger door, he stopped, and fidgeted with the handle. Izabella turned to look him square in the face and regarded his sudden frown.

"Ben, what…"

"Izabella, do you believe in love at first sight?"

"Yes, I do."

"So do I."

"Oh, Ben. Are you telling me…"

"Yes, I am. Yes, I love you."

"I am *deeply* in love with you."

"What's stopping us?" He whipped a long, folded map from his back pocket. "Ever been to Hugo, Oklahoma?"

"No."

"Well, people run off to get married there. You don't have to wait three days. Izabella, will you marry me?"

"Oh… I will."

His frown disappeared. He lowered his head and kissed Izabella for the first time.

She made no attempt to stop him and blushed. "We don't need the map, Ben. I have a GPS in my car. We type in an address and follow the route."

"I know all about a GPS. I'll find a church address on my phone, and we are good for the trip."

"Ready to go?" Izabella tugged at a wisp of fallen hair on her cheek and smoothed it back behind her ear.

Ben tilted his head to one side, displayed a brilliant smile, and winked.

Izabella sucked her breath in sharply and stumbled into the car.

Chapter Three

Susan watched Rick clench his jaw tight.

"What is it? Who called?" Her blood raced, and she tried not to be frantic.

"Tessa is fighting the authorities, refuses to eat. I am still not allowed to see her."

"I'm so sorry, Rick." She gently grabbed his hands. "Let's pray."

Rick bowed his head and slightly squeezed her hands.

"Lord, I lift Rick and Tessa up in prayer. You know their needs. I stand on Your Word, and pray for grace, mercy and a peace that surpasses all understanding for both of them. In Jesus Holy name I pray, Amen."

"Amen. Thank you, Susan, for everything, for being here with me now, for..."

"Don't. You don't have to say anything. This is monumental. This is where I am supposed to be...with you."

"Are you sure?"

"Oh, yes." Susan beamed at him.

"And we begin...come on...I need to get you home."

"And I'll talk nonstop the whole two hour drive."

"Is that a threat?" Rick laughed.

"No way." Susan replied as her thoughts scrambled.

He is the exact opposite of my ex-husband. I can't see Rick ever being cruel, and I can't picture the life he endured with his ex-wife. Their daughter brings him so much grief and pain, but that's his daughter, and he loves her. I know how strong I love my own three kids, grown and happily

*married. Thank God for them all. I can't imagine having a
wayward one. Lord, help me with Rick's daughter, and I
haven't heard from my kids for over a month. Guess they
will always live out of state…that is their home… let them
still be okay…*

"Did I hit your mute button? Haven't reconsidered,
have you?"

"Never. A lot has changed in a short time. A lot to
think about. Look at what's happened this year not
only to us but to Texas. Do you think River Town will
bounce back from the wildfires and severe drought?"

"Lady, you are talking to a realtor who loves this
area. Yes, I think it will explode with the right
development. In fact, I am checking into it with my
banker, guess it's the contractor coming out of me. I
built houses with my Dad when I was younger, and his
business was still thriving."

He glanced at Susan and raised an eyebrow. "I want
to develop a new subdivision. The area I want to
purchase has one lot I'd love to build on for personal
reasons." He gave a sly smile. "It has a hidden creek on
one side and the river on the other. I can already
picture all the other houses I want to build and sell. It's
a buyers' market."

"Your excitement shows. Working out the details
must be challenging."

"Yes, and hopefully, rewarding." He winked, and
Susan tilted her head displaying a half-smile.

Dazzling orange and pink shades of the setting sun
surrounded them as they chatted and left the park.

"We'll be driving through Jacksonville, next. Want
to stop there and eat at the Dairy Queen?"

"Yes. The combo drink with three tacos will work for me. Thanks, Rick."

"Sounds good to me as well, then onto River Town."

◆

Moonlight filtered through sparse tree tops illuminating the lawn. Rick surveyed Izabella's home for signs of lightly glowing windows.

None.

"Susan, I am reluctant to leave you. She's not here. It's pitch-dark in the house."

"Hmm. There is my car, but Izabella's is gone. Maybe she had a date. Guess that would explain the parked truck in front of us."

"You don't recognize it?"

"No, and this is making me jittery." Susan thrust the door open exiting Rick's vehicle. "Come on, I'll unlock the house. Let's check it out."

Rick yanked a flashlight from under the seat and rushed to join her. Susan hurried and shoved the wrong key at the lock and the set of keys dropped to the threshold. Trembling, she retrieved them, and the keys jingled while she finally unlocked the door. Susan stepped back and cast a glance at Rick. "I don't know if I can do this."

"Move over." He cautiously pushed the front door and for a split second, he jumped as it squeaked.

"I'm supposed to be the nervous one," Susan teased and flipped the light switches, flooding the room with a startling brightness.

"Are you suggesting this is an awkward rescue?" Rick stopped scanning the living room and offered Susan a warm smile. "Behave," he teased and charged off to the side hallway.

"Well, there is only so much I can do at a time like this." She said half-aloud.

It's too quiet in here.

She wrapped her arms around her chest, and treading lightly, peeped into an adjoining room.

At least the place isn't ransacked…where is Izabella?

"Hey girl, all's clear." Rick returned to Susan, and she caught a whiff of his aftershave.

"Thank you, Prince Charming." She inhaled slowly filling her senses with the smell.

"Ah, you must remain skeptical, my dear, I have ulterior motives."

"Oh, Rick, I am delighted about our future together."

"Me too." He lowered his head and plopped a kiss on her cheek. "Got to go. Counseling needs to be scheduled, and I'll start scouting out a place for us." Ambling to the door, he paused and turned toward Susan. "Call me when you hear from Izabella."

"I will, I think she's lonesome and is on a date. I'm not worried. She's overdue a carefree evening with someone."

He nodded.

"Uh, Rick…we can talk about Tessa whenever you are ready. You don't have to hide that part of your life from me."

"I know. It's just year after year she goes wild. I've tried so many times to help her, Susan, it's draining. I have to get on with my life. I can't straighten out her bad choices forever."

"We'll face whatever happens to her, together."

His eyes met Susan's. "I love you," he whispered and left.

"Love you, too." Susan managed to say while a lump in her throat formed. Emotions bursting at the seams, and despite being exhausted, she marveled as a cheerful mood engulfed her.

Thank you Lord for bringing Rick into my life.

Susan locked the door and secured the dead bolt. A quick shower, and she withdrew to Izabella's guest bed snuggling in the covers. Overcome by sleep, she sank into the memory foam mattress amid scattered extra pillows. Hours later, a faint sound awakened her and for a moment, she strained to hear any type of motion.

Nothing but the wind.

Content, Susan yawned, regained her comfortable position and drifted back to sleep.

◆

Morning daylight disturbed her. She rolled over and blinked.

Have I forgotten something?

Susan arched her back and lazily stretched until reality returned faster than a flash of lightening. She sprang from the bed.

Izabella…is she home yet?

Both feet hit the floor with a thud. Running from the room, she noticed her long robe. Not missing a step, she snatched it and crammed her arms inside the sleeves. Charging down the hall, she tied the belt around her waist, and the bottom on the robe sailed out behind her.

Entering the living room, Susan jerked the draperies aside over the double window, and gawked at the undisturbed vehicles from the previous night.

No change and no Izabella.

Terror crept along her spine, and she shuddered at the thought of what her friend may have encountered.

An ear deafening knocking sound startled Susan. Someone was at the front door. A brief glance out the window showed a woman in a business suit holding a clip board in one hand.

Maybe it's about Izabella...

Susan opened the door with caution, allowing a few inches to view each other.

"Yes, may I help you?"

"Good morning! Are you Izabella Contrell?"

"No, ma'am, and she isn't here at the present."

"Oh, well, I'm Audrey Duvall from Corner Grocery. I live on the next block and while we usually don't visit employees homes, I wanted to stop in and welcome her. I'm the front-end supervisor."

"Nice to meet you, I'm Susan Penleigh. She will be sorry to miss you. Izabella is so excited about her new job, and believe me, I know how hard they are to find."

"Yes, they are. Wait a minute; would you be interested in submitting an application? We have another opening. Two of our ladies recently retired. I can't promise a job, but we are reviewing applications now."

"I might. I mean it isn't every day a knock on the door brings a potential job offer." Both laughed at the remark, and Susan shook her hand. "Thank you for stopping by. I will be in your store later this morning and fill out the paperwork. Thanks again."

"You're welcome." Audrey turned and strolled across the lawn to a car parked near the curb.

Susan reflected on her own job situation. *I was fired before the wildfires destroyed the school. I loved my job, in spite of some of the craziness that went on and can't seem to find another one...I've filled out so many applications...have to get something soon. Hmm... if I get this job, maybe Izabella and I can carpool to work...Lord, let her be okay...*

Susan hurried to call Rick. Relieved when he answered the phone, she rushed into the conversation. "Rick, it is impossible to act like this is a normal day. I still haven't heard from Izabella. She could be in trouble or worse yet, a missing person by now. I'm calling 911 and reporting her."

Susan held the phone close to her ear and listened to what he was saying.

"I understand, Rick, but why wait twenty four hours to report someone missing?"

She let him talk and didn't interrupt him.

"I agree. Okay, if that is the law, then l have to wait. I guess I'll go put my application in at Corner Grocery. Izabella has a job there, and I think I'd enjoy working at a grocery store."

Rick spoke for several minutes, nonstop.

Susan's voice rose with excitement. "Financing was approved? You *are* going to develop a new subdivision in River Town! Can we afford it? Can we live there?"

Rick answered, and Susan did interrupt.

"We can? What will be the name?"

Susan waited for his response.

"Hidden Creek... I can't wait." Shaky laughter erupted as she mulled over the idea.

Chapter Four

"Answer, Logan." Adrenaline shot through Ben's veins, and he focused on the telephone. Sweat popped out on his forehead, and he grumbled into the receiver. "Come on, come on."

His brother answered while Ben was mid-air in hanging up the phone. The vigorous tapping of his foot ceased, energy left him, and his body involuntarily swayed.

"Logan? It's me Ben. I need help. I cannot make myself look at her." He flopped in a chair and gripped the armrest.

"Who is she? She is my *wife*. Do you recall meeting Izabella when you were in the hospital? She came with Susan. I married her...last night. Only, she won't wake up, today. What? We did party last night. No, I don't need any more trouble. Don't tell *me* to watch my temper. Yes, I'll try harder to wake her." He slammed the motel phone down.

Ben seethed. He forced himself to abandon the mounting fear gnawing at his insides, and studied Izabella's condition. He leaned forward in his chair and felt the weight of his bloated stomach against the top of his legs. Incapable of compassion, Ben stared at her with curiosity. One arm hung off the edge of the bed, and her mouth was slightly open.

"Izabella. Izabella? Well, la-di-da, you are not so reserved now." He jumped up and tiptoed to the bed. "Izabella, can you hear me? I don't believe you are dying."

I will wake you...where's the ice machine?

27

He wandered out in the hall bringing the ice bucket assigned to their room. Ben located the familiar metal machine around the corner and laughed a low, guttural sound. He promptly lifted the lid and filled the bucket. Within mere seconds, he fled the area and entered the motel room with ice intact.

"Izabella?" He snickered and dumped the bucket of cold, ice cubes on her face.

She sputtered and gasped, rising from the bed with a scowl.

"Ben, how dare you, " Izabella yelled.

"Trust me. It was an act of mercy."

"Mercy? Your definition of mercy is not the same as mine."

"I was worried about you, Izabella. You slept and slept. Here, let me help you." He wrapped his arm around her waist and gently lifted. She slowly got up and stood without his assistance.

"What time is it? I feel worn out and groggy." She hobbled across the carpet and retrieved her watch on the nightstand. "Five o'clock? I slept all day?"

"Yes, and I *had* to consider drastic measures. Izabella, let's put this incident behind us."

"You sound so kindhearted about drenching me with ice cubes." She gave him a playful shove. "I'll get cleaned up, and we can leave."

"Fair enough. It won't take long to get us checked out at the office."

He drifted out of the room, and she grabbed her make-up bag. A hot shower eased the stiff muscles in her back. Energy returned, and she emerged resembling herself again.

28

Ben popped in the room and glanced at her. "Well, good to have you back." He embraced his wife and held her at arm's length. "Rather hasty improvement, my dear."

Izabella shook her head. "Before I took my shower, I looked in the mirror and didn't know the haggard woman I saw, either."

"I am notorious for staying up too late. I must have kept you from getting enough sleep last night. I apologize."

"Ben, I don't remember last night."

"We got married last night." He whirled her around and burst out laughing "No need to get anxious. The pastor will record our marriage at the courthouse, and the certificate will be mailed to your house, I mean, our house."

"My house...my house guest...I forgot about Susan. She must be sick with worry. Where is my phone?"

Ben spotted the cell phone near the television and pitched it high into the air. Her arm shot up, and she caught the phone. "Great catch; I'll go get us something to eat." Ben sailed out the door.

Izabella clicked on Susan's name and hit speaker phone as it rang.

"Hello?"

"Susan, it's me."

"Oh, I'm so relieved to hear your voice. Izabella, are you okay? What is going on?"

"It's so romantic. Ben and I ran off and got married..."

Susan yelled, "Izabella, you don't know anything about Ben. I can't believe you rushed into marriage with him."

"Oh, Susan, don't get so alarmed. I *love* him."

"No, you don't. You are attracted to him. It is a physical attraction. That is all. What happens when the attraction dulls? You don't know if you have anything in common with each other, or share the same values, faith, or want the same future together...nothing. No foundation whatsoever."

"Whatsoever? Sounds serious to me." Izabella giggled. "I *am* in love."

"Okay, so tell me about the wedding. What was it like? Where did this happen?"

Izabella laughed. "We got married last night, and I slept all day. Actually, I don't remember."

"You don't remember?" Susan blurted.

"Calm down. I know you are concerned."

"Where are you, Izabella?"

"...Hugo, Oklahoma in a motel. Ben went after food for us."

"Do me a favor, this is important. Before you leave Hugo, please go back and check out the places you were supposed to be last night. See if any people remember *you*. Will you do that for me?"

"Well, yes, and it's a great idea. I mean, I am a grown woman, and I have a right to find out. If everything isn't on the up and up, Ben will have some explaining to do. Does that make you feel better?"

"Yes, and if you need me, don't hesitate to call...day or night."

"I will if it *is* ever necessary."

"When are you two returning?"

"I don't know."

"Please be careful, Izabella."

"Susan, I assure you, there is no reason to worry. We'll talk later, bye."

"I hope you are right. Bye."

Izabella located her purse and placed her cell phone in the side pocket. She glanced at her left hand and gasped.

No wedding ring...apparently I forgot more than I realized...

A noise at the door drew her attention as Ben entered with several to-go boxes of food. Aroma filled the room, and her stomach growled in response.

"Did you hear that?" She laughed. "I didn't realize I was hungry."

"Sounded like a foghorn to me," he teased and set the containers on the small table.

"Watch out, now." She raised an eyebrow and opened two clear bags of plastic eating utensils, while he doled out napkins.

Ben opened the lids on the boxes exposing two enormous hamburgers with fries and onion rings. "Salt?" He held a small package towards her.

"Yes, a little, please." She tore the edge of the paper and sprinkled it across the fries and onion rings.

They ate in silence for the remainder of the meal. Izabella finished off her last bite and sighed.

"Thank you, Ben, for the best hamburger I've had in a while."

"It was pretty tasty, wasn't it? Sure can't compare to Fuglers Bubba Burger, though."

"On Highway 154 out of Marshall, Texas?"

"Yes, ma'am."

"It is the best, and I love the crispy jalapeño 'toothpicks' too."

"Oh, yes. They set off any meal. Are you ready to ride back towards Marshall, Texas, Mrs. Wakefield?" He pushed his chair from the table and selected a wrapped, wooden toothpick from the pile of condiments.

"No, I cannot leave until some issues are clarified."

"Clarified? What kind of a wisecrack is that?" He stood and gawked at Izabella.

Izabella frowned. "No wisecrack, Ben. I have a night and day that is unaccountable to me. I must find out about it."

"Are you serious? Izabella, do you doubt me?"

"Doubting you is not the problem, Ben. I have never forgotten a day or a night before. It is not an acceptable routine for me."

"So, what are you getting at?"

"I'll return to the places I was at last night." She looked at him without blinking an eye.

He glared back. "So we try to outstare each other? How immature."

"Ben, please be patient with me. What did we do, eat first, and then get married?"

"No, we arrived at the parsonage, married, and went to the restaurant they recommended. Later, we came here for the night."

"Oh, such a special time for us, I want the memory back. Is the restaurant still open?"

"I don't know."

"Well, what's the name of the restaurant? I can look it up and call."

"You know, I drove where they instructed, but the name escapes me."

"That's okay. Let's go there now. Think you can find it?"

"Sure, but I don't know if the same group of employees are working there today."

"We'll find out. We have to start somewhere." Izabella grabbed her purse and walked out to her car while Ben shut the door on their motel room. She slid behind the driver's seat and adjusted the rear view mirror.

Ben climbed in the passenger's side. He caught a glimpse of her solemn face. "Are you feeling well enough to drive?"

"I haven't been ill, Ben. Lead the way, point me in the right direction."

"Turn left, go straight about five miles, and you will see it on the right side of the road. I'll try to help you remember." He tugged at the seat belt, strapped himself in, and Izabella followed suit. She started the ignition, turned to drive on the access road, and expertly merged onto the highway. Ben watched her navigate and remained voiceless for several miles.

"You have acquired excellent driving skills."

"That's from years of being independent. I always said I would not be dominated by a man." She briefly glanced at him and half-way smiled.

"I always said I would not want a submissive wife... how boring." He produced a toothpick from his pocket and stuck it in-between his teeth.

"Is that a fact?"

"Sure isn't a rumor." He chuckled. "Slow down this is starting to look familiar."

"I thought I was the one trying to remember," she teased.

"Woman, your mouth is out of order. This is the restaurant, turn here."

Izabella stopped their banter. Locating a parking space, they hurried inside and sat at a nearby booth. A few customers were eating, and a waitress made rapid strides toward them.

"Good afternoon." She spoke in a cheerful manner as she handed Izabella and Ben each a menu.

"Oh, no thank you." Izabella paused. "I don't know where to begin." She laughed.

The waitress drew her eyebrows together and gave Izabella a puzzling look. "Ma'am? Pardon me, but I don't understand."

"Let me try to explain. We ate here yesterday. Do you happen to remember us?"

"I didn't work yesterday, but Denisha did. Let me get her for you." She walked toward another waitress across the room and briefly chatted.

Denisha, bearing a warm smile, hurried to their booth.

Izabella glanced at Ben, and he choked. His face turned red, and he squirmed in his seat.

"Ben, are you ill?"

He shook his head.

"May I help you?" Denisha stood next to Ben.

He remained wordless.

"Yes, we ate here last night. Do you remember us?" Izabella gushed.

"Of course, I do. Thanks for the large tip. Is this some sort of game?"

"No dear, I am having a problem with my memory. Tell me, did I act funny or walk out of here okay? Did I seem all right to you?"

Denisha exchanged a quick look with Ben. "Oh, maybe I'm not supposed to say anything."

Ben silently stared at her.

"No problem, it will help refresh my memory," Izabella assured her.

"Well, you started out reserved and got louder and louder. You really enjoyed yourself. I did notice you staggered when you left, and your husband had to help escort you to the door."

"She felt faint, so I helped her," Ben interrupted.

Denisha turned to leave, obviously troubled.

"Wait, Denisha, what did I drink?" Izabella took a deep breath.

"Iced tea ma'am, and lots of it. I have to go now." She dashed off.

"See, I told you everything was fine. You felt faint, that's all. Come on, let's go."

Izabella grabbed her purse, and Ben followed her out to the car.

"You put something in my drink, didn't you? I never get loud, Ben, and nobody staggers drinking iced tea." She huffed at him and climbed into the car.

"Take it easy, Izabella, we might have got a bit loud but we were happy. We had just gotten married. I guess you got dizzy, I don't know."

"Why didn't you mention it before we talked to the waitress?"

"I thought I should be discreet. I didn't want to embarrass you."

"How do I get to the parsonage? Anything you want to add before we arrive there?"

"No." Ben burst into the car. "Go straight and turn right at the first red light. You will see the sign on the front lawn." He slumped in the seat while Izabella took off.

In less than five minutes, Izabella parked in front of the parsonage. "It looks vacant. I don't see any cars."

"Maybe they went shopping."

"Go knock on the door, I'll wait here."

Ben departed the car and strolled to the front door. He knocked and knocked to no avail. Quickly, he ran back and slid in the front seat.

"No one is home."

"I want to talk to them." Izabella banged her fist against the steering wheel.

"Izabella, I went along with your quest, but I don't want you upset. Trust me, I love you. We have done all we can here. Now, let's leave and go home."

"...but I want to talk to them."

"...and I want to go back to Texas. We will not wait hours for the couple to return. Adios, sayonara, auf wiedersehen, shalom, au revoir, goodbye..."

Izabella put the car in reverse, and frowned.

You're not funny...and you can't play down the issue...

Chapter Five

Susan couldn't stop the alarming news from repeating in her mind. She paced Izabella's guest bedroom; arms swinging, and rediscovered her Mother Hen instinct.

Humpf... jumped into another struggling relationship...and married Ben. After all the years of being alone, after all the horror of her last boyfriend...that girl draws bad men like flies to a picnic.

She surveyed the room and muttered to herself, "I have no intention of being here when he moves in, and who am I to sit in judgment? Not about to judge, never have, never will; sure not going to start now. I'm the one with Izabella's best interests at heart. Ben does not, and that's a fact, or she'd remember the wedding."

Susan jerked the suitcase out of the closet and threw it open on the bed. Rushing to the dresser and yanking drawers open, she gathered armfuls of clothes and crammed the suitcase to capacity. "Marriage indeed, Izabella, it's more of an escapade," she yelled while her heart pounded.

Retrieving several shoe boxes, she stacked them haphazardly against her chest. Dashing to the bed, the boxes shifted off balance and sent Susan stumbling. "Oohh." Her eyes watered while attempting to rise from the floor. Shooting pains knifed through her right shoulder.

"I'm getting out of here, and I'm getting out of here quick." Moaning, she stood, legs aquiver, and steadied herself before walking.

A few slower trips to the car carrying belongings, and Susan, finally packed, noticed the raging anger had calmed.

How can I help Izabella when she realizes the mistake she's made? I'll help her anyway I can…Lord, I pray Ben and Izabella seek Your direction, forgiveness, and blessing on their marriage. In Jesus name I pray, Amen.

"Back to my own problem," she said half-aloud. "Might be some apartments in the older section of town, certainly don't want a motel room."

◆

Susan slowed her car at the only house on the block with a "For Rent" sign. Hanging off the front porch railing, it was partially hidden from new growth on the row of evergreen gardenia bushes. On long silver chains glistening in the direct sunlight, hung the object Susan remembered from childhood. A wooden swing and situated at the right end of the porch.

How cozy…reminds me of my grandmother's house.

A few feet away three, white, long-backed rocking chairs sat amongst two, tall planters bursting with red geranium plants. The entrance door was directly in the middle of the house with white, wicker furniture of tables, chairs and a bench forming a semi-circle to the left. In the background, an enormous pot plant of pencil cactus leaned against double windows. A delightful aroma of rosemary drifted across the lawn from the potted plant displayed on the wicker table. A pair of ceiling fans mounted over each seating area, hummed, and whirling on low speed, created an enjoyable breeze.

So inviting…

Parking near the curb, she bounded up the steps and knocked on the door. Overwhelmed with nostalgia, the heady smells engulfed her, and she longed to call this home.

"Hello" A young man flung the elaborately carved, wooden door open, and addressed her through the screen door.

"I'm Susan Penleigh. I saw your sign. Is this still for rent?"

"Yes, ma'am, it's for rent... half of it anyway. I'm Lee Miller. This was my mother's home. I had it remodeled into two apartments. I live on one side and rent the other. Would you like to see it?"

"Definitely."

Thrusting the screen door open wide, the squeaks emerging brought by-gone days to life. Flooded with memories from her grandmother's home, she entered this one. Following his brisk lead she turned right in the foyer, and he extended his arm out to an open entrance. Susan eagerly darted into the apartment and flitted from room to room. Stopping to explore the back porch and fenced lawn, she hastily returned a bit disheveled to the foyer.

"Would I have access to the laundry room?"

"Of course. Here's a copy of the lease. Everything is covered from rent to liabilities." He handed her a set of typed pages stapled together.

"May I?" Susan motioned to a chair outside.

"By all means. Help yourself. I'll be nearby if you have any questions."

Susan flipped through the contract and drifted to the front porch as he walked away. Details leaped out at her, most being reasonable, and the price was affordable.

I can do this. I can live here.

Sheer joy surged through her in anticipation. She giggled, raising both arms high over her head, and swayed her body with exaggeration in a spontaneous happy dance. The rush of emotion remained long after the quick dance stopped. Unable to stay still, she raced to the back of the house and found the young man raking leaves.

"I'll take it. This is perfect for me. Completely furnished with two bedrooms, two baths, kitchen and dining area, living room, storage, laundry privileges...when can I move in?"

"Today, if you like." He paused, holding onto the rake handle.

"That works for me."

"Fine, I'll get the key while you sign the pages. I'll need your check with the deposit included."

"No problem."

He returned, and they completed the transaction. "If you need anything, let me know. Otherwise, I do value privacy and you won't see much of me unless it's in passing. Welcome to your new home." He reached and shook her hand.

"Thanks. I value privacy also, and I simply fell in love with this place."

"It shows." He laughed. "And I'm glad you did, Mrs. Penleigh. I was hoping to find someone who liked the charm of an older home. Naturally, it's a special place for me."

"Well, I am thrilled to have found it and moving in won't be difficult at all."

"Great, I'll get back to my raking, then." He turned and left as Susan ran to her car.

Unloading took longer than she planned but within a few hours everything was placed in the correct rooms. The large alarm clock displayed 1:15, and Susan stopped the instant she noticed the time.

Got to run, I'll straighten this later. Need to get some errands done...

◆

A fast trip to the grocery store, and she made her way to the service desk. Only one clerk worked behind the desk, and she had several customers. Susan waited, polite and patient, until it was her turn

"May I speak to Mrs. Audrey Duvall?"

"I'm sorry. She took a late lunch today. May I help you?"

"Yes, Mrs. Duvall told me a position is available. I'd like to fill out a job application."

The clerk slid one across the counter to her and pointed to a metal bench. "You can sit there and return it to me when you finish."

"Thanks." Susan eased onto the bench and carefully filled in the required information. She tuned out as much noise as possible. One hassled woman yelled at her crying children and they continued begging for candy, anyway. Half-way through the second page another distraction occurred when the overhead music developed a skip. All hope of concentrating was now gone. It played the first line of a song over and over until Susan was sure she was the only one who noticed. Eventually, the song was interrupted by an employee calling the manager on the intercom to repair the canned music.

41

Finally, she answered the last question on the last page, and exhaustion swept over her whole being.

She handed the clerk the completed application, smiled and took off with an abandoned, empty shopping cart someone left in the middle of an aisle. Selecting a few items, she hastened to the express line, paid and was out the door in record time.

"Whew...can't wait to get home and relax..."

Susan climbed in her car, and started the ignition when her cell phone rang. She put her car in park, glanced at the caller ID, and clicked on the speaker phone.

"Scott, what a wonderful surprise."

"Mom, it may not be wonderful but it will be a surprise. I need your help..."

"Of course, I'll help. What is it?"

"It's Dixie. We have split. She is so self-centered. Whatever our friends do or have done, she always has to top it and demands being the center of attention. She claims to help others, but steps on her so called friends while climbing up the social ladder. I'm sick of her lies, and her laziness. Mom, I've tried talking to her. She gets worse. She has this smart attitude, and she is never home. I'm tired of her excuses. I've had enough." His words spilled out, and Susan recognized the pain.

"I'm *so* sorry, Scott. She seemed sweet and friendly when I met her." Clutching the phone tighter, she swallowed hard.

"She changed and that's not all. She is nearly eight months pregnant." He hesitated, and his voice turned gruff. "... I'm not certain it's my baby."

"Oh... Scott... I had no idea." She gasped, and her hand flew to her mouth.

"I was told today that I'm shipping out to Afghanistan at the end of the week. Dixie has no place to stay. I know this is a lot to ask you under the circumstances but...could she stay with you?"

Susan's heart pounded in her ears and it took a moment for his request to register. Slow to answer, she pictured a new scenario of herself and her pregnant daughter-in-law living together.

The baby will be here soon....

"How could I possibly turn her away?"

"I knew you'd feel compassion. Mom, I did ask her about staying with you. She said it wouldn't be a problem, but she can be difficult. Maybe she will be better around you."

"Let's hope so. I can't imagine the stress you are enduring. She and the baby will have a home with me. You focus on yourself in a foreign country, and I'll be praying for your safety."

"Thanks, Mom. I knew I could count on you. I already checked the flights. She'll be flying United Airlines and arrive at the Shreveport Regional Airport about eleven o'clock tomorrow night."

"Tomorrow night... I'll be there."

"I wouldn't do this to you, but I have no control on going to Afghanistan."

"I know, I understand. I love you."

"I love you, too. Bye"

"Bye."

Susan choked on the last word.

Chapter Six

The instant Izabella drove the car into the driveway, her shoulders slumped. An unexpected release of tension left her lightheaded.

Home. ..never looked so good...

Twisting around in the seat, she poked Ben in the ribs. He drew a deep breath through his nose and continued sleeping.

"Wake up, Ben. We're home."

He stirred and made catlike stretches. His chest rose as he inhaled, and he raised his head making immediate eye contact with Izabella.

"Home." Both feet hit the floorboard, and his hand reached for the passenger door. "Let's go."

"You must have new found energy. Waking from such a deep sleep and so alert? You are wired different from me."

Ben stepped out of the car. "Well, I should hope so."

Izabella scowled.

Is he insulting me? He doesn't even know I am concerned. All I see is his back while he races to the front door.

Flushed by growing anger, Izabella left her vehicle and slammed the door. She joined him on the sidewalk.

"Looks like Susan went somewhere, her car is gone."

"How much rent is she paying you?" Ben spoke nonchalant while clenching his hands into fists.

"Rent? Susan does not pay rent. She is my guest."

"Uh-huh."

Izabella unlocked the front door, and Ben followed her inside the majestic home. His shoes sunk into the deep pile carpet. He went no further.

Entering the hallway, Izabella heard Ben gasp. She turned and saw him still in the foyer. He lightly ran his fingertips over the surface of an elaborate stained glass window. Impatient, she scowled and crossed her arms. Ben took one look at her and held out his hand. "I'm coming. Don't get upset, we've got the rest of the day."

Izabella pivoted and marched towards the kitchen. She withdrew two chicken pot pies from the freezer and popped them in the microwave. Minutes later she placed them on the table. Ben finally wandered in.

"Lunch smells great. Thanks Mrs. Wakefield, I'll cook something for you, next."

"This needs a few more minutes to sit before its ready. Can you cook?"

"Can I ever?"

She finished setting the table as the timer buzzed. The pot pies, hot and bubbly, didn't take long to devour.

He emptied his plate, scraping the remaining bites onto the prongs of his fork. Not a speck was left.

"You know that's the best compliment you can give a Southern woman. I am pleased. Thank you, Ben, for enjoying the meal."

"You are most welcome." He rose, gathered dishes, and loaded the dishwasher. "There is business to take care of, Izabella, we might as well get it done today." He glanced up at her as he added the detergent.

"We do?"

"I need to write checks on your checking account."

"What?" Izabella stormed out of the room. "I don't think I heard you right."

"Come back here. We are a team. We do everything together."

She returned and stood in the doorway, posture stiff and glaring at him. "So, exactly what will you contribute toward this checking account?"

"I am disabled and have direct deposit. A change of address and route numbers for the bank are in order."

"Oh, good. I wondered if I was required to support you." She huffed and remained standing rigid. "Do you have anything else you need to tell me?"

"I get the feeling you are leery of me for some reason. Why is this, Izabella? Are you a domineering woman? Do you need the control a single woman experiences? If so, I am appalled. We are a team. We make decisions together. Or am I wrong?"

She managed to hold her head high. "Don't try and turn this around. I am not guilty, don't address me as if I were. I have nothing to hide."

"Neither do I. Shall we go to the bank?"

"Yes, I'm ready." She grabbed her purse, and they walked out to the car.

He didn't answer my question. Does he have anything else to tell me? It is possible I am overreacting...I need to give the guy a break...

◆

Ben sighed with relief and considered a quote from his favorite comedian.

How sweet it is...

"Izabella, we are on the right track. Even the banker congratulated us on our marriage."

"It's all about trust, Ben. Don't ever let me down."

"Hey, that works both ways. We earn each other's trust."

The sun was setting after a long, calculated evening at the bank. Izabella slowly led the way from the car to the house. Rubbing her arms she abruptly stopped and faced him.

"Then why is fear clutching at my heart?"

He carried a bucket of Kentucky Fried Chicken, he had insisted they purchase on the way home, and handed her a bag.

"You are independent, not familiar with teamwork. You need to think of us and not yourself." He swung the front door open and walked with a swagger to the kitchen. "Stop thinking as a single woman, you have to let that go. I *am* your husband."

Izabella presented Ben with a weak smile and sat the bag on the counter.

"Now, that's more like it. Let me help." He sat the bucket of chicken near the bag and removed the containers of mashed potatoes and gravy. Corn on the cob was next. Izabella set plates on the table, passed out napkins and eating utensils. Ben grabbed two plastic bottles of water from the fridge, and they sat at the table.

Thirty minutes later, after they ate the desert of fried apple pies, Ben mellowed and caressed Izabella's hand.

"You have no idea how happy you have made me."

"Thanks, Ben. I am exhausted by our emotional swings today. I am hopeful we reach a pleasant routine, soon."

"We will. Do you mind if I retire to the recliner and watch T.V.?"

"No." Izabella eyed the exit door and sighed. "I am going to bed. I am done."

Not waiting for a reply, she escaped down the hallway. Yawning, she showered and within minutes sank into bed.

Hours later, Ben slipped under the covers. Izabella, deep in slumber, didn't stir.

Sometime during the early morning, a tremendous sound echoed outside.

Ben bolted from the bed, adrenalin rushing. He lunged across the room and flung the draperies apart at the double windows overlooking the driveway.

He watched in dismay while two men jacked up his truck and pushed it onto a flatbed trailer. His heart sank. Staring but not seeing, he was vaguely aware of Izabella's screams. She had joined him at the windows.

Repossessed. They got away with my truck...

Gasping for breath, Ben succumbed. He hyperventilated and broke out in sweat.

"*...A panic attack...I must be having a panic attack.*"

Izabella jerked his arm, pulling him back to reality. Drained, he focused on her, and his senses gradually returned.

"My truck was repossessed." He uttered.

"We'll deal with this later. Come on back to bed."

She put her arm around his waist and escorted him away from the windows. The men and Ben's truck were gone. He climbed in on his side of the king size bed, and Izabella pulled the covers over him. The air conditioner hummed, and he lay speechless.

Izabella sobbed, walked to the opposite side and slowly tossed the covers back. She lay in the dark and gradually hushed.

No one moved or spoke. After an hour, Ben rolled over, his breath warm on Izabella's face.

"I can't sleep. I need a stiff drink. Where is the whiskey?"

"Are you serious? I don't drink. I don't have alcohol in my home."

A low laugh from Ben filled the room.

"Well, you're going to..."

Chapter Seven

Susan strained to listen. Her mood lightened as Rick spoke.

"Lady, in my book, you made *the only* acceptable decision. I'm proud of you."

"Thanks for your encouraging words. I had to call you. Good thing I rented an apartment when I did. At least I do have room for Dixie and the future baby."

"It *is* good you're living there. A large house and a pleasant neighborhood; you can't go wrong. Have you asked the landlord's permission for Dixie to move in also?"

"Yes, I made a special trip to ask him in person earlier today. Thankfully, he had no objection so it's okay."

"At least that worked out fine. I'll wait until you girls settle in, then come over and check on you."

"Great. I'm getting excited now that the initial shock is over. My goal is for Dixie and I to get along with each other, and ultimately help her take care of herself."

"With her and your son separating, it could turn into an awkward situation for you." He paused. "Don't let anything come between us, either."

"That won't happen, and where did those encouraging words go?" She chuckled.

"Okay, okay, you got me there. Oh, have you heard any more from Izabella?"

"No, I haven't...not yet. I do have to cut this short. Got a lot to do."

"Glad you are feeling better, Susan, and I've decided I don't need to be a two hour drive away from you. The boys will be fine here at the farmhouse in Tyler. I'm moving to the River Town Inn."

"Rick! We can spend more time together!" Susan gushed.

"Yes ma'am, you can count on it."

He ended the call, and her mind whirled.

◆

Spotting the United Airlines plane on the runway was easy enough. Her heart skipped a beat, though, while it taxied closer. Susan advanced to the gate, anticipation mounting as questions raced through her mind.

Will Dixie resent my help? Still be friendly?

Susan bit her bottom lip and slightly shook her head.

Lord, help me, I can't do this alone. I pray all doubt be removed from me. I stand on Your Word and my faith is strong. In Jesus powerful name, I pray. Amen.

Standing off to one side, she searched each face when the passengers embarked.

No, not her...or that one either...wait...that can't be her...

Head cast down, a very pregnant young woman emerged. Her long, brown hair badly needed brushing. She wore wrinkled clothes—obviously forgotten after the drying cycle ended. No one's clothing could get that wrinkled while traveling on a plane for a few hours.

"Dixie?" Susan spoke softly.

A too-quick smile appeared, and her slumped shoulders slightly straightened. "Mrs. Penleigh? Is that you?"

"Yes, it's me." Susan edged closer and timidly hugged her. A surge of protectiveness overcame Susan as she pictured the immaculate, easy-going young woman she met years ago.

Poor girl. She shows signs of depression, and doesn't even know it.

"Come on, let's gather your luggage, and get you home." Susan's arm lay across Dixie's back, and she guided the girl forward.

"This is my first time to be in Texas." Dixie announced while they walked.

"Well, I promise we won't go bull riding tomorrow." Susan grinned.

Dixie laughed heartily.

Her eyes have a new sparkle…thank You, Lord…

The drive to Susan's apartment was quiet, due to the late hour of the night. Both went to bed upon arrival, totally exhausted.

◆

After breakfast, Susan completely moved Dixie into the largest bedroom where she had slept. They unpacked and made a list of what was still needed. The grand tour was given of the entire apartment. In the laundry room, Dixie's words rushed out excitedly. "I have a lot clothes to clean. Can I use the washer right away?"

Instructions were given, she retrieved the clothes, and soon a load sloshed in the machine.

"Care to rest outside on the porch? We can find something to drink and take it with us." Susan motioned to the front of the house..

"I'd like that."

Meandering into the kitchen, they chose bottled water and a raspberry tea. Susan grabbed a few napkins and led the way to the front of the house.

"Don't mind me bringing up the rear." Dixie shuffled her feet approaching the porch. "My ankles swell and throb by the end of the day."

"Sorry to hear that. Do you watch your salt intake?"

"I watch everything. Take vitamins. Drink water. Eat vegetables." She lowered herself in a wicker chair and examined her fingernails. "I used to have pretty nails. Can't afford to have them done now."

Susan reached for an ottoman and placed Dixie's feet on top of it. "You know what? I can't afford to have my nails done, either, but I do have a variety of polish, two types of remover, and clear top coat. Want to try?"

"You mean, do each other's? Oh, Mrs. Penleigh... that sounds like fun."

"It does, doesn't it? You sit here. I'll be right back." Susan sprang to the screen door and entered the house. Glancing back, it tugged at her heart to see Dixie sitting all alone and smiling.

◆

The small tray held so much more than nail polish and beauty aids...a perfect opportunity for bonding.

"Light tangerine will be fine, if you have it." Dixie reached for the emery board and smoothed a jagged nail.

"Here, let me see that hand." Susan pulled a chair closer and applied the requested polish. "I'll put a clear coating on top. Do you like tiny, silver sparkles?"

"Yes." She paused. "Mrs. Penleigh, you have to be wondering about me and Scott. I don't know what he told you, but I am not going back to him." Her voice wavered, "No one can live in a strained relationship."

"You don't have to, and I'm relieved you want to discuss it with me."

"Well, I want to thank you for letting me stay here. As soon as the baby comes, I'll be on my way."

Susan gasped. "I hope you reconsider. There is no reason for you to leave so soon."

"I want to get on with my life." Dixie's voice rose. "Give me some time to make my decision."

"Of course, I will. I am here to help you. It won't be long, and we'll be very busy."

She squirmed in her chair and exhaled noisily. "Let's change the subject. My burst of energy is gone. Could I lay down now?" Dixie glanced at her light tangerine colored fingernails.

Susan applied the silver, sparkly polish—mostly clear, and she quickly blew on each nail to dry. "Certainly, and I hope I didn't upset you. That's the last thing I want to do."

"Oh, no, ma'am, I'm just tired. Sorry, I don't feel like doing your nails."

"Don't worry about it."

"Who is that?" Dixie blurted, as a truck parked near the curb. Susan and Dixie stared at the young man approaching the front porch. Arm muscles bulging, wearing a white t-shirt and tan camouflaged pants, he made rapid strides. His shaved head glistened in the brilliant sunshine. "Good afternoon, ladies." Lee Miller bounded up the steps.

Dixie suddenly sucked her breath in. Glancing at her, Susan noticed Dixie openly staring straight at the landlord.

"Um, um, um…" Dixie muttered.

Susan ignored Dixie's reaction. She rose from her chair and greeted the man. "Good morning. This is Dixie, my daughter-in-law. Dixie, this is Lee Miller. He owns the house and lives in the other apartment." Susan nodded at her.

"Well, Lee," she gushed. "Nice to meet you."

Extending her hand, Dixie straightened her posture and grinned.

He leaned forward, and they shook hands. Instantly, she boldly grasped both of his hands into hers. He squirmed and stepped back, breaking her hold on him. Lee raised an eyebrow at Susan and hurried inside.

Susan frowned and cleared her throat loudly.

"What a man." Dixie drawled. Rising from her chair, she stumbled to her feet, clumsily knocking her chair over. Never setting it upright, she followed Lee into the house.

Chapter Eight

Izabella tiptoed from the adjoining bathroom fully dressed and groomed. Ben lay in the bed motionless.

Good. Guess he's still asleep.

Feeling along the wall, she eased through the darkened bedroom. Her hand brushed the door frame, and she swiftly turned the door knob. It clicked loudly.

"What are you doing?" Ben flooded the room with light and knocked over the bedside lamp. The bed squeaked while he vaulted to rescue the lamp. With a mid-air nab, he placed it back on the table.

She narrowed her eyes at him. "I am going to work."

"Wait, I'll drive you." Blue jeans lay nearby, rumpled on the floor. He sat on the side of the bed and fumbled with a pants leg. "It's wrong side out, give me a minute."

"No, I don't have time to haggle, and I won't let you ride around all day in my car."

"I said I'd drive you. Why would you even consider I'd ride around all day?"

She made sweeping arm gestures as her voice rose, "Well, what else would you do? Your truck was repossessed. I'll be at work. I don't need this stress."

Running out of the house, she rubbed her temples as pain shot across her forehead.

I've got to calm myself.

Approaching the car, a sign of relief escaped her lips. Her demeanor improved until she formed an image of Ben sitting home and watching television the entire day. Disturbed again, her pulse raced. Muttering, she drove to work.

First day on the job, and I won't let him ruin it. Susan was right. I shouldn't have jumped into this marriage...

♦

Izabella entered the store with shoulders straight and held her head up. The service desk, bustling with customers and employees, held her attention as one woman manned the desk. Izabella noticed the name tag, 'Audrey Duvall, Front End Supervisor.' Standing in line behind two others, Izabella overheard instructions spew from the woman.

Talk about being curt and multi-tasking...

"Here is your refund, Mrs. Harless. Someone didn't enter the correct price into the computer. T-bone steaks *are* on sale this week."

The customer nodded and took the money. "I knew that was not the price you advertised. Thank you for taking care of the problem." The woman smiled graciously at the supervisor and left.

"Maggie, I don't see what time you went to the restroom." She grabbed a notebook lying on the counter and studied the page.

"Mrs. Duvall, I don't like writing my name and the time when I go to the restroom, and when I return. It is embarrassing. Customers approach the service desk and glance at the notebook. It sits here open all day."

"Can't be helped, we have to follow company rules."

Maggie pressed her lips together tightly and hesitated. "It is a personal matter, Mrs. Duvall. No disrespect to you, but I have heard some customers snickering while they read the notebook entries."

"Then don't stay gone so long. Go on back to your register."

Turning her back on Audrey Duvall, Maggie avoided looking at Izabella. Paling slightly, she mumbled and hurried away.

Izabella stepped forward and the phone rang. Audrey held her hand up at Izabella and shot a warning look her way while reaching for the phone.

"Good morning, Corner Grocery. How may I help you? Certainly. Let me redirect you to the health and beauty aids department. One moment." She transferred the call and glanced at Izabella.

"You must be the new girl. I'm Audrey Duvall."

"Izabella..." She paused. "Contrell."

"Punctual, I like that. Give me your handbag. I'll lock it in the safe."

Pitching car keys into her purse, Izabella handed it to Audrey who hurried behind a partition. Hearing a series of metal clicks assured her it was indeed in a secure place. Audrey returned to the counter and pushed the swinging door open, leaving the service desk.

"Come on; let's get you to a register." She steered Izabella towards the row of checkout lanes.

"Amanda, Iris, Danielle; meet Izabella," she called out as they walked by. The three checkers nodded and continued scanning groceries. Several customers waited in line. Another lane was open at the far end. "Maggie is working the express lane. Twelve items or less, remember that. Don't let anyone push you on the amount, either."

"I won't."

They reached the express lane counter, and Audrey whirled to face the checker. "Show Izabella what you are doing. Let her watch for a few hours before I put her on another register."

"Yes, ma'am."

"Mrs. Duvall? May I see you a moment?" A middle-aged man wearing a name tag on his jacket appeared at the end of a nearby aisle clutching a clip board.

"Yes, Mr. Shafer." She hastened to him.

Exhaling loudly, Maggie glanced at Izabella. "Nice to meet you. Welcome aboard, oh, and that is our store manager."

"Thanks, I haven't met him yet." Izabella paused. "I might as well tell you; I don't know where to begin or how to do anything. I am so afraid of making an error."

"Don't worry. Hands on mistakes make a lasting impression rather than someone giving you instructions. We all learn the hard way, here."

Shaky laughter erupted from both women.

"Well, I guess I'm ready." Izabella positioned herself next to the trainer.

Maggie raised an eyebrow. Leaning closer to Izabella, she barely spoke above a whisper.

"We are timed for speed. The minute you start an order, the timer begins. It is important to scan the items quickly. Whoever is faster is scheduled more work hours for the following week."

Izabella sputtered in a louder voice. "I have never noticed anyone checking groceries at record speed. I only recall the chatting between the customer and the checker. Doesn't seem like it's going fast when you have to wait your turn."

"Sshh, let me explain. Greet your customer; ask if they found everything they were after, and if they have any coupons. Each customer is unique, and I enjoy treating them as a special person. Some of them I know well enough to call their children by name, but although I really like them, I can't consider this a social hour. I have other customers waiting." Maggie smiled. "I sort bar-coded items together in their shopping cart and group all produce in another area while I talk to them. Don't start the register until you are focused on the items and not the customer. At that point, you rush through the process and quickly turn the register off, or pause to receive cash or a check. Routine is 99% of it. Oh, and you must memorize a coded number for each item of produce. We don't simply weigh something and type in $1.99 a pound. The code is typed in and then the produce is weighed."

Groaning, Izabella shook her head. "What a system."

"It's business." Maggie shrugged.

"Oh, here comes a customer." Izabella perked up. "You work, and I'll watch."

"Not just any customer; that is Mrs. Raney. A more genuine Christian can't be found! With her, it's not about being number one, or making more money, or securing exclusive contacts for her business; but striving to encourage and help those in need. I have utmost respect for her as a sister in Christ."

Mrs. Raney's order was scanned, bagged and paid for. In minutes she left. Mr. Shafer and Mrs. Duvall approached, and he placed meat packages onto Maggie's counter. Devoid of emotion, and silent, he nodded at Mrs. Duvall.

"Double bag these, Maggie, and hurry."

"Yes ma'am." Reaching for the plastic bags, she quickly dumped the packages inside and returned them to her supervisor.

Izabella crossed her arms and observed.

A tall man dressed in khaki pants and a black polo shirt strolled towards Mrs. Duvall. In one swift moment, she passed the package to him, and he darted out the exit door. The supervisor and manager turned without speaking, meandering from the check-out area.

"Wow, three family size packages of T-bone steaks. I guess a lot of customers were charged the wrong price." Izabella blurted.

"Why do you say that?" Maggie frowned.

"Another customer received a refund for being overcharged this morning...but this guy didn't get a refund, just the meat..."

"Izabella, do you have a health card to work here?"

"No, I don't. No one mentioned it."

"Neither do I, and don't worry about it...that *guy* is the health inspector."

Chapter Nine

Susan seethed at the thought of Dixie chasing after the landlord. She breathed heavily with her chest rising in anger, and struggled to keep her temper under control.

Lord, I'm trying to be a good witness of faith, love and kindness; but it looks like I'm now a soldier fighting off an enemy. I stand on Your Word, Lord. So...II Timothy 2: 1-3 applies to me...and...without judging... I hope to teach her II Timothy 2:22 if her lust continues...in Jesus Holy name I pray, Amen.

Laughter bubbled from Dixie at the opposite end of the hall.

"I've never felt a man's head without hair."

"I've never had a pregnant, married woman feel my head." His deep masculine voice rang out in contrast to her childish exclamations.

"Soon to be a divorced...pregnant woman." She chimed in.

"Oh. I'm sorry. How painful for you."

"One can't live like a fish in stagnant water." Dixie sighed.

"Life is what you make it... choices are important."

"I realize choices are important by all parties involved, but it doesn't hurt to dream."

"And set goals to reach those dreams." He added.

"Uh huh." Dixie, suddenly restless, couldn't stand still.

Fascinated, he gazed at her unaware of Susan's advance.

"Dixie, come on, I want to show you something." Susan caught up with the pair and stood with both hands on her hips.

The young woman stuck her lips out in an exaggerated pout and moaned, "Oh, right now?"

"Yes."

Lee laughed. "I'll see you later." He sauntered further down the hall and entered another room.

Susan ushered Dixie down the hall to her apartment door. Deciding to postpone confrontation, Susan refrained from mentioning Lee Miller. Dixie crept along, keeping a distance from her mother-in-law.

"I have envisioned a nursery in the spare bedroom. Cheerful, perhaps a light yellow color; what would you like?" Susan swung the door open and scooped magazines off a table in the foyer.

Dixie eased her heavy body onto a couch and leaned her head back. "Please, no pictures from a magazine. "

"We can get ideas…"

"Not my style. Do whatever you want; it's your home, not mine."

"Dixie, home is where you make it. It's a feeling in your heart, and I want you to experience it. You, the baby, and I can be so happy here. Give us a chance."

"I am not comfortable at *any* home. I guess that is unacceptable behavior."

"Dixie, this doesn't have to be difficult."

"It won't be. We will all be happy. Light yellow is cheerful for a boy or a girl. I suppose I might as well get a sonogram and find out the gender."

"I took the liberty of making an appointment with the best OB/GYN physician in town, tomorrow at 1:00."

"Thanks for finding me a doctor and letting me stay here. Picking out names will be a relief. As the due date for the baby gets closer, I am overwhelmed."

"I'm looking forward to helping. Without prying, I must admit; I had hoped you, my son, and the baby could be a family."

"No." She fixed her gaze on a stain in the carpet.

It occurred to Susan more may be happening than she was aware of, or at this point in time…could even understand.

◆

"It's a girl…oh, what am I going to do with a little girl?" Dixie held onto the sonogram picture shaking her head in slow motion.

"Pink hair bows, dainty sundresses, and tiny tea sets…fun times are right around the corner. A new enjoyable world is opening. How exciting. I'm so happy for you." Susan gave a heart-felt smile. With love flowing, she leaned over and patted Dixie's shoulder.

"Don't. I could easily have had a little boy kicking tires and climbing trees. Either child still won't be raised with both a mother and a father. So unfair."

"One step at a time, Dixie. God has plans for our future, and we can pray for His guidance. We pray for His will to be done and not ours."

"I forget to pray, too busy."

"I can't live your life, but I can try to help you."

Dixie's quivering voice spoke volumes; "I know, and I appreciate what you are doing. I am unhappy with *my* life. End of discussion." Visible tremors coursed through Dixie's body and Susan's eyes widened as she watched in shock.

"Okay, enough said. Stress is dangerous and so unnecessary. We'll finish this later." Susan opened a closet and wrestled with a long box, tugging it to the center of the room. Glancing at Dixie, she was relieved to see the new calmness in her daughter-in-law. "Young lady, we have a project. How are you with tools?"

Dixie stood and traversed to the box. "I can't tell one from the other. Afraid I won't be of much help. Love the picture, though." She ran her fingers across the image of a baby crib on the length of the unopened box.

"I was hoping you'd like it. Regulation size, passed safety tests—a crib that will last."

"Thanks, and it has the antique charm of days gone by. Looks like something my grandmother might have used."

"It even swings. The white wicker is not as fragile as it appears. This crib is solid." Susan paused to smile. "And adorable." Pulling the contents out, she sat with everything scattered on the floor, unfolded the instruction sheet and studied it. Carefully opening small bags of nuts, washers, and bolts; Susan scanned the area. "I thought I brought the tool box. Ohh," she groaned, and rose from the floor. "Middle age is catching up with me." Susan gave Dixie a half smile, walked back to the closet, shuffled boxes until finding the familiar black case with a handle. "There it is. Scott bought this for me years ago, and it still comes in handy."

Grabbing a Phillips screwdriver and a few items from the bags, she faced Dixie. "Will you hold the side and corner piece together while I start assembling?"

"Let's have Lee come over, and he can put the crib together."

"No, this won't take long, besides it's easy."

Susan had two bolts in place when Dixie frowned and the sections began shaking.

"We can stop if you are in a strain." Susan looked directly at her and watched in amazement as rage abruptly overtook Dixie. She moved closer and placed her face within inches of Susan's. Baring her teeth, she yelled in a voice full of hate, blasting away at Susan. "Stop trying to help me. I'm sick of this. Do you hear me? Get out of here. Just go… now! Go on!"

Susan gasped. "Dixie, this is my home."

The pieces fell hard on the floor as Dixie dropped them, stomped out of the room and down the hallway.

I can't believe she yelled right in my face, and telling me to leave…Lord help her…

Susan heard Dixie's voice raise to a shrill, high pitch.

"Lee? Lee where are you?" she ranted.

A distant voice responded. "What is it, Dixie? Are you okay?"

"Susan hurt my feelings. She wouldn't do what I wanted her to do."

"Settle down. Wait for me on the front porch, and I'll talk to Mrs. Penleigh."

Once again, Susan heard echoes of footsteps in the hallway. One set of footsteps walked away. Another set, heavier, stopped at her door, and hesitated.

"Mrs. Penleigh, it's me, Lee Miller." Loud pounding on the door vibrated in Susan's head.

She went too far. She crossed the line, and his knocking is out of order.

Flinging the door open, she frowned at the landlord. "I overheard both of you. Come in."

"I don't want to intrude, but Dixie is so deeply hurt. I simply want to help." He cocked his head to the side and held his hands up in defeat. "Maybe I am wrong to get involved, but she is so emotionally torn up."

"She manipulates, Mr. Miller. Have you ever heard of a need based relationship?"

"No ma'am."

"Do not give what is holy to dogs; nor cast your pearls before swine, lest they trample them under their feet, and turn and tear you in pieces. Matthew 7:6 in the New King James Version of the Bible. That is a good example of what I am referring too."

"I'm trying to understand."

"Do not give of yourself to those who don't have church inside of them. Jesus says you are giving what is holy to those who have no room for God. They can't get happy unless they are with worldly things, and they will not submit to any authority. It's their way or no way. Dixie got all she could from me, and now, she wants to get what she can from you."

"Give her a break, she just needs a friend. I'd really like to help."

"Do you attend church, Mr. Miller?"

"No."

"Then you won't be able to help her. It is a spiritual matter. Good versus evil. Right versus wrong. Light over darkness. A street-smart, sexual woman using an honest, naive man for her own material advancement."

He sighed and glanced at the mess on the floor.

"What is this?"

"Her baby crib we were putting together."

67

Lee squatted and gathered a few parts. "Hand me the screwdriver, please."

Susan bent to assist in the assembly. He applied pressure to each section and quickly had all bolts, washers, and nuts in place. With a grunt, he tightened them again. "That was for being extra cautious."

"Mr. Miller, you should also be extra cautious with Dixie. She is out on the front porch waiting for you, true, but she's waiting for you to pamper and console her."

"She is a grown woman, Mrs. Penleigh. I see her as a fragile bird with a wounded wing, and I do intend to see her."

Chapter Ten

Izabella inserted her card in the time clock to leave and the tenseness in her body relaxed.

Some first day at work this turned out to be. Wonder what Ben did while I was gone? Maybe wash a load of clothes...I doubt it...

Absent-mindedly, she drove home; going through the motions of familiar turns until arriving. *"He must have company. I don't recall anyone with a new, royal blue truck. Look at the chrome wheels...definitely high dollar....*

Discovering the front door wouldn't open, she twisted her key in the lock and entered. The house, eerily quiet, remained as she had left it. Coffee cups still on the counter, crumbs lay near the toaster. Izabella searched for signs of Ben but room after room proved futile.

A glance into the den seemed normal enough, at first.

Bottles? On my mother's handmade oak hutch?

Sprinting to the antique piece of furniture, Izabella snatched at several of the bottles. Whiskey, vodka, tequila, wine, mixers for the alcohol; some had been opened. Many sizes of glasses adorned the smaller shelves of the cabinet.

Izabella felt her blood boil.

"Be-uh-nn." Shrieking, she emptied her lungs and trembled with anger.

No answer.

Hastening toward the patio, she noticed the bathroom door ajar. A brief survey showed the commode seat was raised, but no Ben. Muttering under her breath, she rushed on. A warm sensation spread over her face and quickly alarmed her.

My blood pressure is racing...got to slow my pace...calm down...

Staring through a nearby bay window, Izabella stopped; stiffening at the sight of Ben asleep on the patio in a chaise lounge chair. She shoved on the door and barged outside.

One hand gripped his arm, and the other slipped behind his back. Tight-lipped, she yanked on his upper torso, jerking him into a sitting position. Ben gazed at Izabella without speaking. Weak and probably drunk, he fell back into the lounge chair.

"So how was your day, Ben? Want to talk about it?" Izabella stood over him with her arms folded.

Struggling, he managed to sit upright, and blinked at her. "Something on your mind?"

"What's blue, expensive, and parked out front?"

"My truck, do you like it?" He straightened his shirt and ran his hands through his hair. "I must have dozed off." One leap, and he was on his feet. "Come on, I'll show it to you."

"No, thank you. I'm not interested." Izabella noticed a muscle flinched in Ben's arm.

"Do I have to guess why you mentioned the truck?"

"We never planned on purchasing a truck, Ben. How did you finance it?"

"Details, details... just like a woman; always asking questions."

"Ben..."

"Okay, I got a great deal. Put $5,000.00 down and the payments include insurance. Package deal with free oil change, can't beat it."

"You had $5,000.00 to spend on a truck?"

"No, you did. It was a cash advance from your credit card."

"No. It's not true. I can't believe it. That has 25 % interest, Ben." Izabella's voice grew shrill as she paced the floor and breathed nosily through her nose. "How could you do this to me? It will take forever to pay it off. You can't even make monthly payments on the truck."

"I need transportation. You were upset with me this morning, remember? Wouldn't let me drive you to work in your car."

Izabella held her hand up in the air. "Enough. I won't argue with you. Get your liquor, your clothes, and get out of my house."

"You can't mean it. I have no place to go." Ben quickly changed from pitiful to indignant. "How dare you treat me this way? What kind of a woman are you?"

"Spitting out angry words has no effect on me. It's like water running off a duck's back. How dare you try to turn this around to make me the bad guy? You can stay in the garage tonight, and I want your house key. I will file for an annulment...you are history." Izabella's heartbeat raced and spots flashed in her vision. She stood solemn and erect, though inwardly shaking and waited for him to leave.

He pitched his house key at her feet, turned to leave and didn't look back.

Izabella breathed a sigh of relief and gently rubbed her throbbing forehead.

The sound of glass bottles clinking together followed him as he left the den. She heard the side door to the garage slam shut.

Must have taken his liquor out, first.

Izabella listened for Ben to walk to the bedroom to gather his clothes. He made several trips, and thankfully, the side door shut violently for the last time. Minutes felt like hours as she waited. Satisfied Ben wouldn't return, she locked all of the doors and went so far as to lock herself inside her bedroom.

◆

A restless night behind her, Izabella awoke with mixed feelings. The painful memory had played all night in her mind like a rerun movie. Rolling on her side, she fluffed her pillow, and prayed. Ready for the day, she felt the Lord's strength, and knew she could face anything.

I won't hide from Ben, and I won't let his actions ruin me either. I need to make an appointment with an attorney...and a loan officer at the bank...

No longer groggy, she hurried to dress, made her way to the kitchen and brewed coffee.

The mellow ring of the doorbell suddenly echoed throughout the house. Its pleasant ding-dong sound betrayed the danger that may wait on the other side of the door. Izabella's heartbeat increased quickly, nearly exploding. She froze and felt rooted to the spot. Her leg muscles tightened as fear drenched her now clammy body.

The doorbell rang out merrily again.

She held back a scream and shook.

Get a grip, he can't get in. It may not even be Ben...

Izabella forced herself to tiptoe into the living room. A tiny part in the drapes would let her know if it *was* Ben at the door. She leaned forward to peep when the door-bell rang again. She jumped and almost fell into the window.

"Izabella, it's me, Susan. Izabella, are you there?"

Shoving the drapes wide apart, her eyes welled up when she saw her friend. She flung the door open, ran to Susan and sobbed.

"Susan, oh Susan, I'm so glad you are here." A quick hug and Izabella's cries turned into moans.

"What is wrong? " Susan frowned and grabbed Izabella's arm. "Come on, we need to talk." She led Izabella back into the house.

"Lock...lock the door." Izabella stuttered. "It's my nerves. I'm an... emotional mess." She inhaled loudly and her shoulders shook. The tears ended. "My fears got the best of me. I couldn't deal with this, I'm sorry."

"Deal with what? And don't be sorry, Izabella. We are not perfect. Now, what happened?"

"Ben. He's out in the garage. I thought he was trying to break into the house."

"I thought he lived here with you in the house."

"Not anymore. Let's get some coffee, and I'll unscramble the story of Ben."

In silence, they walked to the kitchen. Izabella filled two cups with the steaming brew, and handed one to Susan. Motioning towards the stools at the other end of the counter, they quickly sat, and each took a sip.

"I have to give credit where credit is due. You were so right about Ben." Her posture sagged as she pronounced each word slowly. "I should not have rushed into marriage with him. Each of the few days we've been married gets worse and worse."

"Sometimes we do things our way instead of seeking God's will. His way happens when He has it happen and *if* it should happen. We get in a hurry and do what we want, regardless. I am just as guilty, Izabella. I took my daughter-in-law into my apartment and didn't pray for God's will or guidance. I was in too big of a hurry to help her, I thought I could ...now we both need help out of a nightmare this has created."

"You always mean well, Susan. I'm sorry it backfired."

"I'm just saying we all make mistakes. Don't be so hard on yourself."

"Point taken. Ben turned out to be the smooth talking, silver-tongued devil we were warned about from our mothers. Only this is my second round with one. What's that old saying? Fool me once, shame on you. Fool me twice, shame on me." Izabella chuckled. "Ben didn't discuss his plans with me. Yesterday, he withdrew $5,000.00 from my credit card for a down payment on a new truck. My den sported a well-stocked bar...overnight...on my mother's antique hutch." She stared into her coffee cup and shuddered. "I threw him out. He spent the night in the garage." Raising her head to make eye contact with Susan; she blurted, "The last thing I said to him was that I wanted an annulment."

"It pains me to mention this, but you may not be married to him. Legally, if he committed fraud, it could help you. Let me refresh your coffee." Susan rose and refilled the cups.

"Where do I begin? I mean, the man is still in my garage."

"I suggest an attorney. Mine will talk to you over the phone; first consultation is free. He may be in court, but he checks his messages during recess. You *will* hear from him."

"Would you please call him for me? I can't think straight."

"Of course. Where's your phonebook?"

Izabella bent from her stool, yanked a drawer open, and grabbed the book. "Here." Susan snatched it, and immediately thumbed through the pages. "There he is, Frank Harrison, Attorney-At-Law."

She keyed the number into her cell phone and glanced at Izabella. "It's ringing," she whispered.

"Hello? This is Susan Penleigh. I'm calling for a friend of mine. She needs a consultation with Mr. Harrison. Yes. Yes, I understand. This concerns a questionable marriage where one party spent money without the other's knowledge. Her name is Izabella Contrell. Yes, ma'am. She will call him at 10:00 this morning. Thank you."

"You're all set." Susan retrieved a ball-point pen from her purse and circled the attorney's name and number in the phone book.

"Susan, I'd be lost without you. True, I *am* nervous, but I'm so ready to get this rolling. Now, let's get back to your daughter-in-law. What's going on?"

"We had an argument yesterday. I thought we could put the baby crib together. Instead she clings to my landlord. Dixie is man crazy…and pregnant…and she and my son have split. He is in Afghanistan, and she needed a place to live. She is alone and the baby will be here soon...and...Scott doesn't think it's his baby."

"A baby, oh Susan, I don't know what to say. No wonder you wanted to help. So, was she in agreement about staying with you?"

"Yes. I asked permission from the landlord, also. He was okay with it. I have an apartment on one side of his house, and he lives in the other side. Who would ever think she'd be after him and be so manipulating? Can you believe she went so far as to yell in my face?"

" How rude. Did you apologize to the landlord for her actions?"

"Are you kidding? He encourages her. She only sleeps in my apartment. They spend all their time together. I rarely see her anymore."

"Strange."

"Strange, indeed. I had pictured us preparing for the baby...what a rude awakening."

"Did Scott think you two could get along with each other?"

"He had told me she could be difficult, but she seemed so sweet years ago when I met her."

"Is she excited about the baby?"

"Hardly mentions it. She did take a sonogram and found out it is a girl."

"Susan, does she have *any* family or close friends?"

"No. I felt so sorry for her at the airport when she arrived. Dixie looked like a scraggly ragdoll, limp and tossed aside. I don't know what to do now, but I do have to be at work soon. Don't forget to call the attorney."

"I won't, and I return to work day after tomorrow. Glad I can sort things out today, and glad you came over."

"Me, too. Let's pray before I leave."

Both bowed their heads, and Susan led the prayer.

"Dear Lord, guide us in our times of trouble. We pray for forgiveness where we have failed you, and thank you for all of our many blessings. Protect us from our enemies, Lord, and we pray for Christians to be placed in their pathways, so they may open their eyes to you. In Jesus Holy name we pray, Amen."

"Amen."

Izabella walked Susan to the front door and cautiously opened it. Turning her head to the left and right, she sighed. "Ben must still be in the garage. His truck hasn't moved."

"Good. Lock the door, and call me if you need me. I work all day tomorrow, so try my cell phone if necessary." Susan advised.

"I will, and thanks again."

Susan nodded and went to her car.

Izabella clicked the dead bolt in place and walked past the kitchen. She continued down the hall toward her bedroom when a light flashed behind her. It flooded the entire area.

"What on earth was that?" She muttered half aloud and scanned the walls and ceiling carefully. A chill shot through her body. An outdoor game camera...a motion activated camera....to watch for deer at deer feeders, sat in the on position and was securely mounted in the corner of the hall near the ceiling. A small, red light blinked constantly...it *was* recording activity!

Ben is a deer hunter...this must belong to him...it sure wasn't here two weeks ago when I dusted and removed cobwebs from the house...what's he trying to do, see who is coming in here?

Anger exploded from Izabella. "This is an invasion of my privacy, Ben," she yelled with no regard to her safety. Running to a closet, she grabbed a broom and hurried to the camera. One strong swipe with the broom and the camera light went out. She clobbered it again until it dangled from the mounting bracket. Satisfied she had destroyed it; she took a deep breath. Thoughts ran through her mind. Fuming, she shook with rage.

I took a shower late last night. Did I cover myself before going in the hall to my room? Was the camera there, then? Was it here this morning when I let Susan in? Or was it installed while Susan and I were talking?

"You had better still be in the garage, Ben, and I have an attorney," she yelled even louder.

Chapter Eleven

Susan couldn't keep yesterday's conversation with Izabella off her mind.

Lord, I pray for ministering angels to guard and protect my friend, Izabella. In Jesus powerful name, I pray, Amen...and maybe someday we can work here at the store together, instead of each working three or four different days a week...but I am thankful for my job...

She hummed as she wiped her register and work area with sanitizer.

I love my job...

Excitement from the special sale still whirled in her head. Other cashiers had hinted today would be busy—what an understatement. They sold over four hundred frozen packages of butterfly shrimp before her shift was over. A few customers were still shopping, but the crowds had dwindled, and their happy chatter was gone.

The front-end supervisor bustled to her counter.

"Mrs. Duvall, today was exhilarating," Susan gushed. "I've never moved so fast in my life. Greet a customer, scan the items, take their money, bag their food and greet the next one. Non-stop."

"It *was* fast. You did well with your training this morning. Let's close your lane and count your till." Audrey Duvall pulled the tray of money out from the bottom of the register in one swift motion. "This won't take long." She turned, and they walked to the service desk. "Wait here," she advised her employee. Audrey entered her work area and carried the till behind the partition.

A low groan rumbled deep in Susan's stomach. Spotting the candy racks in each check-out lane, she considered a selection for a snack on the drive home.

"Mrs. Duvall, do you mind if I go clock out?"

"No, go ahead. Hurry back."

Susan rambled down the aisle to the employee break room. With a brief smile at other co-workers, she located her time card, clocked out and returned quickly. Mrs. Duvall stood behind the counter at the service desk sorting through a stack of papers.

"Mrs. Duvall..."

"Oh, Susan, you may leave now. Your till was fine. Here is your purse. Remind me to issue you a locker tomorrow."

"Yes. I will. Thank you." Susan hurried to stand in line at the express lane and scanned the candy racks. She picked a chocolate bar and pitched it on the counter.

"Great timing, I don't have to wait my turn. I think the customers are gone." Susan laughed, and the cashier grabbed the candy bar calmly examining it.

"You are one of the new girls, aren't you? Hi, I'm Iris."

"Nice to meet you, Iris, I'm Susan."

Iris lowered her voice and glanced about the store. "Uhh, Susan, do not buy this. Hold it up to the light, and you will see a small pin-size hole in the wrapper, several of them. This candy has bugs. Slip it back on the rack while we're alone, and I'll tell you about it."

Susan cautiously looked at the wrapper. "I see it. I see what you are talking about." She shoved it into the carton displayed on the rack. Whispering, she frowned at Iris. "Why is it for sale when it has bugs?"

"It's all about Mr. Shafer's monthly profit and loss report. He sets the thermostat on the air conditioner so high in the summer that the candy melts. Notice we have small electric fans on our registers?"

"Yes, but I don't understand what you are getting at."

"The candy gets wormy. Mr. Shafer has the night stocker boys roll the candy racks into the freezer at night. He said the twenty below temperature in the freezer kills the bugs, and the candy can still be sold."

"Yuck. That is sickening. This store sells candy with dead bugs in it?" Susan felt her stomach contract.

"Yes. Mr. Shafer gets a bonus for keeping costs down. He does the same thing with dry bags of dog food when they get weevils. He has the night crew pull every bag off the shelves, freeze them overnight, and return them in the morning. He said dead bugs are protein and won't hurt animals, either."

"Iris, I don't know if I can be quiet about this."

"You have to be. Besides, no one here will back you up on the story. We desperately need our jobs. You *will* see the night crew following Mr. Shafer's orders when you work late at night. I had to warn you."

"Thanks Iris. I had no idea." Susan nodded and left the store. The more she thought about the candy and the dog food, the queasier her stomach became. Reaching the sidewalk, she stopped and gagged.

"Susan, are you all right?"

She twisted to one side and felt her face flush. "Rick...you couldn't have come at a better time."

"Are you sure?"

"Yes. How long were you behind me?"

"Long enough to hear you in distress." He looked her straight in the face and half-way smiled.

"Now I am embarrassed, happy, but embarrassed."

"Don't be embarrassed, it's just me, Rick. Do I need to call a doctor?"

"No. It was work related. We can talk about it later. I'm fine."

"Okay. So, Ms. Susan…I have a lot to discuss with you." He circled his arm around her waist and started to walk towards his truck. "Care to ride with me for a while?"

She quickly fell in step with him and slid her arm across his lower back. "I'd love a ride, thank you, kind sir."

They burst out in laughter, and he helped her into the vehicle.

"Big changes going on, my dear." He jumped in, started the engine, and drove away from the store.

"Well, tell me, show me." Susan glanced at him with a wide grin.

"The new subdivision is coming along right on schedule. Land is cleared, and utilities are going in. Paved roads, curbs and sidewalks are next. Thought we'd pick out the lot our house will be built on." He raised an eyebrow. "Since ours will be the first house going up."

"I can't wait. This is finally happening. Yes, oh, yes." She drew her hand into a fist and shook it in the air.

"My sentiments exactly, I don't think I can wait. That's what I wanted to talk to you about. "

"I love a surprise."

"Prepare yourself, we are almost there."

The trip was short. He slowed and angled off into the landscaped entrance. Rows of survey stakes sporting orange tape were scattered across the subdivision. A slight breeze ruffled the dangling ends of tape tied around each stake.

Susan raised her head and peered through the windshield. "Looks so inviting. What sizes are the lots?"

"They vary from one acre to three-fourths of an acre."

"Hmm, I like that, Rick. Large enough to not feel cramped."

"Room enough to stretch and breath...and get on with our life." He shot her a solemn look and continued driving. "It won't be long, and we can decide on a location." Winding closer to the river, Susan gasped when they went around the curve.

"Oh, Rick. Is that the creek on the other side of the road you mentioned earlier?"

"Yes ma'am, and I was hoping you'd like this area as much as I do. The main road winds around to form a circle." His voice rose with excitement. "This short road coming out of the circle is a natural peninsula...right here inside the subdivision." Stopping at the end of the road, they climbed out of the truck. Another breeze sent Susan's hair flying across the side of her face. Rick raised his hand and eased the hair back with the brush of his fingers.

"Love it?"

"Love it. We found our place...right here at the end of the road." Susan squeezed his hand, and he quickly kissed her twice.

"Susan, we could marry now. I can move in with you until our house is built."

"Call the preacher. Make the counseling appointment for us, and ask if he can marry us next week."

"Okay, and we have to obtain a marriage license at the courthouse." He raised his arm and studied his watch. "It's too late today. Let's plan that for tomorrow morning. I'll try to schedule the counseling, also, for later tomorrow."

"Great. Oh, and Rick, I have to ask the landlord if you can move in."

"I'll ask him, man to man."

"Dixie is with him constantly. Talking to him may be like walking on eggs."

"Why put it off? We can go back to the store, get your car, and I'll meet you at the apartment. Susan, I have been praying for this, and if it's His will, it *will fall in place*."

"I agree." Susan blinked repeatedly as moisture clung to her eyelashes. "I've been praying for us for a long time. I'm so thankful God has sent me a Christian man to share my life with and together, we can serve God."

Rick could not speak at first. He uttered a prayer, and then drew Susan to his side. "No one is more thankful than I. God put you in my life. Susan, we are so blessed."

They hugged and shared a peaceful silence until Rick finally drew away from her.

"Ready?"

Susan beamed. "Ready."

Hand in hand they strolled to the truck and were soon driving to Susan's new job.

"Stop in the middle of the store's parking lot when we arrive."

"Will do." Minutes later, he zipped into the lot and came to a halt near her vehicle.

Stepping from the truck, she unlocked her car and wasted no time getting it on the road. Rick gave her some space and followed at a safe distance.

Susan was not surprised that Lee Miller's truck was not at the apartment. She drove all the way up the driveway to the garage, and Rick parked at the curb. Both exited their vehicles, and Rick met her on the front porch.

"We've got the whole place to ourselves." Susan declared. "I have no clue what they do or where they go."

"She's still living with you, isn't she?"

"Only spends the night. Dixie and Lee are inseparable any other time."

"Is she preparing for the baby?"

"Not to my knowledge. So far a baby crib is assembled. No diapers. No supplies." Susan opened the flap on the wall mailbox and withdrew a stack of mail. She tugged the chain hanging from the ceiling fan and stood under the quick whirl of fan blades.

"Have a seat. We'll wait for them here."

Rick winked at her and relaxed in a love seat. Susan sorted through the mail.

"Oh, here's a letter from my son, Scott." She opened the envelope, scanned through the pages, and sighed.

"Scott is still in Afghanistan. He wants the baby's physician to do a DNA on her, and send the results to his Marine base. They have his DNA and will do the paternity test." She glanced at Rick. "I bet *that* goes over big with Dixie." She flipped a page over and read the P.S. "He wants to know how we are doing. Guess I better try to call him." She inserted the pages back into the envelope.

Rick stood and paced the length of the porch. "So, he doesn't think the baby is his?'

"No, he doesn't. I have so much to tell you. Helping Dixie was a mistake, and I stumbled upon a serious issue at work."

"We will work it out together. Susan, do you think Dixie wants the baby?"

"No, I do not."

"What do you know about the landlord?"

"Very little. Oh, look, here they come."

Both quit talking. The approaching truck slowed and parked behind Rick's truck.

Dixie was enormous. Lee had to help her out of the passenger's side of the vehicle. He held her by the arm and walked each step with her to the porch.

"Hello." Rick descended the stairs and shook Lee's hand. "I'm Susan's fiancé, Rick Yeager." He glanced at the very pregnant young woman. "You must be Dixie, nice to meet you."

She snickered, and Lee drew his mouth in a tight line.

"I'd like to talk to you, Lee, if you have a minute." Rick focused directly on the landlord.

Lee and Dixie glanced at each other and sat in the love seat. "Sure, man. What's up?" Lee stared at Rick.

"Susan and I are getting married. Do you have any objection to my moving in with her here at the apartment?'

Dixie sucked her breath in noisily and scowled. The entire gesture was wasted on Lee. He never took his eyes off of Rick.

"Plenty of room. No problem, Mr. Yeager."

Dixie whimpered, and Lee turned to look at her.

"It's getting hot out here." She whined.

Lee helped her stand and slowly escorted her to the front door.

Rick hurried and opened the door for them. "Pardon me, Ms. Dixie, but why aren't you thinking about your baby?"

"What's it to you, anyway? It's none of your business." Dixie glared at him.

"Oh, but it is my business. It is as long as you are living with my fiancé."

"I don't have to listen to this." Shifting around, she frowned at the landlord. "Come on, let's go."

Dixie drew her hand back, slammed the door on Rick and escaped down the hall with Lee.

Chapter Twelve

Furious, Izabella yelled louder than a child having a tooth pulled, "A camera… how dare you, Ben?" Pent up inside, the frustration of her days in Hugo, Oklahoma blasted forth as well. She doubled over hugging her sides and moaned loudly in agony. Slumping to the floor, she burst into tears until anger took control, again. "How dare you?" She screamed and leaped from the floor. Hurrying, she peered out the window and saw Ben run from the garage to the house.

His pounding on the side door startled her, and she drew her breath in sharply.

"What's going on? What's all the commotion about?" He demanded, and his fist hit the door harder with each strike. Bam, bam, bam, the sound echoed throughout the neighborhood like repetitive thunder.

She unlocked the dead bolt, grasped the handle, and swung the door with such force it hit the outside wall. "Must you persist in beating my door so violently?" A vein throbbed in her neck, and she felt her pulse quicken.

Ben stood with his mouth hanging open.

Irritated, Izabella's index finger shot up. She stepped forward and wagged it straight in Ben's face.

"Don't you ever…ever… put a live video camera in *my* home."

Parting his lips in a slight smile, Ben leaner closer; emitting a deep, belly laugh.

"Don't you dare laugh at me, Ben Wakefield. Get your stuff out of my garage and get off of my property."

"It was a joke, Izabella. Can't you take a joke? I mean, who in their right mind would want to see you in a video? " Throaty laughter erupted briefly until he swayed and couldn't stay still. "I'm not being rude, Izabella, I'm being real."

"You are intoxicated, and let me tell you something, buddy boy, I have an attorney." She saw his face immediately pale.

"Get out, and watch your ugly attitude." She jerked the door shut so fast a puff of air whirled upward to her face. He shuffled away and disappeared inside the garage.

Chin held high, Izabella stood at the window near the door with an alert gaze. Minutes later, Ben reappeared on the sidewalk carrying folded clothing on hangers to the truck. After several trips, he emerged with large trash bags stuffed to capacity.

His body language left no doubt as to his state of mind. Ben slung bags into the bed of the truck with such a fury; he resembled a pitcher throwing a hard ball at a baseball game.

And which one of your choices brought this on? Reap what you sow, Ben.

She heard the engine race and observed the truck weave from side to side while he backed it out of the driveway with uncontrollable rage. He shifted gears and roared off down the street. She left the window and entered the kitchen. The wall clock displayed 9:55 A.M.

What a relief, I can call the attorney. At least Ben did something right, he left before I missed this 10:00 appointment.

She retrieved the phone book from the counter, and in making the call, experienced calmness long overdue.

Thank You, Lord, for Your presence and guidance.

She clicked the speaker phone on and eased onto a stool.

A perky voice rang out. "Good morning, Harrison and Harrison Law Firm."

"Mr. Harrison, please. This is Izabella Contrell."

"One moment."

Izabella listened to the instrumental music while the call transferred.

"Frank Harrison, here. How may I be of assistance to you, Mrs. Contrell?" The pleasant male voice spoke distinctively with authority.

"I'm in a predicament. I have no record of being married, but my husband assured me we were married in Hugo, Oklahoma a few weeks ago. I don't remember it, and that's not like me to forget an important event like my marriage ceremony."

"How well do you know him?"

"Not near as well as I should. I've learned enough about him in the last few days to want an annulment."

"No problem. I'll contact the courthouse in Hugo, and see if a marriage license was filed. What is his name?"

"Benjamin Wakefield."

"I need his social security number, and his birth date."

Izabella exhaled deeply. "I don't have either of them. He does have a brother, Logan. He lives here in town."

"Can you get the information from the brother? I'm assuming you'd rather not talk to your husband at this time."

"If Logan has it, yes, I think he would help me." Izabella paused. "Mr. Harrison, I had Ben leave. I told him I don't want him on my property. He has done some things I don't feel I should be responsible for."

"Such as?"

"Without my knowledge, he got a cash advance from my credit card for $5,000.00, and used it for a down payment on a new truck."

"You two didn't discuss this transaction?"

"No, we did not."

"Did he forge your signature?"

"No, I added him to my bank account and credit cards."

"Ma'am, you gave him permission to use your money when you included his name to your accounts."

Izabella frowned and blurted. "...But we might not be married, couldn't that be fraud?"

"Married or not, you legally added his name to your accounts. I'm sorry, but I can't help you there. If I find out you two are *not* legally married, then you don't need an annulment. He could also claim you are his common-law wife."

"I don't care what he claims. I want to know once and for all if I am married."

"That I can do. My service fees are reasonable. Contact my secretary about the options. Call the bank and the credit card company. Remove his name before it gets worse, and let me know about his identification."

"I will, and thank you."

"You are welcome, and I'm glad to help."

Izabella ended the call.

Thumbing through the phone book, she called customer service at her bank. "Oh great, an automated menu," she mumbled out loud. Numerous prompts later, she spoke to a person. "I want to remove someone from my account."

Izabella listened to the bank's procedure and agreed to appear in person to fill out a form. Another phone menu later, and she finally talked to someone at the credit card company. "I do not have a claim, but didn't know what other option to try. My only concern is to remove someone from using my card."

A well explained procedure was related, again.

"I don't have a fax machine to obtain your form. Could you send it to my bank in care of the customer service department?" She rubbed the back of her neck while waiting for an answer.

"Wonderful! It's Caddo Credit Union in River Town, Texas. I'll be there within thirty minutes, but I don't have their fax number."

Izabella laughed. "You are so right. It *can* be found on the internet. I'll get it and call you back. Are you sure? You don't mind finding it? Well, thank *you.*"

◆

Shaking hands with the customer service manager, Izabella completed her transactions. Both forms from the bank and the credit card company were signed, notarized, and as required by the last institution, faxed back.

"I'm done. Ben is history!" She vented, climbing into her car. "Now, where is Logan?"

Seizing her cell phone, she considered calling Logan instantly.

No, too much traffic. I need to concentrate. I'll focus on Logan when I get home.

To her amazement, Izabella drove block after block through town, greeted by green lights at each intersection. Mindful of never having a traffic ticket, she glanced about in preparation of a sudden red light. An older model sedan was following too close. If she had to stop, it would rear-end her car. The next intersection loomed ahead; the light was green, and she floor-boarded the gas pedal.

There! The sedan caught the red light and is no longer riding my bumper.

She veered east and arrived home before the daily five o'clock congestion erupted on the roads. One vehicle zipped past her as she attempted to pull into her drive-way. Izabella glanced at her wrist watch.

Yes, it is officially five o'clock.

Parking her car, she strolled toward the back of her home. The patio loomed ahead. Enjoying the solitude, she flopped into a chair and dug the cell phone out of her purse. With no plan on how to begin this possibly awkward conversation, she typed in Logan's number.

He answered immediately. "Hello?'

Izabella's adrenalin rushed at the sound of his voice, and her body tensed.

Calm down…he can't control his brother…

"…Logan? Hi… it's me, Izabella. We need to talk." She stammered.

93

"Well, Izabella, Ben *won't* talk. He moved in with me this morning. What is going on?"

"I told him to get off of my property. Logan, I've never met a more self-centered person in my life, or one who can change so drastically. His behavior is awful."

"What did he do?"

"Number one, he lost my trust. I still don't know if we are married or not. I don't know if he drugged me, and I do not remember the wedding ceremony. Are you aware he is an alcoholic?"

"No, I am aware he drinks."

"He drinks a lot and every day. Did he mention how he bought the truck he's driving?"

"Ben is not talking about anything. I know he is on disability with a fixed income. How did he manage buying a new truck? Did he talk to you about it?" Logan demanded.

"We didn't discuss the purchase of a new truck. I came home from work and saw it in the driveway. He took $5,000.00 from my credit card for the down payment on it. We didn't discuss that, either. Can you imagine what the monthly interest will be? I am sick about it. Still can't believe he did that to me."

"Well, I wondered where he got the down payment." Logan inhaled and exhaled noisily. "I'm sorry this happened, Izabella."

"So am I, and I hired an attorney. Ben can't take $5,000.00, and run and hide. He needs to be responsible for his actions."

"Oh, he will be. You are a decent woman, Izabella. I can't make it up to you on how you were treated, but I can and will pay off the $5,000.00 on the credit card."

"Logan! I don't expect any monetary help. It's not your debt."

"You don't deserve being stuck with that. He's my brother, and he will pay me back. I assure you, it may take time, but he will repay me the entire amount."

"How can you be so sure? I won't let you do it unless I am convinced *you will* be reimbursed by him."

"I heard the same remark from his ex-wife, Savanna. She was as concerned as you are. Ben paid me back then, he will pay me back now."

"Savanna? Ben has an ex-wife?" Izabella felt her stomach flutter.

"Ben took her money for financial investments. Lost a bundle, but Savanna had no clue. One day she discovered the bank statement was way off from her checkbook balance. She confronted Ben, who was nonchalant about the whole situation. Instead of writing checks like she normally did, she had no choice, but to charge any services she required. Eye exams, oil change on the car; I could go on and on. So, yes, I helped her also. Paid off her credit card, and Ben did pay me back."

"I had no idea. Logan, thank you for your kindness. Thank you for helping both me and Savanna. I don't know if you can help me with another problem, though. My attorney needs Ben's social security number and date of birth to find out if we *are* married."

"I'll mail you the identification on Ben and the check. It's the least I can do."

He ended the call, and Izabella stared at the phone.

How incredible...thank You Lord Jesus, and thank You for Logan.

◆

Logan barged into the spare bedroom. Ben, lightly snoring, was sprawled across the bed, completely dressed and still wearing boots.

"Get up!"

Ben gave an unfocused gaze toward his brother. His head tilted to the side. "What?" he drawled.

"How can you do a woman that way? How can you live with your conscience? Or do you have one?"

Ben wrinkled his brow. "Women are witches. They are all witches."

"Did you drug Izabella on that trip to Oklahoma?"

Ben covered his ears with his hands.

Logan grabbed Ben's leg and flung him to the floor.

"You will pay me the money you took from Izabella's credit card..."

Chapter Thirteen

"I'm not familiar with this courthouse." Susan muttered while pausing to read a notice taped to the main entrance.

"It's the usual warning; no knives, no weapons beyond this point." Rick advanced to the double glass doors, and they automatically swung open. Joining several people standing in line, they waited to be inspected. The checkpoint station resembled a large foyer in a home. A sheriff's deputy manned the desk. Each individual in line went through a metal detector. Women would place their purse and keys on a tray at the counter. He'd open and rummage through the purse, then hand it back. Always courteous, he'd smile while motioning for the person to enter the hall behind him. Men went through the same procedure with their billfolds and keys when it was their turn. The line moved smoothly until the deputy nodded at two officers standing nearby, who patted down a man. With nothing illegal in his pockets, or on his person, he was swiftly released.

Susan and Rick went through the inspection, quickly and without incident. Glancing about in the massive hall, they spotted several elevators. One had its doors open and was empty. The lighted arrow above it pointed up, and they hurried to catch it. Stepping inside the elevator, Rick bumped into a biker dressed in black leather pants and vest. Chains hanging from his side, added to the man's rough appearance.

"Pardon me." Rick made eye contact and moved aside.

"No sweat."

More people rushed into the elevator. Susan squeezed past a couple and stood next to Rick. The doors closed, and the biker did a double take at Rick.

"Hey, bro; isn't Tessa your daughter?"

"Yes, she is."

"I thought so." He grunted and watched the floor numbers display while they zipped along. Fourth floor neared, and the elevator slowed. The doors sped open. Rick and Susan had to walk past the biker to exit. His tank top shirt couldn't hide the red, white, and blue eagle tattooed on his entire back.

Rick nodded at him as he and Susan stepped out.

"Later." The biker replied. The elevator doors immediately shut.

Rick and Susan stood in the empty hall with nothing but the sound of whirling hydraulics as the elevator shot upward.

A muscle quivered on her face. She absent-mindedly rubbed it and cleared her throat. "Do you know him?"

Rick placed his hand behind her back, steering her towards the information plaque on the wall. "No, and put him out of your mind." Scanning each office and room number, he stood straight. "There it is; County Clerk's office, room 415."

Susan glanced at him and noticed the creases at the corners of his eyes. With a warm smile, he lightly moved his feet in an impromptu tap dance.

"Ready for this?" He held his arms out and laughed.

"You are as nervous as I am," she blurted. "Of course, I'm ready." Her heart swelled at the sight of him clowning. She approached him with ease. "Lead the way."

Walking side by side, the only sound came from their muffled footsteps on the worn carpet until discovering room 415. Rick tugged at the heavy solid oak door, and Susan stared in amazement. The county clerk's office expanded across the entire half of the fourth floor. At least thirty people bustled from one area of desks to rows of ledgers and maps.

"Reminds me of a library," Susan half muttered.

"You should get out more." Rick teased.

Susan bent her arm and quickly poked her elbow at his side, but he dodged, and her elbow had no target. He regained his stiff posture as an employee rose from her chair.

"May I help you?"

Susan stifled a smile, and Rick stepped forward projecting his voice. "Yes, ma'am, we want a marriage license."

"I will need both of your driver's license. The application for a marriage license is $67.00 in cash. No checks."

"What?" Susan turned away and covered her mouth.

"It's okay." Rick placed his hand under her chin and gently maneuvered her face to look at him. He raised one eyebrow and winked.

Warmth radiated throughout her body, and she beamed.

He reached for his billfold, dug out a one hundred dollar bill, and handed it to the clerk. She gave him thirty-three dollars, a receipt, and handed him the application. "You may have a seat and fill it out now, if you like." She motioned to the row of chairs against the entrance wall.

"Thank you, we will."

Names, addresses, and other pertinent information were written. Questions carefully answered, the application was finally complete. Rick lunged to the desk.

"Here you are." He shoved the form to the clerk and glanced at his watch.

"Almost lunch time," she chatted. A fast review, and she stamped a seal upon it. Returning the form to Rick, she nodded, "We'll file this after the minister completes his part."

"We're done?"

"Yes, sir, and congratulations."

Grabbing her purse, Susan jumped from the chair and scrambled beside Rick. He walked beside her, and they strolled out of the room.

"Lost in thought?" Susan gave his hand a squeeze.

"Who me?"

"Anxious would be an understatement. I know we both want our wedding soon, but it's important to have it done correctly." He stopped in front of the elevators and remained close-lipped as others gathered to catch a ride. The doors abruptly flung open and once again they were pushed inside. Everyone was crammed shoulder to shoulder and in the midst of strangers, Rick held Susan to his side.

Someone against the side wall mumbled, "This really does feel like packed sardines in a can." A few chuckles erupted, and Susan sighed with relief when they reached the ground floor.

"Let's go eat. We have plenty of time to make our counseling appointment with Pastor Williford at 1:30.

"I am so ready." Susan felt her face flush. "Rick, I don't know how to say this, but I never thought I was claustrophobic until today. I have to admit, I *was* getting light-headed the last time we were in the elevator."

"It *was* too crowded in there. Could be your empty stomach didn't help matters, either."

"Whatever it was is not going to ruin our day."

Stepping outside the building, both blinked at the bright sunshine. Heavy traffic crowded the downtown area.

"Any preference on lunch?" Rick squinted while they waited for the light to change.

"Yes, Sweet Sabine's...delicious food with healthy choices."

Darting across the street to the parking lot, bells rang out from a church located two blocks away, signaling the noon hour.

"Where is the restaurant?"

"Here on the courthouse square around the corner."

"If we hurry, we'll beat the local workers. Come on." He seized her hand, and they sprinted down the sidewalk. Minutes later, Susan motioned to Rick.

"See the orange metal planters mid-way on the next block?"

"Uh-huh."

"That's it. The owner grows herbs in the planters on the sidewalk in front of the restaurant."

Nodding, they took off sprinting again.

Arriving at Sweet Sabine's, they bent over to catch their breath, and entered with laughter. Making their way to the counter, Susan raised an eyebrow at the clerk.

"I'll have my favorite; the Courthouse Croissant with stuffed baked potato salad, and a Peach Bellini tea."

Rick looked at Susan as the clerk wrote the order.

"What's the Courthouse Croissant?"

"Bacon, turkey, cheese and avocado—*delicious!*"

The clerk handed Rick a menu. "Some men prefer our Big Tex sandwich, if you'd like to try that."

"Okay, and I'll have the rest of what she's having."

"It won't take long, and you can sit anywhere."

Susan led him to the tables near the windows. "I love this place, so much charm and character."

Rick glanced back at the counter. "Were those homemade iced cupcakes?"

"Yes, you'll have to try one."

He picked up a snow globe on their table, and a wide smile lit up his face. "Haven't seen one of these in years, homemade snow globes...bright, and shiny." He held it up, shook it vigorously, and watched the tiny, white particles dance around.

"I knew you'd like it here. The color scheme invites a happy evening."

Thirty minutes later, Rick complimented the owner on a terrific lunch. He and Susan had to leave and rushed to the counseling appointment.

Traffic slowed several blocks before their destination. Sirens approached behind his truck, and Rick jerked at the steering wheel, pulling his truck off the road. One police squad car, two sheriff deputy patrol cars, and one state trooper flew past him. Sirens continued blaring and traffic was at a standstill.

Speechless, Susan watched in shock while officers barricaded off the block ahead of them.

"Some fugitive must have escaped." Rick finally spoke as deputies walked to each parked vehicle and talked briefly. Using hand signals, they guided every car and truck to turn around and leave.

Anticipation grew when armed snipers arrived and ran toward the barricades. An officer approached Rick's truck, and Rick rolled his window down quickly.

"Sir, ma'am; I have to ask you to leave for your own safety. We'll help you turn around."

"Of course, officer. Is it a hostage situation?"

"I'm not allowed to discuss it." The officer stood back from the truck window. "Now, if you'll pull forward and swing wide open, you should have no problem."

"Thank you, officer."

Susan glanced at Rick. "I'd rather not say it, but we just missed our counseling appointment."

"We can reschedule. Whatever is happening here could make tomorrow's newspaper."

"My gut feeling is strong. I know Tessa is incarcerated, but I feel she has something to do with this."

"So do I."

Chapter Fourteen

Who would ever think I welcome the familiar routine of work?

Izabella shifted her weight and pushed hard on the heavy cart of boxes. It began to move, slow as molasses, but it was rolling.

One more aisle to go.

Cashiers also stocked between peak times of checking customers. Izabella's duty today was removing out of date spices and maintaining a full product line on the shelf.

Cinnamon sold out fast. Since the River Town Gazette printed the numerous ailments that improved by a mixture of cinnamon and honey, both were being bought several times a day.

Ripping a case open with a box cutter revealed a higher price than the shelf tag displayed. She examined the date on the box and the page of new price tags. Definitely a price increase.

Only one employee programed prices into the computer, Mira Foley, and she worked upstairs.

Izabella closed the box cutter, crammed it inside her uniform pocket, and retrieved the pricing gun. Walking briskly, she made her way to the back of the store. Passing the ice cream section, she spotted Danielle, also stocking.

"If anyone looks for me, I'll be upstairs giving Mira a price increase," she announced and stepped up her pace.

"Will do."

Izabella reached the stairs and started to climb to the second floor landing. It held one long, narrow office recently converted into two. Mira's office was first. A door to the right of her desk opened into the back office; that of Mr. Shafer, the manager.

I sound like an elephant charging up these stairs...so unprofessional...

Instantly, she stepped lightly and continued up the stairs.

Posture erect, shoulders squared, she opened Mira's door. Impatient to complete her task, Izabella shook her head upon viewing both the desk, and Mira's chair. They were empty. Something moved out of the corner of her eye, and Izabella spotted Mira embraced with Mr. Shafer in his chair...in his office.

They left his door open...

Backing out, completely silent, Izabella tiptoed down the stairs.

What have I stumbled upon? I can't believe this...

In a daze, Izabella continued tiptoeing until nearly at the bottom of the stairs, when someone called her name. She jumped and felt every nerve in her body twitch.

Danielle stood staring at her. "I take it you found Mira."

"I ...uh...didn't get to talk to Mira. She was busy."

"Izabella, everyone knows about Mira and Mr. Shafer. Did they see you?"

"No."

"Good. Knock loudly on the door next time. Oh, and be nice to Mira, she makes our work schedule."

"What an incredible work environment." Izabella shook her head and both employees returned to stocking.

Within an hour, Mrs. Duvall summoned Danielle and Izabella to their registers. Lines were long and the shopping carts were loaded. Izabella opened her check-out lane and was bombarded with customers. Trying to concentrate on the correct procedure, her mind only repeated flash backs of Mira and Mr. Shafer upstairs.

I won't have the fastest speed today...so what...I'll enjoy the customers.

Izabella kept her smile and listened attentively to the customer's needs. Calling stockers to her check-out lane, she'd inform the co-worker what the customer couldn't find. In their racing to bring the item to her, Izabella experienced a team feeling of pride, and customer after customer sailed out of the store, happily laden with bags of exactly what they were trying to find.

Exhausted, Izabella's shift ended, and Mrs. Duvall carried the till to the service desk, as was her habit. Once again, the money was correct, and Izabella received a thumbs up sign.

"Oh, wait. Someone left this for you and said it is very important." Audrey Duvall handed her a long white, envelope.

"Thanks." Unhurried, Izabella went to the employee break room, opened her locker and retrieved her purse. Tired, she shoved the envelope into a zippered compartment on her purse, and left.

I can't wait to get home...

Upon arrival, she grabbed envelopes from her mail box, and noticed one from Logan. Tearing it open revealed the check to pay off her credit card and the information on Ben. She stuck the check inside her purse to later deposit. Quickly calling the attorney, she gave him Ben's identification information.

There! Business is taken care of...the attorney can start investigating if Ben and I are married... I can deposit this check and pay off my credit card...

Entering the house, she slung her purse on the kitchen counter, walked straight to the living room, and collapsed into a heavy-cushioned recliner. Jerking the wooden lever, the foot rest shot forward, and she quickly situated her feet.

Oh, what a relief...

The instant she leaned her head back to relax, someone knocked at the door.

Her body refused to move. It was almost numb. Izabella savored the moment. Her elevated legs were not throbbing, neither were her feet. Logan had sent the check. It was a moment to treasure.

The knocking intensified.

Locating the wooden lever, she reversed its position. Forcing herself, she lunged from the chair, and crossed the living room to the front door. Smoothing her hair in place, she peeped out the window.

Susan and Rick...wonder what's going on...

"Hey, what a surprise!" Izabella swung the door open and greeted her friends. "Come on in."

"We're not interrupting anything, are we?"

"No, you two are always welcome." Izabella escorted them to the patio. "Care for spiced, iced tea?"

"Izabella, I can't resist your special brew of tea." Susan turned towards Rick. "You will love it."

"If you say so."

"Have a seat... get comfortable. I'll bring the tea." Izabella offered and took off.

"Let me help." Susan rushed to follow.

Rick sprawled out in a lounge chair and observed the massive plants Izabella had scattered around the patio.

The women returned with one tray of three frosted mugs of spiced tea and another tray of homemade cookies.

Rick graciously accepted his refreshments and sampled them quickly.

"Excellent, thank you, Izabella, but let me ask you one question...are your plants real?"

"Yes." She chuckled. "Most men don't pay any attention to them."

"Susan and I will soon be selecting plants. I've never noticed them before, but now they stand out wherever I go."

"Selecting plants?" Izabella frowned.

Susan stood and moved closer to Rick. "We have an announcement to make...we're getting married."

Rick glanced at Susan and beamed.

"Oh, Susan... Rick; I can't think of a better suited couple. I am so happy for both of you."

"Thanks, Izabella, but there is more." Rick hinted.

Izabella glanced at Susan. "I want you to be my maid of honor."

"Of course, I will. I can't wait. When, tell me when?" Izabella gushed.

"Next week. We still have to talk to the pastor, and we'll let you know, then."

Rick got to his feet. "We decided not to put it off any longer. We can marry now, and I'll move in with Susan until our house is built."

"That's where the plants come in." Izabella blurted.

"Yes, now you understand." Susan nodded.

"I hope you don't think I'm prying, but Dixie will also be there..." Izabella frowned.

"She isn't planning any future. We don't know what to expect, but whatever happens, Susan and I will face it together. " Rick raised an eyebrow and reached for Susan's hand. "Ready to go?"

"Yes, it's late."

"Well, I'm happy you stopped in and told me the great news. I can't wait for the wedding." Izabella walked them to the door. They hugged and said their goodbyes.

Locking the door, Izabella was still filled with joy about her friends' announcement. She went to the patio and brought the tray of cookies and tea to the kitchen. Spotting her purse on the counter and remembering the long, white envelope from work, she unzipped the side compartment and removed it. She strolled to the living room, sighed deeply, and flopped back into the recliner. Carefully opening the envelope, she removed the only page. Curious, she quickly unfolded it and at first, her mind couldn't comprehend.

Ben...a letter from Ben...

Shocked at this discovery, she dropped the letter, and it fluttered from her hand into her lap.

Alarm flooded her being. Retrieving the page, she read it slowly, letting each word soak in.

Dear Izabella,
I know I have done wrong. I will do everything possible to make it up to you. Please forgive me. I will be at your house tomorrow evening to talk about this.
I love you,
Ben

Devoid of emotion, Izabella wadded the page and envelope into a ball and threw it in the trash.

Nope...we are done...

She felt her blood pressure rise as anger took control.

He's got a lot of nerve...

Chapter Fifteen

Half asleep, Susan straightened her legs in one long stretch and flexed her toes. The whirl of blades on high speed from the ceiling fan soothed her. Aware of a slight chill on her shoulders, she pulled the covers, drawing them close to her neck.

A distant clanging disturbed her morning of sleeping an hour longer than usual. Rising on her elbows, she tried to focus and listen.

Must be Dixie...sounds like she's in the kitchen.

Yawning, Susan settled back in bed and closed her eyes, enjoying the cool breeze on her face.

What a special visit Rick and I had with Izabella yesterday. I knew she'd agree to be my maid of honor...what's scheduled for today? Counseling...oh yes, we had to reschedule...wonder if they caught who they were after...

She tried to dismiss the thoughts flashing through her mind but no use. They came one after the other until she was completely awake. Jumping from the bed, she dressed and made her way to the kitchen. The noise continued but was muffled. Susan stopped in the doorway, gazing in disbelief at Dixie.

"Mopping! Am I dreaming?"

"Burst of energy, Mrs. Penleigh, and it's a 'Swiffer Sweeper.' I'm using a wet refill." Dixie glided the sweeper around stool legs without banging into them. Pausing, she stood erect holding onto the handle. "Smells good, too."

"Yes, it certainly does. What is that smell?"

"Gain... exactly like the detergent... same fresh clean scent." Dixie reached in her pocket and crammed three sticks of gum into her mouth. Never losing eye contact, she chewed, blew a bubble out and popped it.

Susan, being at a loss for words, nodded.

"Lee bought the 'Swiffer Sweeper' kit for me. We went shopping yesterday."

"I realize Lee is a friend of yours. Thanks for cleaning the floor. I guess the kitchen ends up with more spills than any other room."

Dixie snatched the refill box of disposable cloths; placing it, and the sweeper inside the closet.

"Lee is helping me name the baby today. He bought me a book of baby names to select from, and we both have our favorites."

"I had hoped to help you." Susan blurted.

"Well, I haven't felt civil. Lee is another matter, entirely." Dixie raised an eyebrow and drew her mouth into a tight line.

And you are so enjoying this...no wonder my son warned me...

"Don't wait up for me tonight, I might be in late." Dixie slipped out of the room and Susan soon heard the front door slam. A male voice could be heard, mingled with Dixie's. Peeping out the window, Susan observed a private moment between Lee and Dixie as they made eye contact and shared a smile.

Susan returned to her bedroom, reached for her Bible and daily devotional book.

Now I can start my day, then get ready for Rick...

◆

"Come on Rick, I'm ready to go," Susan muttered to herself. "The River Town Inn isn't that far away. I imagine you are getting tired of staying there. I know I would." Pacing the deserted porch, she recalled how Dixie and Lee couldn't quit looking at each other before leaving.

"Sickening, and no, I'm not judging…just saying…sickening…" Susan muttered to herself and glanced down the street for any sign of Rick's truck.

And how can this possibly work out with all of us soon living here together? She gets irritated with whatever I say, I cannot please her…she doesn't want me to…she wants drama …wants male attention…

Susan wandered to both potted geranium plants and removed the old, dried blooms. Enjoying the remaining bright red flowers that barely stood above the dark green leaves, she checked each plant and pulled off several leaves that had yellowed. The distinct smell of geraniums drifted across the porch and Susan took a deep breath.

The act of sprucing up the plants had a calming effect on her. She noticed the gardenia bushes were loaded with buds about to open and strolled to the right end of the porch, resting in the swing. The peace was overwhelming, and Susan silently prayed.

Dear Lord, I can't help Dixie. I can't even talk to her. She doesn't know she has to submit herself completely to You, in order to receive Your blessings and promises. Lord, I stand on Your Word and pray she comes to know Romans 10: 3, James 4:7-8, prays for forgiveness and prays to be saved. In Jesus Holy name I pray, Amen.

Leaning back in the swing, the gentle sway relaxed her even more. Rick's truck approached, and she felt a flutter in the pit of her stomach. She grasped her purse, and skipped down the porch steps, meeting Rick at the curb. He flung the passenger door open and beamed.

"I guess you are ready to go."

"Yes, and I can hardly wait for our wedding and life together." She pounced onto the seat, leaned over and kissed him right on the lips.

"Well, I don't know what brought that on, but I'm sure happy about it. I can't wait to check the pastor's schedule and see when he can marry us. Who knows, it might be next week."

He changed gears and drove back into the street, whistling. Content, Susan glanced out the window and smiled at nothing. They reached their destination, and she considered the actual counseling session for the first time.

"Rick, do you know if he's going to talk to us or teach us something?"

"Probably both. I'm sure there is a process for couples before they marry."

Pastor Williford opened the sliding glass door and invited them into the parsonage. The session began in prayer, zipping along with questions, reading scripture, and discussion. Ending in prayer, the counseling was well received by all. Rick stood to leave, and Susan tugged at his arm. Darting a glance at her, he smiled and cleared his throat.

"We want to set the date, Pastor Williford. When are you available to marry us?"

"Well, Mr. Yeager... Rick, may I call you Rick?"

"Yes sir."

"I suggest having the wedding immediately after the morning service not this Sunday, but next Sunday. We will have time to print the announcement in the church bulletin and everyone can plan for it. We have done that before, and the whole congregation was included. That is, if it's agreeable with you and Susan." He squinted at the couple.

"This is where we will be attending church." Rick looked at Susan.

"I like the idea of our church family sharing our wedding." Susan nodded.

"Okay, it is official." Pastor Williford shook hands with the couple. "Congratulations."

"Thank you, sir." Rick ushered Susan out the door, and she turned and waved excitedly at the pastor.

He grinned at them while they climbed into the truck and drove away.

"Can you believe this? It is going to happen so soon." Susan gushed. "There is no way my son can give me away, but he'll be proud to meet the one whom I have chosen." She hesitated a moment, and glanced at Rick. "What do you think about M & M?"

"Perfect! Matt and Mead McKinley, Matt can be my best man, and Mead can give you away. What better beginning in our new life but to start out with them totally in our family?"

"When our home is built, they could live upstairs. I'd love it."

"So would I. I've missed them. They are nearly done remodeling the farmhouse I bought in Tyler. Now, they can live with us as a family and work out at the subdivision. Plenty of houses to build there."

"I can't wait. The brothers are so special to me. I'll never forget them living at the refuge shelter and helping fight the wildfires."

"They are equally special to me also. Their days with no caring family are over." Rick nodded.

"I agree."

Susan and Rick glanced at each other and shared a smile.

They approached an intersection as the light turned red. Rick stopped and scanned the newspaper stand placed near the corner on the sidewalk. He gasped, did a double take at the headline and said half-aloud, "Tyler Bank Robber Still On The Run."

The light changed to green. Rick's tires squealed as he made a U-turn. Susan braced herself to keep from falling while he slid into a parking space across from the yellow newspaper stand. He ran to it, dug into his pocket, and dropped coins into the slot.

Quickly pulling the glass door open, he retrieved the newspaper, scanned over it and returned to the truck.

"What is going on?" Susan looked at him, wide-eyed.

"Your gut feeling, it was correct."

Rick's face turned a light ash grey as he shook his head.

"It's them. It's Tessa and the biker from the courthouse."

"Let me see."

He held the front page toward Susan, and she stared at the mug shots.

"You are right." She waved her hand at the paper. "Take it away; I don't want to see their pictures anymore."

Rick repositioned the newspaper and scanned each column. "His name is Mack Reynolds, and he is still on the run."

Susan chewed on her inner cheek and frowned.

"Here we go; this is what I'm after, the details of the robbery." He spoke matter-of-factly, displaying no emotion. "They entered the bank together. Tessa rushed to a female teller, shoved a bag at her, demanding money. Mack stood near the door, waving his gun at everyone. Eye witnesses said it didn't last but a few minutes. The teller filled the bag, handed it back to Tessa, and the pair left. The teller then collapsed and died of an apparent heart attack. Authorities are waiting on the autopsy results." He paused, rubbed the back of his neck and reexamined the newspaper. "It states that Tessa Yeager was caught running behind the bank. She was arrested and is being held on $500,000 bond. Mack Reynolds remains a fugitive and was nearly apprehended yesterday. He is considered armed and dangerous."

"So Mack could be the reason the law enforcement officers barricaded the street, yesterday. What was he doing at the courthouse earlier?" Susan leaned toward Rick and frowned.

"Don't ask me. It's amazing someone didn't recognize him."

"I don't know. He had a skull cap on his head, wore all the biker garb, and his beard was bushy. He resembled many other bikers, but has a tattoo of a red, white and blue eagle on his back." Susan shrugged. "Who would believe he is still on the run, and Tessa is still sitting in jail?"

"I've bailed her out my last time. She has to be responsible for her own actions." Rick folded the paper and crammed it under the seat.

"How about grabbing a quick bite to eat? I need to get back to the subdivision. Several contractors are hard at work out there."

"Okay with me. I want to call Izabella, and I have plenty to do at the apartment. Clothes don't wash themselves." A half-smile slowly appeared as she turned her face up to Rick.

"They don't take themselves to the dry cleaners, either." He teased.

Susan gave him a good-natured shove. "I'm glad we aren't letting Tessa and Mack ruin our day."

Rick raised an eyebrow. "That won't happen."

Chapter Sixteen

Izabella considered Ben's letter for the umpteenth time since opening it late yesterday evening. After a sleepless night of tossing, her head throbbed from stress.

What gall he has...at least I don't work today...I need time to think...call my attorney...

At nine o'clock, she phoned the law firm.

"Mr. Harrison, please."

"I'm sorry. Mr. Harrison is in court today. May I take a message?"

"No, that won't be necessary. I'll call later." Izabella laid the cellphone on the counter, frowning.

"Did I ever eat last night?" She wondered aloud and remembered events from the previous evening with Rick and Susan's visit, and later opening the awful letter. Realizing she didn't eat, Izabella charged into the kitchen suddenly starved.

I'll never let him irritate me again. He will not get the satisfaction of making me angry.

Gently laying three pieces of bacon across a rack, she placed the plastic rack and tray in the microwave. Whole grain bread was dropped into the toaster, and apple butter retrieved from the fridge. Carefully, she scrambled two eggs, adding one tablespoon of diced onion, two tablespoons of shredded, sharp, cheddar cheese, and two tablespoons of milk.

Ms. Organized with the zip-lock bag of diced onion already prepared...I can do just fine by myself...thank you...

Humming, she removed the bacon in three minutes, poured the grease from the tray into a metal container, and pulled the lever down on the toaster. The egg mixture went into a hot, stainless steel pan—without a Teflon coating, and stirred briskly until it was fully cooked.

Scooting the pan to a cool burner, she retrieved the toast, and placed the two pieces on a plate.

No nasty margarine, no thank you, and my arteries thank you...

In a happy mood, she added a huge dollop of apple butter, the bacon, and folded the eggs onto the plate. She sprinkled course, restaurant-style black pepper, and a dash of light salt on the eggs, looked around and frowned.

Reaching into the fridge, again, she poured a glass of 2% milk—ice cold. Finally, she sat down at the counter, and ate her breakfast, savoring each bite.

My treat for the weeks of having oatmeal for breakfast...before Ben arrived...and my treat for Ben being gone...

Cleaning the kitchen didn't take long. She loaded the dishwasher and put everything else where it belonged. The trash was full so she placed it in the outside receptacle and rolled it to the curb.

During a leisurely walk back to the house, Izabella decided to spend the day taking care of business. She drove to the bank, deposited Logan's check and hurried home. Bills needed to be paid soon, and she had clothes to wash. Entering her home, she gathered the stack of mail on the desk and retrieved her checkbook. Concentrating, she quickly had the utility bills, phone bill, and the entire credit care bill paid. Humming a happy tune, she strolled back outside, placed the return envelopes in the mail-box and raised the flag. The phone rang when she was half-way to the front door. Out of breath, she answered it on the third ring.

"Hello?"

"Mrs. Contrell?"

"Yes."

"I'm Ovella Ferguson, an assistant with the Harrison and Harrison law firm. Mr. Frank Harrison is still in court, but he requested I contact you about the results of his investigation."

"Does he have any information?"

"Oh yes, ma'am. No marriage license was filed on behalf of you and Mr. Ben Wakefield."

The small cellphone slipped from Izabella's grasp, and she felt her heart pound in her ears. Speechless, she hung her head in shame.

"Mrs.Contrell? Are you there, Mrs. Contrell?"

"I'm here."

"Bookkeeping will send you a statement of Mr. Harrison's services for $125.00."

"If you can give me the account number, I'll mail him a check now."

"Certainly, it's 95037."

"Thank you, Ms. Ferguson. This sure was fast. Please thank Mr. Harrison for his help. "

"I will, and it doesn't take long when we have social security and driver's license numbers. If we can be of further assistance to you, don't hesitate to call."

"I do appreciate the offer. Thanks again."

Absentmindedly, she crammed the cellphone in her pocket, and rubbed her arms in dismay.

Not married...we were never married...oh Lord, help me through this...

Slump shouldered, she went to the kitchen and wrote the check with a shaky hand. She searched the phone book for the address, and stared at the envelope.

How could I have been so naïve...so gullible?

Izabella wrote the address on the envelope, slipped the check inside, sealed and stamped it. Pouring a steamy cup of coffee, she carried it, and the envelope outside to the mail box. The red flag was still raised, and she quickly inserted the envelope in the box. Taking a sip of the hot brew, her resolve grew with each step back to the house. She stood near the front door when the dreaded royal blue truck suddenly appeared and raced up her driveway.

"Ben." She uttered under her breath and straightened her posture.

Raising his head, he spotted her outside and brought the truck to a screeching halt. Thrusting his driver's door open, he leapt from the vehicle and sprinted towards Izabella.

"We need to talk. Let's go inside." He stopped directly in front of her and stared.

His unkempt appearance startled her. Uncombed hair, rumpled shirt not tucked into his pants, and a day's growth of whiskers shadowed his face.

"No."

Ben held his mouth in a tight line and firmly laid a hand on her shoulder. "Oh, yes you are."

"Take your hand off of me, or I'll call 9-1-1."

"Don't threaten me." His fingernails dug into her shoulder, and she tried not to flinch as she fumbled in her pocket for the cellphone.

Still making eye contact with Ben, she hit the speed dial button for emergencies. He gasped at the sight of her phone and reached for it.

"9-1-1, what's your emergency?" The dispatcher demanded.

Her strength was no match for him, and he overpowered her. She struggled to keep the phone. He drew his fist back and punched her below an eye, cutting into her skin with his graduation ring. Izabella yelled out in pain, and Ben jerked her arm behind her back.

"9-1-1, what is the emergency?" The dispatcher demanded.

"I'm being assaulted by my ex-boyfriend," Izabella hollered and twisted away from Ben as he snatched at the phone. The coffee cup slipped from her fingers and fell.

"What is your location?" The dispatcher waited and realized the caller was unable to give her address. Still listening, she quickly looked up the address and sent help.

The phone sailed through the air, and Izabella's heart sank. Instead of going after the phone, Ben lunged at Izabella. She ran across the lawn with him chasing after her. Gaining speed, he got close enough to grab her arm, throwing her off balance. She tripped, and they wrestled on the ground. Abruptly, she felt his hand grab onto her ankle. Kicking her foot, she fought Ben and tried to stand, but it was useless. He continued holding her ankle and began dragging her toward the front door of the house.

Sirens screamed through the neighborhood, and Izabella cried with relief.

She listened, the dispatcher heard us in the background, and she sent officers...thank you...thank you...

Upon hearing the sirens approach, mere seconds passed and two patrol cars approached, traveling at a high rate of speed; one parked in the driveway, and one remained at the curb. With lights still flashing, each officer exited from their car. They approached Ben with caution. His mouth fell open, and he immediately released his hold on Izabella.

"Ma'am," the officer made eye contact with Izabella, "come over to us."

Izabella ran to the officers as they gave Ben instructions.

"Drop to your knees, cross your ankles and interlace your fingers on the top of your head."

Silently, he complied and did not resist arrest. One officer handcuffed him while another looked at Izabella. She brushed dirt off her clothes and trembled.

"Do you need medical attention, ma'am?"

Her voice shook. "No, and thank you for getting here as fast as you did." She glanced at Ben and saw him sitting in the back seat of a patrol car.

He's in custody...thank You, Lord...

At that moment, he snapped at the nearest officer. "Hey, you are making a big mistake. That is my wife. We are just having an argument."

"Ma'am, is this correct? Is he your husband?"

"No, he is Ben Wakefield, and I am Izabella Contrell."

"Do you want to press charges, ma'am?"

"Yes, I certainly do. I don't ever want to experience another attack."

"We'll need you to make a statement."

"I can do it now." She looked at Ben again and felt no sympathy.

An officer addressed Ben solemnly. "You have the right to remain silent ..."

Izabella overheard the officer giving the Miranda Rights to Ben and watched the second officer take pictures of everything, including both her and Ben. He also wrote her statement as she recalled what had happened.

As both officers left, Izabella had one last glimpse of Ben. He remained sullen.

Chapter Seventeen

Susan completed her morning devotional and contemplated having another hot cup of coffee when an aroma wafted through the apartment. She hastened from her bedroom and entered the kitchen.

Dixie, her back to Susan, stood in front of the stove.

"Oh, there is no mistaking that smell, definitely bacon. How tempting."

Dixie spun around, clearly startled, and her face flushed. "Oh hi, Mrs. Penleigh."

"Hi yourself. Good to see you busy. I had bursts of energy before each of my children were born."

"Well, it's still a bit early for me. I can't seem to get enough to eat, though."

"Your due date may be closer than you calculated. Want me to help with the food?"

"No, I'm nearly done. I'd invite you to grab a plate, but this is for me and Lee. We are eating out on the front porch, today."

"Well, that's okay. How nice to have breakfast there." Susan headed out of the room. She hesitated, turned and leaned against the door frame. "Oh, did you two decide on a name for the baby?"

"Yes, we did, it's Venita Irene Penleigh. Her initials spell: V.I.P. and she *will* be a very important person."

"She certainly will. How unique, V.I.P. and what a beautiful name." Susan waited for Dixie to turn from the stove again, made eye contact with her, and gave her a warm smile.

Dixie froze. "I...I have to go outside now." She stammered and retrieved a tray from under the cabinet.

"Enjoy your morning." Susan escaped to the bedroom.

Wow, that was as close to friendly as we have ever been...

Hearing the front door slam twice, Susan decided she would have the kitchen to herself, again. Darting back in, she glanced at the coffee pot, and muttered to herself. "I can't believe I forgot a cup of coffee."

"I can't believe it, either." Rick stood in the doorway with a half-smile on his face.

"Rick, you're here!" Susan ran to him.

"In person." He quickly hugged her, and planted a kiss on her forehead. "Lady, where are the cups?"

Susan, excited and embarrassed, looked down to hide a grin, snatched two cups from the cabinet and poured their coffee.

"Have a seat." She beamed, nodding at the small table with two chairs. Carefully, she sat the cups on the table and flopped in a chair. Rick sprawled in the other one.

"What a surprise."

"I thought you'd like it."

They sipped the coffee, and Rick raised an eyebrow. "Want to go with me this morning to see the progress at the subdivision?"

"Are you kidding? Yes, of course."

"So we stroll pass King Kong and Ms. Spiteful... excuse me, King Kong and *Ms. Pitiful*, in order to leave the house. How is that working for you?"

Susan straightened her posture, and stifled a smile. "I admit it is awkward at times but it is working. You're descriptions are right on target by the way."

"Thank you. I don't call people names, but occasionally cartoon characters or movie heroes come to mind. Private joke, you understand?"

"Absolutely, and I see how it can soften the blow from someone's verbal attack."

"Well, there you go. Instead of a lady rushing through the check-out line yelling at you, for instance; you could picture the road runner pausing to beep at you."

Susan chuckled. "Brings a whole new perspective to dealing with stress."

Rick rose and took the coffee cups to the sink. "Life is full of daily choices. You can decide to make it a great day or not."

Susan got her purse and keys. "Let's start our great day off chatting with King Kong and Ms. Pitiful."

"I'll try to be as serious as possible." Rick assured her.

"And I'll try not to have a goofy smile."

"No, don't say goofy smile. I'll think of Goofy the cartoon character, and when I look at you, *I'll* end up with a goofy smile. We will be serious and cordial."

"Lead the way."

They left the kitchen and hurried out into the hall. Daylight filtered through the screen door at the end of the hallway. Rick and Susan walked at a fast pace and suddenly frowned. The sound of Dixie and Lee's loud voice's echoing from the front porch could not be ignored.

"I think they are becoming hostile," Susan whispered.

Rick pushed on the screen door and its squeaking grew more prominent as he opened it wide. He and Susan stepped out on the porch perfectly serious. Lee and Dixie stopped snapping at each other and stared at Rick and Susan for a brief moment.

"Hey, you found her." Lee motioned towards Susan.

"Yes, thanks for the directions." He lightly held Susan's arm and ushered her across the porch to the steps.

"We'll see you both later." Susan addressed the couple and descended the steps.

"Well, we might not be here when you return," Dixie stammered.

Lee scoffed. "That is, if we can agree on a movie for later. Talk about a debate, it was almost tooth and nail."

"It wasn't that bad," Dixie sang out.

"How did you two agree about the details of your upcoming wedding? What is your secret?" Lee followed Rick and Susan down the steps and stood on the lawn.

"God comes first. Susan is second. It's the same with her." Rick nodded.

"That's right. God is first. Rick is second. We'd love for you both to join us in worship sometime. Pastor Williford is going to marry us...not this Sunday, but the next Sunday."

"I know the church. Mother was a member and often spoke on not being self-centered. Thanks for the invitation, we'd love to come." He turned to look at Dixie. She smiled and seemed to relax.

Rick and Susan waved and entered the truck.

"Lord, I am the clay, and You are the potter. I am Your vessel, use me for Your purpose. In Jesus powerful name, Amen." Susan proclaimed and scooted over on the seat, closer to Rick. "Do you see how God works?" She blurted. "We were having harmless fun, not hurting anyone or anyone's feelings. Then... bam... we suddenly have an opportunity to witness and invite them to church."

"Feels good... thank You Lord, thank You, Lord!" He squeezed her hand making eye contact, and they shared a warm smile.

◆

Entering the new subdivision, Susan gazed from one area to another.

"This place is a beehive of activity. I had no idea." She immediately turned her head for another view.

Dump trucks unloaded and left as road graders spread the mixture on the new road. Rick finally stopped near several workers and rolled his window down.

"Keep this up, and you might get a paycheck." Rick teased.

One man grinned. "Coming along, right on time."

Rick nodded and backed out.

"Don't want to get in their way. Feel like walking?"

"Sure."

He drove on a dirt trail and parked the truck near the river.

"Come on." He helped her down from the cab. Rick pointed to the thick woods and sighed noisily.

"Feral hogs have been discovered a mile from here. They are all over Texas now. I have no choice but thin the woods and set traps. One was reported to be over four hundred pounds and came charging from the woods toward a landowner. Fortunately, the man escaped unharmed."

"Oh Rick, how scary!" Susan's face quickly paled, and she leaned against the truck. "I don't want to go walking."

"It's not that bad. Hunters and trappers are in the area taking care of the problem. The wild hogs can't take control."

Susan flinched, and Rick changed the subject.

"Hungry?"

"Yes, I am. How about you?"

"Starved. Any place you have in mind?"

"I can't recall anything after having the wild hog conversation." She chuckled.

"Sorry, I didn't mean to frighten you. I do want you to be informed."

"I'll take informed, any time."

"Works for me. Pizza okay?"

"I'd love pizza."

Entering the truck, Rick winked at Susan, and she scooted closer. They leaned against each other as Rick drove off. Leaving the subdivision, he honked the horn at the workers and all waved.

"Happy?" Rick lowered his voice.

"Couldn't be any happier. How..."

Rick interrupted her. "How about me? Well, I am feeling like a giddy young man on my first date." He smiled at her, and Susan noticed his laugh lines crinkle from the corners of his eyes.

"Thanks, I am impressed."

They enjoyed a pleasant silence for the remainder of the drive. Rick drove into the parking lot and circled the pizza restaurant twice before finding a parking space.

"Must be good." He commented as they entered and selected a booth.

The waitress approached, and Rick and Susan spoke in unison, "We want the buffet."

Rick shook his head. "We went from first date to old married couple in ten seconds."

"Well, let's try another one. Water?" Susan queried Rick.

"Two waters, please." Rick spoke to the waitress.

They burst out laughing and enjoyed the meal. Susan talked non-stop, and Rick listened to her with a glowing expression on his face. Leaving the restaurant, they walked through the parking lot, both smiling at nothing.

"Here you go." He grabbed her arm and helped her in the truck.

He made rapid strides to the driver's door and eased inside.

"Let's go back to your apartment; the front porch is calling my name."

"What's the term they use in the service, R & R?"

"Rest and relaxation; yes ma'am, our number one priority today." He put his arm around her shoulder and using his left hand, expertly maneuvered the truck from the parking space.

Susan leaned her head against his shoulder briefly, and pulled back. "No distracting you while you drive." She glanced at him. "So, about the front porch…"

"I have plans…" He looked straight ahead.

"Shall I guess?"

"No, it's a surprise."

"One hint?"

"I have plans." Rick flashed a smile.

"Such a broad statement, thanks a lot. I can be patient." She squirmed in her seat and glimpsed out the side window.

"Well, I can't. Anticipation is mounting…can't wait to see your reaction to my surprise." He pressed his lips tightly together.

"You are trying to keep from smiling."

"No, I'm not."

"Rick, you just missed the exit." Susan squinted at the glare on the exit sign.

"Oh, I'll be so glad when we are married, and I don't have to drive to see you. It seems I spend as much time sleeping at the River Town Inn as I do driving this highway."

Susan opened her mouth to say something, and then thought better of it.

He carefully made his way to the nearest frontage road, turned back and reentered the highway. "Excuse me for blowing off steam. I get frustrated when it seems there aren't enough hours in the day to do what I want."

"We all have to vent, sometimes. I can't count the times I've been talking and drove right past the place I had planned on going."

"You are only saying that to make me feel better."

"No, it can happen. We are human and don't concentrate sometimes."

"Well, we'll both try harder to focus when driving. Thankfully, neither one of us has had a car wreck."

"Or truck wreck."

"You don't say truck wreck, my dear."

"It does sound weird. Anyway, I agree with the 'try harder' and yes, I certainly am thankful." She flipped a loose strand of hair from her face to behind her ear, and nodded.

◆

Approaching Susan's neighborhood, Rick slowed his vehicle. Traffic was light. He glanced at Susan. "Wonder if Lee and Dixie are at home?"

"We'll soon find out."

The house came into their view, and Lee's truck was parked in the driveway.

"Surprise, they are here." Susan gazed out the window. "Only not on the front porch."

"Possibly having a leisure afternoon on the back lawn, who knows? Maybe roasting hot dogs on the grill."

"It may sound doubtful to you, but I am glad they enjoy each other's company."

Rick parked his truck on the street close to the curb, and they exited. "I think we'll both be glad to see them in church." He retrieved a slender package from the tool box in the bed of the truck.

"Oh, yes, more than anything." Susan glanced at the package. "What is that, a roll of posters?"

"Could be." He reached for her hand, and they rambled over the lawn. Tall scraggly patches of Bahia grass brushed against their legs. Black seeds on the top of the stalks clung to their pants legs, and Susan paused to flick them off.

"I hope we don't end up with this in our lawn."

"It takes over quick. Lawn maintenance companies actually spread the seeds from one lawn to another. The seeds fall from the mowers. As long as we do our own mowing, we can lay St. Augustine grass sod and not worry about it."

Susan nodded. "I like St. Augustine."

They skipped up the steps, reached the porch and settled in the chairs. Rick gripped the package and held it in the air. "Ready for your surprise?"

"Show me!" Susan lunged forward in her chair, and Rick ripped the end of the package open, pulling out a long, rolled paper. Spreading it across the table, Susan looked closer at it and yelled," House plans!"

"Yes ma'am, three sets to choose from."

"You said you had plans..." Susan beamed.

"The first one has a built-in greenhouse, a sun room, open kitchen, L-shape living room with fireplace, dining room, three bedrooms, two bathrooms, and laundry room downstairs. Master bedroom, sitting area and bath upstairs. Four car garage."

"Sounds wonderful, but too large."

"I agree. Number two has the master bedroom downstairs, large walk-in closets, seating area, and huge bathroom all on one side of the house. Open kitchen, large pantry, L-shape living room with fireplace, dining room, utility room, laundry room, a sun room, extra bedroom and bath. Upstairs has two bedrooms and one bath, and a game room. Three car garage." Rick paused. "What do you think of this one?"

"Show me how it's laid out. I think we may have found the right one."

Rick ran his finger over the drawing and pointed out each room. "I can see us living in this house, and both M & M having their bedrooms upstairs. Privacy for all of us, I like it."

"So do I. No need to keep looking." Susan glanced at the plans again and nodded.

"Done deal?"

"Done deal. You can roll them back up, but be careful of ours. Don't let anything happen to it." She stood and walked around the porch. "I can't sit still. I'm so excited!" She laughed and threw a fist into the air."Woo-hoo," she hollered and ran up to Rick.

"Your eyes are sparkling, lady. Welcome to our new life." He lifted her up, quickly swinging her around, and their laughter filled the air.

"Mrs. Penleigh, Rick; hurry, it's Dixie."

Rick stopped and put Susan down. They stared at Lee, momentarily speechless.

"She is having pains."

All three rushed into the house. Charging down the hall, their footsteps sounded like an army of men wearing heavy work boots. Bam, bam, bam, they ran into Lee's open apartment doorway.

Dixie sat on the couch, held her belly with both hands and moaned.

"It hurts," she wailed.

Susan knelt beside her and felt her forehead. Lee stood just inside the door visibly shaking.

"Rick bring my car around. We are taking her to the emergency room. My keys are in my purse on the porch."

He took off, and Susan glanced at Lee. His complexion paled, and he kept swallowing hard.

"Lee find the phone book. Call the hospital and tell them we are bringing Dixie Penleigh in to the E.R., and she may be having her baby."

Without a word, he too left the room in a split second.

Susan noticed Dixie's purse on the floor and grabbed it.

"You will be fine, Dixie. We live close to the hospital. Rick will be here soon with my car. You don't have any fever so that's good."

Dixie nodded her head and took a deep breath.

Rick darted in and glanced at the women. "Let me help you up, Dixie. We'll go slow."

She whimpered. Rick put his arm around her for support. They slowly inched across the room and down the hall. Descending the front steps of the porch was awkward. Susan brought Dixie's purse and retrieved hers. Finally, Dixie was in the car, and Susan jumped into the back seat with her. Rick started the car and drove away.

Dixie laid her head back against the seat and emitted a low moan.

Susan gently ran her hand across Dixie's hair, and it seemed to calm her.

"Where is Lee?"

The question jolted Susan.

Lee has disappeared. I don't remember his truck following us...I don't even remember him coming outside...

"We didn't have time to talk to Lee. He hurried to call the hospital."

"Oh, that is right." She bellowed out again as another pain shot through her body.

Rick stopped at the E.R. entrance, and an attendant approached the car with a wheel chair.

"Penleigh?"

"Yes, and she is ..."

"I know. We received the phone call."

Dixie was carefully removed from the car and placed into the wheel chair.

"Go with her," Rick yelled to Susan. "I'll give her information to the admitting desk."

Susan turned, pitched Dixie's purse to Rick, and darted after the attendant and Dixie.

A security officer entered and glanced at Rick. "Sir, you need to move your car. They can wait for the information."

"Yes, of course. I wasn't thinking."

Rick left, toting the purse and found a parking space. He had to walk a half mile back to the E.R. entrance. Out of breath, he managed to locate Dixie's I.D. and insurance card in her billfold. He gave those to the admitting clerk and completed the necessary paperwork.

Exhausted, he slumped into a chair in the waiting room holding Dixie's purse on his lap.

Two hours later, Susan entered the waiting room, accidentally banging her purse into the doorway. The commotion startled Rick. He sprang from the chair and hurried towards her. "You look tired. Any word from the doctor?"

"It has been a long day... pleasant, but long." She exhaled a deep, gratifying sigh. "Yes. He thinks its false labor pains but wants to keep her overnight in case he's wrong. She is almost asleep. I'll come back and check on her tomorrow. They have my phone number if they need me."

Rick yawned. "I'll go get the car."

"That's okay. We can stroll to the parking lot."

Rick smiled, and they slowly made their way to the vehicle. He drove Susan back to the apartment and walked her to the door.

"Here's Dixie's purse and your car keys." His voice thickened. "I'm beat. I'll be going straight to the Inn." He kissed her and ambled to his truck. Opening the driver's door, he twisted to one side and yelled at Susan.

"Wonder what happened to Lee?"

"I think it was too much for him."

Chapter Eighteen

Izabella dressed for work, thought of her friend and glanced at the wall clock.

Five after eight A.M., Susan should be up by now.

Grasping the cell phone, she clicked speed dial for Susan's number. Quickly pressing the speaker phone, she drummed her fingertips on the dresser and waited. Susan answered on the second ring.

"Good morning, girl!" Izabella's voice bubbled. "I didn't wake you, did I?"

"No, I finished breakfast about an hour ago."

"Good. Listen, I work the ten till seven shift, today. Mind if I run by, and we chat a bit? I need to talk to you about something. Hope you aren't too busy."

"Fine. All I have to do is check on Dixie later this morning, and I don't work until tomorrow. Come on over."

"I'm on my way." Izabella snatched her name badge from the dresser and pinned it to her uniform. Sailing out the door, she took off in her car and arrived at Susan's apartment in less than ten minutes.

Izabella, while parking next to the curb, spotted Susan on the porch swing. Hurrying, she crossed the lawn and skipped up the porch steps.

"How inviting, this is so cozy!"

"Thanks, it is relaxing." Susan placed her feet on the floor and stopped the swing. "I'll move over. Have a seat."

Izabella joined Susan on the wooden swing, and they slowly set it in motion.

"I love the creaking sound as it swings back and forth." Izabella's voice lost its power as she paused, and stared down at her feet. " This is so enjoyable, but I don't know if I can ever feel better again."

"Nothing can be that bad. What's wrong?"

Wringing her hands together, Izabella abruptly made eye contact with Susan. "I discovered Ben and I were never married. You were right, I didn't really know him."

"I am so sorry. I know this is hard on you." Susan grabbed Izabella's hands and held them still. Frowning, she motioned to her hands. "Don't let him upset you like this. He may not be here to see your reaction, but he is winning."

"How can I forgive myself?" Trembling, her voice rose in anguish. "I am so ashamed, Susan. We were *not* married!"

"He tricked you. As harsh as it sounds, *deal* with it and move on. At least it is over...he's not bothering you, is he?"

"Not after yesterday, I had him arrested."

"Arrested?" Susan's voice cracked. She released Izabella's hands and waved her own into the air. "What in the world did he do?"

"He became violent...insisted we get back together. I called 9-1-1."

"Izabella, when someone can't dominate you, they will try to destroy you...verbally, or physically. They *have* to be number one, they *have* to be in charge, and they *have* to be the center of attention. That's when *you* stay away from *them*. In this case, Ben didn't win. I'm proud you pressed charges against him."

"Oh, I had to. He was not going to get away with it, and I sure didn't want it to happen again. What I *want* is to get on with my life."

"Izabella, you are getting there. Turn the whole situation over to God, and He'll take care of it. The stress will be behind you."

"When I woke up this morning, I did pray. I even prayed for Ben, and I forgave him. I won't be around him again, but I did pray for his soul."

"Good. We pray for our enemies to know Christ, and if we don't forgive them, God won't forgive us of our sins. Matthew 6:14-15; 'For if you forgive their trespasses, your Heavenly Father will also forgive you. But if you forgive not men their trespasses, neither will your Father forgive your trespasses.' Izabella, true forgiveness comes from the heart, and God knows when it is true. Read Matthew 18:35."

"Thanks for reminding me, Susan. With so many people scheming, hiding the truth, and having ulterior motives; it is important *to* forgive."

"Whoa, what brought on all of those negative issues?"

"Our job. Some people will do anything to benefit themselves at the risk of others."

"Izabella, I agree. We are referring to Mr. Shafer, aren't we?"

"Yes, and it involves so many others. He gave the health inspector three family-size packages of T-bone steaks. Ever notice none of us have health certificates?"

"Incredible. I never realized. I didn't know we needed one." Susan paused and shook her head repeatedly. "He even has us sell previously frozen chocolate candy full of dead bugs."

"Eww! I didn't know about that. How repulsive..." Izabella drew her mouth together and shivered.

Susan stopped the swing and stood by the porch railing. "Did I mention he has a girlfriend? She makes our schedule...I had no idea."

"Welcome to our friendly grocery store." Izabella ran her hand up the chain holding the now still, wooden swing. "You know, I've been toying with an idea. Since the wildfires, our town has bounced back tremendously. I love children, and I'm sure there's a lot of red tape involved, but I want to open my own day-care center."

"Izabella, you'd be a natural...perfect. "

"Thanks, I am checking into it, and pardon the pun, but I may not have to keep my checking job."

"Oh, that was good, and if you need an employee, let me know." Susan lifted a single eyebrow. "It is a shame about our work environment. If you speak up and complain, you lose your job."

The swing creaked as Izabella set it back in motion. "Enough about work. How are things going for you?"

Susan muttered to herself and pointed a finger at Izabella. "You would not believe it. Dixie is in the hospital. Rick and I took her late yesterday. It *is* false labor pains because no one called me during the night about the baby's birth. Oh, and she is *clinging* to the landlord. All of my efforts to help her were dismissed. She only spends the night with me. So she hasn't shopped for the baby, no diapers, nothing, but she did name the baby."

"Tragic. Does she not realize she will have a baby in her life? A precious treasure from God? What did she name the baby girl?"

"Venita Irene Penleigh. Her initials are V.I.P., and Dixie is very proud of that. She said the baby will be a very important person."

"Beautiful name, and how original about the initials. How are you and Rick?"

"Rick and I are spending more time together and getting closer and closer. Our wedding date is approaching fast. Pastor Williford will marry us not this Sunday, but next Sunday. Okay, maid of honor, get ready for that." Susan stated.

"What are you planning on wearing, so I won't match the color?"

"Well, it's going to be at the church. I'll wear a simple light blue dress, and you can wear a pastel green dress. It will be a small wedding, and I can have blue, green, and white in the flower arrangements. What do you think?"

"I think it would be awesome."

"The church is furnishing the reception. I'm so excited."

"I'm so happy for you, Susan." Izabella looked at her watch and exclaimed, "Oh, I have to go. I have to be at work in thirty minutes." She jumped from the swing and fled down the porch steps. "Call me later," she yelled and ran to her car.

"I will." Susan replied.

Izabella's car roared off down the road. She couldn't hear a word Susan said.

Chapter Nineteen

The hospital was packed. Susan edged through the crowded waiting room and approached the admissions desk.

"I'm here to check on my daughter-in-law, Dixie Penleigh. She is in the maternity wing."

"Our system is slow, today. It will take a minute for the computer to reboot." The clerk scanned the screen. "Come on, come on," she demanded. "Oh, here we go." Whirling her fingertips across the keyboard, she glanced at Susan. "Dixie Penleigh is in room 480. Use the elevators near the gift shop, and her room will be down the right hall when you arrive upstairs."

"Thank you." Susan made her way to the elevators. One of the doors opened, and she waited as the people inside disembarked. One elderly woman was rolled out in a wheel chair. She held herself erect and chatted with the male attendant. He had one hand on the patient's I.V. pole, and the other on the wheel chair.

"Have you heard anyone say when I can go home?" Her voice cracked. Turning her head, she briefly looked around. The hallway was busy. Anxious patients and visitors bustled to their destinations.

"Not today, Mrs. Sport. We are going to the radiology department. Dr. Perkins ordered an x-ray. He wants one of your right knee, maybe two." The attendant teased, and Susan watched as Mrs. Sport's eyes gleamed with merriment.

"He is the best doctor in town. I'd go as far as saying the best doctor in Texas." She beamed.

Susan blinked and studied the woman's face closer.

It can't be…is this the same Mrs. Sport who mentored to so many teenagers in River Town?

"Excuse me, ma'am, I'm Susan Penleigh. I worked at the high school before it was consumed by the wildfires."

"I have heard your name before. You were the secretary, is that right?"

"Yes, and I am so proud to meet you. I read the article in the paper about all the years you mentored teenagers. You had such a positive effect on many generations."

"Come see me sometime, and we can talk about it. Do you enjoy flowers?"

"Yes, I do."

"My greenhouse is full of African Violets. I'll show you how easy it is to start a new plant. "

The attendant pushed the wheel chair around and dragged the I.V. pole. It rolled along, and he nodded at Susan. "We have to leave, or we'll be late."

"I'd love to visit sometime." Susan took a few steps with them.

"I live at the corner of Quail Run and Cypress Drive. It's the house landscaped with azalea bushes." Mrs. Sport instructed. She waved, and the attendant wheeled her away.

"I'll come and visit," Susan sang out. The pair happily chatted with each other and continued down the hall.

Susan caught a ride with the next elevator and hurried to locate Dixie's room on the fourth floor. Advancing toward room 480, Susan frowned at the site of a sign on the door. Alarmed, she walked closer, and read the sign, 'No Visitors.'

Hmm...why no visitors? Whose idea was that?

Susan pivoted and marched to the nurses' station in a huff. Three employees each sat in front of a computer and the phone was ringing. One woman hurried to answer it while another noticed Susan and met her at the counter.

"Good morning." She gave her full attention to Susan.

"Good morning. I'm Susan Penleigh. I came to check on my daughter-in- law, Dixie Penleigh. There is a no visitor's sign on her door. What is going on?"

"What room number is it?"

"Room 480."

"Oh, that is because Doctor Adahy is examining her now. If you'll have a seat in the waiting room, I'll tell him you are here for an update on her condition. It's the waiting room directly across from the elevators. We also have another one near the delivery rooms in case Dixie is about to give birth. We'll let you know something soon."

"Thank you."

It's too early for Dixie to deliver...I think she has two more weeks before her due date...

Lost in thought, Susan meandered through the maze of halls and ended up at the nursery. Scanning the babies lined up near the window brought an immediate comfort to her frame of mind. Some had creamy complexions, while others had blotchy red, fat cheeks. Either a mop of hair on their head, or almost bald with fuzz on top; all were so sweet and so beautiful. Two couples awed over one particular baby and glanced at Susan as she stood near the window.

"Can you tell we are new grandparents?"

"Yes. What a darling baby. Congratulations."

They gave a chorus of 'thanks' and turned back to gaze at the baby. Susan strolled to find the waiting room.

Why does Dixie have such bizarre behavior towards me? Why can't she let us enjoy this time together?

Following arrows with information posted at each corner wall, Susan finally returned to Dixie's wing of rooms and found the waiting room. Lowering herself into a chair, she leaned to the side and selected a magazine from the end table. She thumbed through it, and thought again of the nursery full of babies. Filled with sudden nostalgia, she remembered when she had each of her own babies; Scott, Karen and Molly.

All precious...all grown...all with their own individual personalities...I do miss them. Breaks my heart not getting to see them, but the girls made a life in Washington, and Scott's life is in the armed service...

"Mrs. Penleigh? I'm Dr. Adahy."

Startled, Susan stood and shook his hand. "Dr. Adahy... Adahy," she repeated." I don't want to embarrass you, but what a lovely name."

"Why, thank you. I'm Native American. Adahy is Cherokee for lives in the woods."

"I traveled through the Cherokee Nation in Oklahoma when I drove from Washington to Texas. The country is breathtaking." She eased back into her chair.

"That is my home." With a slight smile, he nodded and sat next to Susan.

Facing her, he sighed. "Mrs. Penleigh, I have to be blunt. Dixie has developed a blood pressure problem."

Susan gasped and absentmindedly gripped the armrests of the chair with both hands. Her knuckles turned white.

Dr. Adahy glanced at her fists and frowned. "I don't want to alarm you, but I cannot let the situation bounce from low to extremely high blood pressure. I am forced to perform a C-Section and take the baby." He paused. "Dixie and the baby will have some risk, but it beats the alternative. I will operate immediately."

"Thank you." Susan swallowed hard and felt her chest tighten.

Rising, he briskly walked out of the room.

Susan silently prayed, and trembling, retrieved the cellphone from her purse.

Whom should I call first, and I wonder if I'll still be able to work tomorrow? Can't call Izabella, she's at work now...

Clicking Rick's name on speed dial, she jabbed at the speaker phone button and waited.

"Rick? The doctor is about to perform a C-Section on Dixie. She is having trouble with her blood pressure."

"I'm on my way." The call ended fast, and Susan sat still, thinking. After a moment, a recording from the phone company played, 'if you'd like to make a call, please hang up, and try again.' Clearing doubt from her mind, she clicked for a dial tone, and decided not to work her shift scheduled for the following day.

She dialed the store, and after selecting options on the phone menu, Mrs. Duvall finally answered.

"Mrs. Duvall, this is Susan Penleigh. I'm at the hospital. My daughter-in-law is having her baby. There are complications so I won't be able to work tomorrow."

She listened to her supervisor. "Thank you for understanding. Oh, could you tell my friend, Izabella about it during her break?" She paused. "Thanks again. Yes, I will keep you informed. Goodbye."

Susan stared at the television mounted on the wall. The local news channel was on, but the volume was too low. Frustrated, she tried straining to listen, but it was useless. Scanning her surroundings she searched for a remote but couldn't find it. She did spot a drink machine in the corner, and dug a dollar bill from her purse. Halfway to the machine, Susan accidentally dropped the dollar. Her breathing accelerated while she bent over and retrieved it.

Calm down…get your water and be patient…

Breathing loudly, she slipped the dollar bill in the slot and depressed the button for bottled water. Standing on one foot then the other, she heard it falling and watched the opening at the bottom of the machine. The second the bottle landed, she snatched it, and ran out—directly into a group entering the waiting room.

"Ummph." A nurse grabbed her chest and stared wide-eyed at Susan.

Susan, overwhelmed with embarrassment, tightly clutched the plastic bottle. Realizing the sudden warmth on her face was seen as crimson, her embarrassment worsened, and her voice weakened. "Oh, I am so sorry. Are you okay?"

"Yes, I'm just surprised. That was quite a powerful blow. And you?"

"No physical damage done. Restless, and a wondering mind is no excuse, but that is what happened." She observed the other people. "Sorry for the intrusion."

"Nothing to worry about." One woman stated as they meandered to a row of chairs.

"Well, here is the waiting room." The nurse frowned and motioned to the program. "How can anyone hear the news? I'll be back and adjust the sound." She entered an office across the hall and returned with a long-handled screwdriver.

"Someone got off with our remote so we improvise." She announced and darted to the television. Quickly popping the side control-panel open with the tool; she reached and turned the volume higher. "Got to run." The nurse held onto the screwdriver and left.

"Thanks for bringing us here," one woman yelled.

"See, she's taking the tool with her, probably going to check on a patient." One man laughed. "It happens to all of us. Get in a hurry and don't think straight. Can you imagine how the patient will react when she charges in the room with the screwdriver in her hand?"

Someone chuckled, and Susan had to smile. "We do have our moments. She could have been annoyed with me for bumping into her, but she wasn't, and I'm thankful she was so considerate to stop what she was doing to fix the television."

"So true. With so many rude people just working for a paycheck nowadays, it's refreshing to see someone go above and beyond their job description to help customers." An older woman spoke and fingered her necklace.

"Things have changed since I retired." An older man joined the discussion. "If we give a recommendation to her superiors, she may get in trouble for straying from her duties. Yes, sir, things are different with this generation." He raised his head to watch the news and everyone grew quiet.

Susan reflected on his words, and on today's events. Her stomach knotted, and she avoided further conversation. Studying the T.V., she tried to focus on what the news anchor was saying.

Rick walked into the waiting room at that moment. Susan sprang from the chair and rushed to him. He embraced her and neither spoke.

Susan trembled and remained silent.

"Is everything okay?"

"Yes, I'm just totally drained. It's been stressful." Susan laughed nervously.

He answered with a small nod, and rubbed the back of her shoulders, holding her close.

Susan let the relief sink in. Her body sagged against him, and her legs went wobbly. Using humor to lighten the moment, Susan whispered," I am literally falling...I feel as weak and shaky as a thirteen year old on her first date."

Rick glanced at her in disbelief, noticed the worry shadowing her face and instantly became alarmed. He walked her to the nearest row of chairs positioned against all four walls. Helping Susan into a chair, he then slipped in the one next to her. Concerned, he regarded her carefully. "Are you sure you are okay?"

Susan squirmed in her chair. "Yes, I am okay. It *has* to do with hormones or something. I haven't felt so emotional or vulnerable in a long time."

"Even Superwoman has limits. Aren't you supposed to work tomorrow?"

"Superwoman? No, no, that is not me." She shook her head and a warm smile appeared on her face. "I was supposed to work, but I called in and explained the situation to my supervisor. She was wonderful about it."

"Good." He hesitated and nodded solemnly. "Superwoman."

Susan bit her lips to keep from smiling, and it didn't work.

Rick winked at her.

"Mrs. Penleigh?" A male nurse stood at the door and scanned every face in the waiting room.

"Here." Susan stiffened, and held her hand in the air.

"Doctor Adahy has begun surgery. So far, mother and baby are doing fine. I will be giving you progress reports."

"Thank you." Susan sat upright and watched him leave.

"Lean back and relax. We may be in for a long evening and night." Rick shifted his weight in the chair. "Try to sleep."

Susan curled up in the chair and rested her head upon his arm. People were scattered about the room in various stages of rest.

An hour passed. The hum of voices from the television continued as some snored and others played games on their smart-phones. Rick observed the wall clock often. Susan slumped in her chair and was sound asleep. An unspoken hush settled over the room. Another hour passed when it occurred to Rick that Susan may have to quit her job and take care of the baby.

Rick dozed for a while, and awoke slightly, feeling his head bobbing. Yawning, he positioned his hand over his mouth, sat at attention, and noticed someone enter the room.

Wearing scrubs, Dr. Adahy wearily veered towards Susan.

"Mrs. Penleigh?"

Susan stirred. She sucked her breath in as she awoke and recognized the doctor.

"Dr. Adahy. What has happened?"

"I apologize for not keeping you informed. We had two emergencies and some of my staff were needed in other operating rooms. Dixie's condition is stable. The baby is indeed doing well. A preemie baby for sure. She will remain with us, and according to her weight gain, should be able to leave in about two weeks. That is if my calculations are correct. I want the new medication for Dixie to take effect before releasing her. She is still sedated, but you may visit the nursery to see the baby. Don't let the tubes scare you. The baby is on oxygen for precaution. I have her heart monitored also."

"Oh, I'm so thankful. They will both be fine, and I can't wait to see the baby." Susan beamed.

Rick seized her arm. "Wait. Did you tell the doctor about the test?"

Susan felt her face flush and turned as the doctor spoke.

"What test, Mrs. Penleigh?"

Reaching in her purse, Susan took out a large, yellow envelope.

"My son, Scott, doesn't believe he is the baby's father. He is in the Marines and is stationed in Afghanistan. He wants you to do a DNA on the baby and send the results to his doctor at his base. They have his DNA and will do a paternity test. The information is in this envelope."

She thrust the envelope towards the doctor, and he accepted it.

"Is Dixie aware of this request?"

"No, I don't think so."

"I will discuss it with her and handle the paperwork."

Chapter Twenty

"I need to see your driver's license." Izabella bent over the counter and studied the customer's check.

Unsnapping her billfold, the woman handed the card to Izabella, ducked her head and spoke in a low voice. "Who is that girl in the low waist short-shorts and halter top?"

"Where?"

"She's squatted by the candy rack, carrying a hand-held machine."

Izabella straightened and instantly spotted the girl. "Oh, I see her now, looks like she is ordering."

"Well, who is she?"

"I don't know. I'm new here, and I haven't noticed her before."

"Dressed so skimpy, you'd think everyone would be pointing at her. How can she be allowed to work without wearing a uniform? The rest of you wear one."

"She may not work here, but for another company, or she's doing a survey. Who knows?"

"I plan on finding out. What a disgrace to show so much skin in a public place. I thought this was a respectable business. Where is your manager?"

"He isn't here."

"I want to report this to someone. Who is available that will talk to me?"

"Mrs. Duvall is at the customer service desk. She is our front-end supervisor."

"Thank you, and I'll push my own grocery cart there. I don't intend to leave today without some answers." The customer bustled directly to Mrs. Duvall.

Izabella greeted a new customer who approached the check-out lane. Forcing herself, Izabella refrained from stealing a glance at the service desk. Conversation between the irate customer, and Mrs. Duvall was constant but muffled.

I can't dwell on their encounter...whatever happens is out of my control...

Being her usual cheerful self, Izabella waited on customer after customer as they continued shopping non-stop all morning. She kept up with the pace until the majority had left. At the first sign of a lull, Audrey Duvall hurried to close Izabella's and Amanda's lanes.

"Go on break while you can. Fifteen minutes, ladies."

Halfway back to the service desk, she turned and marched toward Izabella.

"Wait a minute. There is something I want to tell you."

Jumping to conclusions, Izabella flashed images of worse case scenarios through her mind. Adrenaline spikes raced her heart and pounded in her ears. Feeling rooted to the spot, she waited for Audrey Duvall's return, yet wanted to hide. Engulfed in fear, Izabella knew without a doubt, the irate customer from this morning had caused waves large enough to sink her job.

"Your friend, Susan Penleigh phoned. Her daughter-in-law is having the baby today." Audrey seemed content, and with an unhurried walk, returned to the customer service desk.

Izabella could still hear the pounding inside her ears as anxiety decreased, washing over her in pure comfort.

"Wow, great news," Amanda sang out.

"No joke." Izabella agreed and gave a silent prayer of thanks.

"I'll meet you in the break room. Pit stop first." Amanda raced off.

"Okay."

Wow indeed…no more letting doubt and fear take over…I can only hope everyone experiences peace like I now have …I need to spend more time with positive and like-minded people…I need to get back in church…hear the Word…cultivate and enjoy the fellowship…the more Word that goes in us…the more Word comes out of us…and the more peace we experience…

Izabella sighed, entered the break room, and sat with her feet elevated in another chair.

Full of energy, Amanda sailed into the room with a cold drink in her hand and flung her long, auburn hair away from her face.

"What a morning, but I prefer staying busy. Sometimes hours creep by so slow you nearly forget what day it is."

Izabella burst out in laughter. "Well, I've never heard it put quite that way."

"I've worked here for five years, and it's always the same situations. Only change is different faces and a different day." Amanda sprawled on a bench and leaned her head back.

"If I hadn't witnessed something out of the ordinary today, I might agree. It nearly ruined my day."

"What?" Amanda leaned forward and made eye contact with Izabella.

"A customer noticed some girl wearing shorts, and a halter top, and wanted to know if she worked here. I told her I was new and didn't know. Bottom line was: the customer wanted to complain about the girl so I sent her to Mrs. Duvall."

Amanda shot from the bench and paced the floor. Wide-eyed, she looked at Izabella in shock. "Do you have any idea who that girl is?"

Izabella shook her head. "No. I told the customer I wasn't sure she even worked here."

"Our manager, Mr. Shafer... well, she's one of his girls."

"Enough said. I take it you are not referring to his daughters if he has any."

"Not hardly. Her name is Misty, and I think her hair is red this week. Anyway, she is one of Mr. Shafer's girlfriends that work here. She also has an elderly boyfriend who helps pay her bills. He is white-headed and on social security. I feel sorry for him. He walks around in the store with his mouth hanging open while he buys her groceries." Amanda cleared her throat. "Have you got a clear picture of the kind of person Misty is? I'm not judging her, simply stating facts. Her children sleep in Mr. Shafer's front, upstairs office while she works all night. She takes them to school when she gets off work. I have seen them climb the stairs wearing their pajamas, all scrubbed and showered, with Misty carrying school clothes on hangers. She feeds them before coming to work."

"How did this situation materialize?"

"The night crew missed seeing Misty and a young man for a few hours one night. This is when Misty was first hired. Anyway, the couple was caught in the boiler room this particular night ...I don't think I have to say what they were caught doing...and it was reported to Mr. Shafer. He fired the young man and kept the girl. Thus, we now have Misty as a full time employee."

"I'm sorry. I have to back track...in the boiler room?" Izabella frowned.

"Yes, the boiler room."

"Doesn't he worry about his wife coming here and seeing what is going on?"

"No. She can't drive. The only time she is here is when he brings her. Everyone is pleasant to her. She even bakes for us on special occasions, furnishes food for parties, birthdays, and major holidays. She is very sweet, and very happy."

Izabella paused. "...As a Christian, my heart naturally goes out to the victim. I'll pray for her. How sad, she is living a lie."

"But she doesn't know."

Izabella hung her head. "That doesn't make it right. I suffered through something similar, and believe me; people can change so drastically, you hardly recognize them."

"Who was he?"

"...Ben Wakefield."

Amanda grabbed Izabella's arm, and she sputtered. "Logan Wakefield's brother?"

Izabella briefly squeezed her eyes shut. "Yes, how do you know them?"

"This is my hometown, and no, we didn't attend school together. They are both years older than I am. Ben made the paper often, always in trouble. Logan believed his stories of innocence until the incidents became worse. Ben finally married and left town."

"Well, he returned, and met me." Izabella hesitated. "...I usually don't talk about my private life, but I pressed charges against him."

"Good for you."

"Thanks." Izabella glanced at the wall clock. "Break's over, got to run."

"Catch you later." Amanda nodded and threw her canned drink in the recycle bin.

Rushing back, each worked with enthusiasm. In between customers, they chatted with each other while cleaning their work areas. Another employee sauntered by, dark-haired and tall. Amanda waved at her.

"Sonya, I want you to meet Izabella."

Sonya approached Izabella with an upturned face. "Welcome to our world." She laughed.

"Thanks, Sonya. I'm learning more than I ever knew existed about a grocery store."

"We'll all be glad to give you tips on procedures or help with produce codes. Don't be shy to ask."

"I won't. Maybe I can help you with something, someday. Nice meeting you."

Sonya flashed a smile, and the brunette took off to the express lane.

"Did I mention I've only been blond for a month?" Izabella whispered to Amanda, and hesitated. "And I haven't heard one dumb blond joke yet. I guess the dumb thing to do would be changing my hair color to red."

"Watch out." Amanda stifled a smile as Audrey Duvall rushed to Izabella's counter.

"Your shift is over. I'll count your till. Go ahead and clock out." Mrs. Duvall grabbed the till from the register and hurried back to the service desk.

Izabella glanced at Amanda. "Talk about a close call, that won't happen again. I learned my lesson."

Amanda nodded. "Time and place for everything. Been there and done that..."

"...and got a t-shirt." Izabella finished the familiar saying.

"No." Amanda took a deep breath. "I got fired."

"Ouch! I'd better go clock out and stop talking." Izabella's lighthearted mood disappeared as fast as it arrived. She escaped to the break room and located her time card. Shoving it into the time clock, her thoughts wandered.

Standards may be slipping here, but mine can't. I have my own to uphold...not the place to have fun...

Walking in a slow, steady gait, Izabella passed the service desk, and Audrey Duvall gave her a thumbs up sign, again. Nodding, she left the store and decided to run by the hospital to surprise Susan. It was 7:15 p.m., and Izabella was certain Susan and Rick would be there.

She inquired about Dixie at the information desk and made her way to room 480. A 'No Visitors' sign hung on the door. Izabella strolled to the waiting room, and it was empty. Muttering to herself, she followed the signs to the nursery. Discovering only four babies there, she observed one at a time and quickly went to the next. After three babies, and none having the Penleigh name, she walked briskly in anticipation to the other end of the nursery. There she was, by herself; away from the others, no one watching her or admiring her features. Much smaller than the others, she was attached to a monstrosity of tubes and wires. Standing still, Izabella continued her gaze at the fourth baby and felt a lump develop in her throat. Glued to the window, Izabella's unexpected love soared for the tiny Penleigh baby, and after twenty years of pain in her own life, joy had returned.

Chapter Twenty-One

It was 7:30 in the morning. Rick thought about last night and being with Susan at the hospital. Time would tell the results of the paternity test—alarming or not.

Rick drove his truck through the familiar streets to Susan's home and parked next to the curb.

"We're here, guys."

M & M had dozed and quickly stirred in the back seat.

Thrilled to surprise Susan, Rick was almost giddy as he stepped from the vehicle. Matt and Mead opened the passenger door and leisurely exited the truck, stretching their arms out and yawning.

Scanning the area, Matt didn't hesitate and sprinted to the porch. Putting a finger over his lips, he sprawled into the wooden swing, raised his legs and quickly leaned back—starting the swinging motion. Rick and Mead hurried across the lawn and took their positions. Mead sat on a wicker chair, and Rick leaned against the railing.

I am so ready for us to be a family...

He glanced up the street watching neighbors start their cars and leave their driveways. A bird chirped merrily and more joined the serenade as Rick and the boys absorbed the peaceful morning. The sweet aroma of flowers hung in the air, and Rick's senses heightened. Silently, he sneaked to the door. Standing on his toes, he peeped in the front door window, and not seeing anyone, turned and shook his head at Matt and Mead.

164

Matt waved both arms at Rick, grabbing his immediate attention, and leaned forward in the swing. "Go ahead and call her," he whispered.

Rick seized his cell phone and clicked on Susan's number. His pulse rate grew faster as the phone rang. Energized, he struggled to sound nonchalant when Susan answered.

"Hey, lady, I'm not calling too early, am I?"

He nodded and listened.

"Well, take your coffee to the porch and enjoy the morning. I thought I'd pick you up. We can talk to Dixie and check on the baby. I guess we'd better shop for diapers and everything else today." He listened to Susan, again.

"Sounds good to me. Okay, bye." He ended the call and crammed the phone into his pants pocket. Hearing footsteps approach from inside the house, Rick stepped lightly, and resumed his position by the railing. "She's coming," he snapped, and M & M straightened their posture.

The screen door squeaked as Susan shoved it open. She instantly saw the three visitors on the porch, and a yell shot forth from her lungs in the highest degree of volume attainable. Grinning, she wiggled, and did a happy dance; sloshing coffee from her cup, but held on to it, absent-mindedly.

Rick and the boys ran to her and hugged—all speaking rapidly at the same time.

"This is incredible, guys. I'm overwhelmed!" Susan beamed. "...and we're all here together."

"I told the boys we had something to discuss with them." Rick winked at Susan.

"Definitely, but first I want to thank you boys for being here. It's no easy task to leave Tyler, drive two hours, and arrive here at 7:30 in the morning. Rick tells me you are almost finished with remodeling the farmhouse there."

"We still have scrap material to haul off." Matt sighed. "After the usual cleaning, we'll be done."

"That's right." Mead added.

"How would you two like to work here in River Town, next?" Rick squinted with a probing gaze.

"Sure." A sly smile appeared on Matt's face, and he put his hands on his hips. "That is if Mrs. Penleigh wouldn't mind cooking every now and then."

"Oh, I love to cook, and you guys could see your friends here." Susan sat her coffee cup on the wicker end table.

"I'd like that, and I'd even cook sometime." Matt laced his fingers behind his head and thrust out his chin.

Mead chimed in, "Tyler was great, but it's not like being here. Where would we stay?"

"I'll get you a room at the River Town Inn, that's where I am now."

"Now?" Matt frowned.

Susan leaned against Rick. He put his arm around her shoulders and cleared his throat. "We have an announcement to make."

"We're getting married," she blurted.

Matt jerked his head back. "What?"

"I knew this was coming!" Mead gave a playful shove at his brother. "What did I tell you?"

"You sure did. This is amazing." Matt deepened his voice. "Ladies and gentleman, your attention, please.

May I present, Mr. and Mrs. Rick Yeager." He thrust himself between them. "… and to think, I knew them when…" He paused and pointed at Mead.

Mead frowned and continued. "…when…when all else failed, and they stuck out like a sore thumb, and they couldn't help noticing each other, and the price of gasoline sky-rocketed, and he drove day and night to see her, and…"

With a wide grin, Rick held up his hand. "Enough."

Laughter erupted, and Susan shook her head.

Rick took a deep breath and walked closer to the boys. "We want both of you in the wedding. Also, we'd like for one of you to be my best man and the other to give Mrs. Penleigh away."

M & M nodded and grew solemn.

"Now, there are more plans to discuss. The timing worked out great on the farmhouse. You two can go ahead and finish it. We have a whole new project ahead of us. I am developing a new subdivision, and we will be building houses. The first house to be built is ours, and I want us to start on it right away."

A hush fell over the group as the boys stared at Rick and Susan until Matt blinked.

"Did I hear you right? Did you say *our house?*" He and Mead quick exchanged looks in total amazement.

Susan spoke first. "We want you to be part of our family if you'll have us. We'll build our home together, you'll each have your own bedroom, and more home cooking than you can stand."

"Yes, oh yes." The boys choked out their responses in unison.

They interlocked arms and had a group hug, much stronger than the last one. After patting each other, they broke apart.

"This is one day I'll never forget." Susan wiped an escaping tear off her face.

"None of us will, Mrs. Penleigh." Matt reflected.

"She won't be Mrs. Penleigh long, and we are hoping you will call us something less formal."

Words rushed from Mead instantly. "In case the pitter-patter of little Yeager footsteps end up running around here?"

"Oh…no." Susan sputtered. "We aren't planning on having any babies. The only people here with Yeager for a last name will be Rick and I."

"Now, *I'd like that,* being a Yeager, that is." Matt stated.

"You would?" Rick gasped.

"I'd be honored to be a Yeager. I could have my named changed."

Rick blinked rapidly. "Matt, *I'd* be honored for you to have my name. I never expected this. I think you should take your time and really give it a lot of thought. This is an important step in your life."

"I want to be a Yeager, too. We'll become the Yeager family with a Dad and Mom." Mead straightened his posture.

"We've made up our mind. Could you check into it for us?"

"I will." Susan beamed. "I have an attorney."

Rick raised an eyebrow. "You got the job, my dear." He turned to the boys, and at first, his voice broke. "Today… will be the first of many family discussions." He hesitated, and his voice rose in strength. "You have heard about my daughter, Tessa. It's time you found out about Dixie. She is Mrs. Penleigh's daughter-in-law. She had a baby girl yesterday, and we aren't sure who the father is. Mrs. Penleigh's son, Scott, is in Afghanistan, and they are getting a divorce. Dixie is man crazy so stay away from her. She is after the landlord, Lee Miller, and is nothing but trouble, believe me."

"Point taken." Matt glanced at Mead. "You got that?"

"I got it."

"Anything you want to add to the discussion?"

"No, we don't have any girls in our family." Mead laughed, and Matt slapped at him and missed.

"Too funny." Rick tried not to smile and didn't quite make it. "Okay, guys, let's round 'em up and move 'em out!" He cocked his head to the side and winked at Susan. "That means let's hop in the truck and get this show on the road... pilgrim."

Susan's hand flew to her mouth, and she chuckled." I don't know who I am marrying now, Gil Favor on "Rawhide' or John Wayne calling everyone a pilgrim."

"Get in the truck, woman." Rick bounded down the porch steps. Susan and M & M followed.

They dashed across the lawn and climbed in Rick's truck. Susan, contented, could not stop smiling.

"First stop will be the baby at the hospital, then Dixie." Rick started the ignition and drove off.

"What is the baby's name?" Matt inquired as he glanced at the passing neighborhood.

"Vinita Irene Penleigh. Her mother is proud of the initials; V.I.P."

"She will be my first baby to meet...a very important person indeed." Matt said half-aloud.

◆

The curtains were pulled together tightly at the nursery. The new Yeager family decided to try room 480. Upon seeing the sign, they stopped and walked back to the nurses' station.

"What's the deal with the 'No Visitors' sign for room 480?"

"Oh, I think Mrs. Penleigh wanted to cat-nap today." The nurse smiled.

"So, we *can* go in?"

"Yes, ma'am."

"Thank you." Susan pivoted and sailed down the hallway. Rick and M & M were close behind. She tore the sign off the door, and still grasping it in her hand, shoved the door open.

"Dixie, how are you feeling?"

"Zapped. I had no idea my energy would be gone."

"Oh, it will return. Have you seen your baby, yet?"

"No, I've been too weak to walk. I've been told she is hooked up to a heart monitor, has an I.V., and is on oxygen. So she can't come here, poor little thing."

"We can get you in a wheel chair and wheel you to see her." Susan stared boldly at Dixie.

"Oh, no, it would hurt so badly. I am in a lot of pain and have many stitches."

Susan heard someone snicker in the background. Glancing behind her, she saw Rick and M & M standing together.

"Where is Lee? Have you seen him?" Dixie rose up on an elbow and frowned at Susan.

"No, I haven't seen him...don't have a clue where he is, or what he's doing."

Dixie whimpered.

"I'm sorry you don't feel well. I wanted you to meet my fiancé and our two sons."

"I'm tired." Dixie shut her eyes and rolled over, turning her back to Susan.

"Seems you don't want company, so we'll go now." Susan motioned to the others, and they silently left.

◆

A stroll through the local baby department filled two shopping carts. The soon-to-be Yeager family didn't know when Vinita would arrive home, but wanted to be sure she had what she needed, and then some.

M & M headed back to Tyler. Rick and Susan were determined to see the baby, soon.

Chapter Twenty-Two

Startled by the jingling ring tone, Izabella snatched her cellphone, clicked the speaker option, and turned up the volume.

"Mrs. Contrell?"

"Yes, this is Izabella Contrell."

"I'm Ethan Brady, Assistant District Attorney. May I have a moment of your time?"

"Of course." Izabella's heart raced. "I suppose this is in reference to Ben Wakefield?" Fidgety, she wrapped a loose curl around her finger.

"Yes, ma'am. Based on the evidence we'll offer Mr. Wakefield a plea bargain."

"What would that be?"

"He'll have one year probation and ninety hours community service. If he doesn't complete the arrangement, his probation is revoked. In that case, he'll be incarcerated for twelve months."

"This is the best news I have heard in a long time. I'm sure Ben's going to decide too many people will be watching every step he takes, and he'll leave town."

"It's hard to say how Mr. Wakefield might feel, or what he may do."

"I know, Mr. Brady, but he will have to deal with disciplinary measures, and I thank you for that."

"You are welcome, ma'am."

Izabella instantly ended the call and sighed deeply with relief.

Thank You Lord... thank you Mr. Brady...and goodbye Ben...

Pouring a steaming cup of coffee, Izabella pondered the dramatic turn of events. For the first time in days, she walked to the outside patio and sank into a chaise lounge chair. The three-inch padded cushions seemed to ease her mind as well as her body. She took a sip of the hot brew, and her tension disappeared by small degrees.

Safe...I feel safe...as if I finally departed from a ship no longer caught in a raging sea...

She set her cellphone and coffee cup on the side table. Stretching out on the lounge chair, she leaned her head against the top cushion and gazed at the clouds. Two men popped into her mind; Theodore Hilton and Ben Wakefield. Reflecting on the two men she had been romantically drawn to during her life, she involuntarily shuddered. Theodore had passed himself off as a single man captivated by her supposed charm. Actually married, and conniving to obtain her parents river-front property, she recalled the moment he poked a gun into her side on the stairs in her parents' home. She had struggled to obtain the gun, and the anguish on her parents' faces burst into plain view, as majestically as a wide screen movie...painfully playing again and again.

And now...I can no longer conceive...no more babies...and he is in prison...

Raging seas indeed...

And Ben, waltzing into my life...literally sweeping me off my feet...after any material possession he could get from me...anything I worked hard for...anything I saved toward my old age years...and he pretended to marry me ...ended up dragging me across my front lawn...

No, I won't be making a trip out to sea again...I am too happy being by myself...

"Izabella...Izabella?" Susan yelled, "... There you are!"

Flinching, Izabella jerked her head toward the side of the house. Susan briefly stood on the sidewalk; a happy smile glowed on her face, and she hurried to the patio.

"Well... hello. What a surprise! Pull up a chair." She sat up and her mood lightened immediately. "What's going on?"

"Ha! Too much...I could settle for soothing peach tea and a lazy afternoon."

"Well, you are at the right place. I have both." Izabella threw her legs over the side of the chair.

"No, don't move. I'll get the tea."

"Susan, *you* are my guest." Izabella insisted.

"Your uninvited guest." Susan chuckled. "It's past time for someone to do something for you without ulterior motives."

"I can't believe this...a true friend and a mind reader! Okay, go get the tea." Izabella settled back into the chaise lounge, laying with her legs outstretched.

Susan frowned. "I *will* bring the tea, but I'm not sure about being a mind reader." She sauntered to the rear entrance of the house.

"You will when you hear what I was recently thinking about," Izabella exclaimed. Flexing her feet, she enjoyed the morning sun's warm sensation upon her whole being. A light breeze engulfed the entire patio with aroma from a nearby rose garden. Izabella took a deep breath and filled her senses with the delightful, mingled smell of Don Juan, Peace, and Jacob's Coat of Many Color's rose bushes.

Susan quietly returned with two iced tea glasses.

"Here you go." She handed one to Izabella and stifled a smile as her friend's whole body jumped an inch off the chair.

"Oh! I didn't hear you!" Izabella gushed, "Guess I was lost in the moment." She grabbed her glass and enjoyed a sip.

"It *is* relaxing here." Susan sprawled into a matching lounge chair. Tilting her head, she made eye contact with Izabella. "So, a mind reader? Come on, out with it, girl."

"I was joking. Neither of us believes in mind reading. It was more like perfect timing. I'd been reminiscing about Theodore and Ben. What awful experiences they were."

"Neither man deserved you, nor was it my timing to suddenly show up, now. It was God's timing for me to be here. You needed someone who genuinely cared about you to be with you today. God gives us a brain to realize who can harm us, and who won't."

"It is comforting to know He has a plan for all of us if we'd simply wait for His timing, and His will to be done. Unfortunately, I didn't wait for His timing or His will with either Theodore or Ben."

"Izabella, God isn't through with you yet. He has a plan, and I don't know about you, but this is an exciting time. Get ready for Him to bless you. I know you, Izabella. You forgive all who were evil towards you, and ask for your own sins to be forgiven, while trying not to repeat them. Izabella, you are a child of

God. People can see Jesus in you. The devil cannot stop you, remember that."

"Thanks, Susan. It is such a relief to be with like-minded people. I'm ready to get back in church. I need to hear The Word of God, and I need the encouragement Christians give each other. That old saying is so true: 'the more Word of God that goes into you…the more The Word of God comes out of you.' I soak up scripture like water soaks into a sponge."

"I'm certain you have read II Corinthians 5:17; 'Therefore if any man *be* in Christ, he *is* a new creature: old things are passed away; behold, all things are become new.' This is one of my favorites." Susan added.

Izabella swirled ice cubes around in her half-full glass as she continued talking. "One with another strong meaning for me is II Corinthians 6:14; 'Be not unequally yoked together with unbelievers: for what fellowship has righteousness with unrighteousness? And what communion has light with darkness?' Of course the answer is none."

"I have to give one more." Susan's voice rose as she quoted. "This is Romans 8:28; 'And we know that all things work together for good: to them who love God, to them who are the called according to *His* purpose.' Once again we go back to His purpose …not ours. His will, not ours. That is why it is so important to pray for His will to be done in our lives, not our will."

"I agree completely. Look at the mess my life has been by doing *my* will. And not God's will."

"Izebella, your life is not over. Like I said before, get ready, girl."

"I am, believe me, I am. I had a call earlier from the Assistant District Attorney, and Ben is mighty close to being out of my life."

"It's already starting. I am so happy for you." Susan finished her tea in one long gulp and gave Izabella a mischievous grin. "And it's started for me, too."

"What? Spit it out! Enough about me, what's going on with you?" Izabella noticed Susan's features seemed to soften as she hesitated to answer.

"...Rick and I and M & M are going to be our own family. M & M even want to change their last name to Yeager. I'll make arrangements for them to meet with my attorney soon."

"Could you repeat that, please?" Izabella laughed. "A new family, a new beginning, oh, Susan, what a blessing..."

"I know," Susan squealed. She stood and squeezed her friend's hand. "To God be the glory."

"Amen! I'm overjoyed for all of you."

"Thanks. I knew you would be, and I do have to run. Errands are mounting as I speak. Don't get up, I will call you later."

"Thanks for stopping by. I am going to lie here and treasure this contentment," Izabella slowly rolled over on her side soaking up the warm sunshine.

Sure feels good on my back...

Nearly dozing off, Izabella frowned at the sound of her phone ringing. She slapped at the top of the side table and retrieved the noisy intrusion. Holding it up in the air, she jabbed a finger on the speaker button and answered the call.

"Hello?"

"Izabella, this is Sonya Taneli from work. Do you remember me?"

A mental picture of the brunette flashed through her memory. "Yes, of course, I do."

"Amanda recommended I call you. She said you are a Christian, and you might be able to help me."

"Um... I'll certainly try, and if I can't we'll find someone who can."

"Thanks, Izabella. I hardly know you, but I am in a difficult situation. It has to stop, and I thought with you being new, well, maybe someone would be afraid of you."

"Afraid of me? I don't understand. What is going on?"

Sonya took a deep breath and continued. "It's Mr. Shafer."

"Oh...I'm sorry if he is bothering you, Sonya."

"It's worse than a mere bother...he...he is coming over tonight, and I don't want him to."

"Why don't you start at the beginning, and I'll be quiet and listen. Take your time, and don't worry, whatever you say will be strictly confidential."

"Well... I worked at Corner Grocery for many years, and then moved away to another town when I married. I was gone for a few years, and we recently returned. Then my husband got a job off shore on a drilling rig. I asked Mr. Shafer if I could have my old job back and resume my original seniority status. He acted fine about it. He said we could work something out." Her voice cracked, and Izabella could hear a muffled sob.

Both fell silent. Izabella waited for Sonya to regain her composure. Catching her breath, Sonya rushed on with her explanation.

"Mr. Shafer walks by me at work and whispers that he is coming over to my house. I keep telling him it would never happen. He assured me it will. Then I got sick with allergies and ran a fever. Yesterday was my first day back at work. He quickly informed me that he would be at my house tonight. I told him, again, *not* to come over."

"So, he hasn't been to your house yet?"

"No, but he said he was going to bring me a can of soup and check on me tonight. He plans on being there at 7 o'clock. I am scared. He won't leave me alone."

"How can I help?"

"I'd like for you to be at my house at 6:30 tonight. When he knocks on my door, I want you to stand inside against the wall. When I open the door, you will be hidden behind it. He walks in, and I quickly announce you are also here to check on me. I close the door and that is when he sees you standing against the wall. Oh, it will be perfect! He will know I deliberately invited you over to stop his harassment, and he cannot retaliate towards you because you are a new employee. He doesn't know who you have as friends in this town that could ruin him if they knew the truth about him. He will have to leave and won't be able to control either of us."

"I'll be glad to help. Where do you live?"

"My house is near the new apartment complex with the swimming pool on the highway. It's a two-story Tudor style, four houses past the apartments on the same side of the street. You will see a winding driveway, and the house is at the back of the property."

"I know exactly where it is. I'll be there at 6:30 this evening."

"Thanks, Izabella. I was hoping I could count on you."

Their conversation abruptly ended, and Izabella heard the distant sound of a dial tone. She blinked and went through the motion of turning the phone off. Running her hand through her hair, she grimaced at the thought of their boss.

Sonya did not agree to private meetings with him to obtain her previous seniority...

Lord, I lift Sonya, and her situation up to You. I pray for strength, and Your guidance. In Jesus powerful name I pray, Amen.

◆

"Thanks for coming." Sonya spoke quietly and invited Izabella inside her home. The brunette's once perky attitude had disappeared. Lines of worry etched across her forehead.

Izabella shook her head and stared at Sonya. "You look awfully tired. Don't let him affect you like that. He is robbing you of your peace, your joy. Can you see the devil in Mr. Shafer? The devil comes to steal, kill, and destroy."

"I *can* see the devil in him. Maybe this wasn't such a good idea, after all. I am so worried about him retaliating. I could lose my job."

"Sonya, there are laws to protect you from his harassment. Believe me, he will not want to address that issue in court."

"You are right. To the public, he is the man who commits himself to helping others in the community. He offers our facilities for car wash fundraisers, gives day old bread and bakery items to the local food bank, and contributes to charities. Most people think he is wonderful...those that don't work for him, that is."

"It doesn't matter how much good he does helping others. As a Christian, we commit ourselves to what God has done—not what good deeds *we* do. When someone trusts Him and receives Him as their Savior, they have a closer relationship with God. His peace will flood their soul, and they are ready to share their Christianity. Someone with evil ways—and that includes ulterior motives—has no idea what they are missing." Izabella glanced at her watch. "We have about fifteen minutes unless Mr. Shafer arrives early."

An abrupt knock pounded loudly.

Sonya flinched, and Izabella positioned her back against the wall directly where the open door would soon hide her.

Izabella nodded to Sonya, and trembling, Sonya placed her hand on the knob. She carefully swung the door open and stopped the door a foot before it touched the wall.

Completely out of sight, Izabella peeped through the slight crack next to the hinges on the door. Sonya cringed at the sight of her boss, who stood with a smile from ear to ear.

"Mr. Shafer, I can't believe you are actually here."

He held a can of chicken noodle soup in the air and pitched it into the seat of a nearby padded couch. "I had to check on my Sonya." He rushed towards her with outstretched arms and Sonya backed away.

"You aren't the only one who came to check on me, Mr. Shafer, look who arrived earlier."

Izabella kicked the door out of her way and burst into the room. The puzzled expression on his face caused Izabella's bravery to grow. She stepped close to him and spoke face to face.

"I'm Izabella Contrell, the new employee at your store."

"Oh, yes, Mrs. Contrell, I do recall hiring you." He narrowed his eyes and stared boldly at her. His breath felt hot on Izabella's face, and she darted to the couch. Retrieving the can of soup, she handed it back to him.

"I'm taking care of Sonya. We won't need this."

"Mrs. Contrell, I am appalled! I thought it was wonderful of me to bring the soup."

"Wonderful, Mr. Shafer? Read Isaiah 9:6. 'For unto us a Child is born, unto us a Son is given: and the government shall be upon His shoulder: and His name shall be called Wonderful, Counselor, The Mighty God/The Everlasting Father, The Prince of Prince.' I could never call *you* wonderful, Mr. Shafer."

Both women watched his face turn red. He sputtered, and fast as lightening, shot out the open door.

Izabella calmly walked to the door, shut and locked it.

Chapter Twenty-Three

Susan mellowed at the sight of the small framed older woman. Mrs. Sport, with her back facing Susan and watering can in hand, didn't realize her new friend had arrived. The sitting area, busy with activity, was exactly as Susan pictured. A squirrel raced up a tree that crowded the front of the house. Reaching safety from the higher branches, it turned and barked at her. Hummingbirds darted to red feeders, each filled to capacity, hanging from the rafters. Massive hanging baskets of Boston fern decorated the wraparound porch. The slender body of a grey and black stripped cat remained perfectly still… in stalking position… as it gazed upward at the hummingbirds.

Mrs. Sport laughed out loud as the cat made a sudden leap in the air and tumbled to the floor.

"Give it up, Rascal, you'll never catch one."

A chuckle erupted from Susan, and Mrs. Sport glanced over her shoulder.

"Mrs. Penleigh, welcome to my menagerie. I have a lot of wild animals here, or at least mine *think* they are. The Yorkie is inside. *He* thinks *he* is a guard dog." She sat the watering can down and smiled warmly. "I'm happy you came. Please, have a seat."

"You have a lovely home. Thanks for inviting me. How are you feeling?" Susan sat on a wooden bench, and Mrs. Sport yanked the long chain on the outside ceiling fan.

"I'm glad to be out of the hospital. Tests showed normal wear and tear on my right knee. They call it degenerative."

"It doesn't sound like you need immediate surgery."

"I know my limits, Mrs. Penleigh, and try not to overdo anything. Maybe I can just keep plodding along as I am."

"Don't we all." Susan beamed.

"Indeed." Mrs. Sport laughed and joined Susan on the bench. "And how are you, my dear?"

Susan sighed and shrugged her shoulders. "As well as can be expected, I guess. I came for advice on handling young women...*troubled*, young women. I know you have mentored many teenagers and have encountered numerous situations concerning their family issues. I trust your judgment."

"I'd be glad to listen. Hopefully, I can give some insight to an underlying problem. Go ahead." She settled back in anticipation, and the cat jumped on her lap, purring. With a few pats across it's back, Mrs. Sport glanced at Susan and smiled.

"It's about my fiancés daughter, Tessa, and my son's estranged wife, Dixie. Both are self-centered and both are creating havoc in our lives." Susan stood and paced the floor. "Tessa has a history of drug abuse and has been in and out of court ordered drug treatment centers. She recently escaped a rehab facility and was arrested for a bank robbery." Susan stopped, and her posture slumped slightly. "The female teller died after Tessa left the bank. I'm sure the stress was unbearable for the older woman. It's difficult to imagine."

Mrs. Sport hung her head. Engulfed in the sharing of personal sorrow, it immediately changed her demeanor. Drawing her mouth in a tight line, she frowned and focused on the cat, gently massaging it's ears.

"Dixie and my son are divorcing. She has little interest in her newborn baby girl. My son doesn't believe he is the father, and a paternity test is ongoing. She constantly wants male attention and will not listen to my suggestions. Oh, she *is* staying with me or was until she had the baby. Dixie's still in the hospital, and my son is in the service, stationed in Afghanistan."

"Sit down, dear. You cannot let this turmoil control you."

Susan stopped pacing and continued with an emotionally distressed voice. "My finance, Rick, and I pray, and we aren't letting the situation defeat us. Sometimes though, deep down inside, I fear we won't have the happy, married life we are looking for."

"Married life is a work in progress. Happiness doesn't just miraculously happen."

"I know, and I don't want to sound as if I am whining, but we can all be vulnerable at times. Fear and faith don't belong together, and I do have a strong faith. I can't and won't let fear control on life. I pray for strength and God's will, and recognize the devil wants to create doubt. I am learning." She reflected. "Rick and I have to handle Tessa and Dixie firmly and go on with our lives. What advice can you offer?"

"Be consistent with both of them. If they don't abide by the law and disregard rules, *they* are responsible for their actions; not you and not your finance. Don't let them turn it around and place a burden on your lives. I'm sure you pray for them but don't let them use you. It sounds like neither is respectful with others' lives."

"They aren't. Rick and I are blessed in so many ways, and I don't want to add to a difficult situation by saying something wrong to them."

"Mrs. Penleigh, the best way to handle them is to be true to yourself. You, as a Christian will be a good example to them, simply in how you live your life. Most of this generation was not raised in church. They do not have to live hopeless lives, though."

"I agree. Have you ever encountered anything similar to what we are dealing with?"

"Not exactly. There was one young man, Mack Reynolds, who was an awful bully. Created trouble everywhere he went."

"Did you say Mack Reynolds?"

"Yes."

Susan cried out, "That is the name of the biker who robbed the bank with Tessa."

"I'm not surprised. As a youth, he was in and out of juvenile detention centers, and ended up in and out of jail when he was older. The majority of teens need encouragement from people who are good role models... and they need positive peers who want a better future."

"So true." Susan sighed. "Thanks for listening. I could stay all day, but I have to leave."

"Wait a minute." Mrs. Sport crossed the lawn to the greenhouse next door and returned with a small plant. "Here. This is an African Violet. Let it get indirect light inside your house. They are easy to care for, and you can stick a leaf in the soil...with part of it above the dirt, and it will root another plant. Start several in the same pot." With a wide smile, she handed it to Susan.. "Come visit anytime."

"I will, thanks again for everything, and I am excited about this plant." She hugged Mrs. Sport and felt a pat on her back. Turning, she sauntered back to her car and left.

What an amazing woman...

◆

Zipping her vehicle through the streets of River Town, Susan tried to focus on the future. The reassuring smile on Mrs. Sport's face kept returning to her mind.

We all need a positive role model...no matter what age we are.

The florist shop downtown was the next stop. The pungent smell of field flowers surrounded her as she entered. A woman engrossed in filling a vase of tall gladiolas; expertly added sprigs of fresh, green fern to compliment the arrangement. Looking over the top of her glasses, resting half-way down her nose, the woman called out, "I'll be right with you."

"No hurry," Susan replied and scanned the shelves of other colorful arrangements. Live carnations... dyed blue...nestled in tiny, white flowers of baby's breath; adorned a blue and white porcelain cradle planter. Susan discovered a wind-up musical key protruding from one end of the cradle. She gently turned it and smiled as Brahms's Lullaby filed the air. On the next shelve were artificial, long-stemmed, red roses tied with a cascading red, velvet ribbon.

She strolled across the room and stopped the instant she saw them...lilies. With an incredulous stare, Susan hurried to the display and bent to smell them.

"Umm." She filled her senses with the sweet aroma.

187

"Lovely, aren't they?" The woman approached wiping her hands on a paper towel. "I'm Twyla Sherman. How may I be of help?"

"Susan Penleigh. I'm getting married this Sunday. I hope the lilies are available."

"Congratulations! Yes, ma'am, the lilies are available. What do you have in mind?"

"We are having a small wedding. I need the bouquet, of course, and the maid of honor's corsage. Three boutonnieres: one for the groom, the best man, and one for who is giving me away. I'd also like an arrangement on the refreshment table in the fellowship hall at the church."

"May I recommend a combination of extra-large lilies intertwined with smaller ones tucked into baby's breath for the bouquet? Smaller lilies would be for the others and an arrangement with both sizes for the table."

"Great idea."

"What colors do you prefer?"

"I can imagine the large, blue lily as a happy splash of color against the white lily and green one. They would complement each other. Do you have enough of them?"

"Yes. Let me work on an invoice. When do you want the order?"

"I can pick the flowers up on Saturday and keep them refrigerated at the church until the wedding."

"Works for me." Mrs. Sherman scribbled on the invoice, added tax, and handed it to Susan.

After a quick glance, Susan nodded. "Price is good. Let me pay you, now." She hurried to write a check, passed it to the woman, and shook her hand. "Thanks, Mrs. Sherman. I'll see you this coming Saturday."

"Saturday will be here sooner than you think."

Susan turned it over in her mind and quietly made her way to the exit. Outside, she allowed time to indulge in the excitement of the upcoming wedding and pictured daily life as Mrs. Rick Yeager. Slipping into her car, she felt her pulse race. "Yes, Mrs. Sherman," Susan muttered, "you are so correct. Saturday will be here sooner than I realize."

My sandy-haired, middle-aged, sweet Rick Yeager is moving in after Sunday. We'll be together for the rest of our lives. M & M will be living at the Inn...right here in town...until our home is built...I am so blessed!

Lord, I pray that Tessa and Dixie come to know You as their Savior. I know M & M have and so has Rick. Thank you for bringing him into my life. In Jesus name I pray, Amen.

Her resolve grew stronger as she drove home.

I'm fully charged, right on target, and no one is bringing me down!

Susan, zipping down the street, nearly passed up her house when she spotted Rick's truck in her driveway. Slamming on her brakes, she quickly drove behind his truck and parked. He stood on the porch, waving. With a silly grin, Susan hurried across the lawn. Rick darted from the porch and met her at the bottom of the steps.

"Not getting second thoughts, are you?"

"No." Susan laughed nervously. "My mind was on us though."

"Good thoughts?"

"The best."

"Great!" They walked up the steps and onto the porch. Rick stood at the front door and paused. "I stopped by to see if you want to check on Dixie and the baby, before it gets too late."

"Yes, and if Dixie isn't civil to us, it's her loss. I want to see that precious baby." Susan's face lit up, and Rick beamed.

"Me too, come on."

They strolled to Rick's truck and took off without saying another word. Arriving at the hospital, they quickly made their way to the fourth floor. Silently walking down the hall and around the corner, they passed the nurses' station near Dixie's room.

"Let's stop and ask how they are both doing." Susan raised her head and looked at Rick.

He nodded and they edged toward the desk.

One of the nurses glanced at them. "May I help you?"

"Yes. I'm Susan Penleigh. How are Dixie and the baby today? Any change?"

"They are the same. Oh, Mrs. Penleigh, Dr. Adahy left a message for you. He sent the results to Scott's military base and said you would know what he was referring too."

"Yes, I do understand. Thank you." Susan and Rick shared a tentative smile and continued on to room 480.

"It won't be long now." Rick squeezed Susan's hand.

"Scott will call me with the results as soon as he gets the report. I can't wait."

Pushing the door open, they exchanged another look at each other.

"No Dixie. Wonder where she is?" Susan frowned and checked the bathroom. "Nope, not in there."

"She can't be far. Maybe she went to see little Vinita." Rick shrugged his shoulders.

"Dixie? I'd be surprised if she did." Susan sighed. "I wish she would take an interest in her baby girl. Well, we came to see the baby too, might as well go now."

They meandered down the maze of halls to discover the nursery had no one viewing the babies. The curtains were open, and both raced to the front of the window, going from baby to baby, until finding Vinita Penleigh.

"There she is! How beautiful!" Susan gushed. Scanning the many wires and tubes attached to the baby, she frowned. "Oh, Rick. I feel like I've been hit with a ton of bricks. I know you've heard that expression before, but for the first time I honestly *feel* it. How overwhelming."

"She looks helpless and probably vulnerable to infection. At least her condition hasn't changed. She isn't worse. We will keep her in our prayers." He grimaced and moved closer to the window.

As if on cue, the baby curled her fingers to form a fist and slowly released the grip.

"She's trying to get my attention. She wants me to hold her." Rick announced and raised an eyebrow. "It won't be long, little girl and you'll be out of there. Keep growing."

Susan placed her hand on the window, gazing intently at the child. "I hope we *can* hold her someday...you never know about Dixie's plans."

A nurse smiled at them and donned a pair of gloves. She walked to Vinita's incubator, and placed a finger into the side opening. Her finger hovered over the baby's hand, barely brushing against it, and Vinita quickly curled her tiny fingers around the nurse's finger.

"Adorable!" Susan mouthed to the nurse through the window, and she gave Susan a thumbs up sign with her other hand. Glancing at the clock, the nurse pointed to the visiting hours sign and slowly drew the curtains together.

"Must be feeding time. Glad we finally got to see her." Rick waved to the nurse, and Susan stood immobile, still gazing at the baby as the curtains closed.

"Perfect timing."

"Shall we try to locate Mrs. Dixie?"

Susan's hands darted to her hips. "Are you kidding? I wouldn't leave without trying."

Rick chuckled. "I tell you what...with those elbows bent like that, you might be five feet three inches tall, but you definitely look like a force to be reckoned with."

Susan whirled around, bouncing her short blond hair across her forehead, and spoke in a soft voice. "I thank you for the support, but the last thing I want to convey is that I am a force."

Rick gave a half-hearted shrug. "It's okay. I would never want you to be a force. I like you just the way you are; a compassionate, confident, Christian woman." He hugged her close and kissed the top of her head. They stepped apart and shared a warm smile.

Wandering down several halls, and making a few turns, they heard the unmistakable laughter belonging to Dixie. High-pitched and loud, it sailed out from a room displaying a sign that read, 'Employee Lounge.'

Rick knocked on the door, and it instantly swung open. A wide smile on his face, one young man looked at Rick. "Do I know you?" He appeared confused.

"No, we haven't met." As Rick spoke, Susan stepped beside him, and at the first sight of Dixie, Susan quickly turned her head away. Dixie sat on a couch, the only female in the room, completely surrounded by men.

Dixie glared at Susan. "Mrs. Penleigh, what are you doing here?"

Susan faced her and spoke with newly found boldness. "We came to visit and were trying to find you. I recognized your laughter so here we are. Certainly, didn't mean to disturb you with your friends."

Two of the men stood immediately. "Our shift starts soon, we were just leaving. Bye, Dixie."

"Yeah, bye Dixie." The other one added, and they fled the room.

"Wait up for me." The young man that greeted Rick hurried out behind the other two.

"Well, girl, you've got my number. Call me sometime." The last man rose from the couch, flexed his arm muscles and winked at her. He nodded at Rick and Susan and swaggered to the door.

Dixie smirked. "We might as well return to my room, they are all gone, now." She stood and her body swayed.

Rick reached to grab her arm. "Here, let me help steady you."

She stepped back, dodging him. Visibly stiffening, she crossed the room and left. Rick and Susan followed her out in the hall, and the heavy silence seemed to drown out even the most minuscule sound a hospital can have.

Room 480 loomed ahead. Dixie slackened her pace, and Susan fell in beside her. Rick brought up the rear as the three progressed down the hall.

Dixie is so bitter, she hurts inside. If I could only reach her…only show her Rick and I are not her enemies…

Sidestepping a portable scale left beside a wall, Susan careened into the side of Dixie, gasping. Dixie rubbed her arm from the forceful impact, and she seized Susan's shoulders.

"Cut it out, Ms. Graceful. Can't you walk in a straight line?"

Susan instantly narrowed her eyes at Dixie, and spoke sharply. "No, sometimes I can't." Exasperated at herself for losing her temper, Susan took a deep breath. She deliberately stared at Dixie, and lowered her voice. "I am not perfect. And you can provoke me all you want too, but I will still pray for your soul. I will pray for you to *want* to know Jesus as your Savior. I don't want you burning in hell for eternity."

"Neither do I." Rick added. "Come on, we can talk, and still go back to Dixie's room."

They exchanged looks with each other and continued walking at a slow pace.

"I don't go to church because I don't like hypocrites, but I think you are genuine, Mrs. Penleigh. Thanks for the prayers."

"Dixie, there are as many hypocrites out of church as are in. Church is for sinners. We develop a

194

relationship with Christ, we share, we lift each other up. The person *not* in church keeps a church from growing. The person *not* in church claims to be a Christian without hearing God's Word. They promote themselves, not God's Word. Think about it."

"I will. No one has ever talked to me like that."

They found themselves at the entrance of Dixie's room, and all three stood awkwardly.

"You have given me food for thought, thank you. I will be released tomorrow, if everything goes okay." Dixie paused and glanced at Susan. "I guess you are aware of the paternity test Scott is paying for."

"Yes, I am."

"Well, then, we have nothing else to say."

"We'll see you tomorrow, regardless of the outcome." Susan responded.

"Thank you. Goodnight." Dixie entered her room and closed the door behind her.

"Goodnight," Susan replied. She involuntarily shuddered, and Rick shook his head, muttering as they left the hospital.

Weary, Susan climbed into Rick's truck. "Take me home, please," she pleaded.

"Lady, we are on our way." He sighed and slouched into the driver's seat. "What a day."

It started raining as they drove to Susan's home. Lightening rippled through the sky as thunder crackled shockingly loud. The rain developed into a raging storm with heavy winds, visibility diminished fast. Rick slowed the truck to a crawl as his windshield wipers raced across the window on high speed. Eventually, they drove out of the storm. Looking in the rear view mirror, the dark sky remained behind them with clear skies ahead.

"Hungry?" Rick shot Susan a quick glance.

"A little."

He hurried into her driveway, and they exited the vehicle. "Let's relax on the porch, and I'll get us something to eat in a while."

"I'd enjoy that. Thanks."

"Come on, let's swing." Rick slipped his arm around her waist, and he steered her to the porch.

Easing into the wooden swing, Rick and Susan leaned back, and they both set it in motion.

The familiar squeak of the swing was comforting. Susan rested completely and leaned against Rick's side.

"I don't know about you, but I am emotionally exhausted."

"Me too." Rick agreed.

Time seemed to stand still as they shared an idle evening. No hurry, no worries, and no intrusions.

"I ordered the flowers today...for the wedding." Susan yawned.

"I can pay for them, you don't have to do it by yourself." He joined her in a deeper yawn, and she half-way smiled.

After yawning again, she giggled. "I guess we are relaxing too fast. I can't quit yawning."

"You are making me yawn. It's all your fault." He teased, and leaned his head back. "Oh, this rocking motion sure feels good."

"It sure does."

Minutes passed, and they dozed off to sleep.

Groggy, Susan thought she heard someone clear their throat. She barely opened one eye and saw two men standing in front of the swing. She quickly poked Rick in his ribs and shot out of the swing, shifting the swing into a sideways movement.

"What?" Rick stirred and rubbed his side, gradually waking up.

"Excuse us. It's just me, Lee Miller. This is my friend, Clayton Vaughn. I…uh…wanted to talk to you about something." Lee wrinkled his brow and waited for Rick to clearly awaken.

"No problem." Rick stood and glanced at Susan. "We were worn out, girl." He grinned sheepishly.

"No joke." Susan blurted, and embarrassed, hung her head.

"Hey, it's okay." Lee laughed, putting them at ease.

"What's this about?" Rick asked. He and Susan leaned against the railing, side by side.

"I don't know any other way to say it, but be blunt. It's about Dixie. She is getting on my nerves. She is crowding me, man. I can't handle it."

Rick answered with a nod.

Susan chimed in. "She seems obsessed with you."

"Hey, that's it, and I am out of here. No way will I ever settle down, that's not my style." Lee paced the porch and shook his head. "She is smothering me, I can't breathe."

Susan hesitated. "Uh… she should be released from the hospital tomorrow if all goes well."

"Fine. Good for her, but I'm not hanging around." He kicked a spiked sweet gum ball off the porch and looked at his friend. "You will be taking care of things here. Cut down that sweet gum tree, it is a nuisance!"

Clayton burst into a wide smile and nodded.

Lee glanced at Rick and Susan again. "I'm going to sell the house and leave town. Nothing to keep me here. If you are interested in purchasing the home, it will be a good investment. Live on one side and rent out the other. What do you think?"

Rick stroked his fingers across his chin. "Not for us, we are already building a new home, but you are so correct. It is a great investment. I do know someone who might be interested." He turned and looked at Susan. "I think this would be super for Izabella's future."

"I agree."

Lee's smile appeared tight. "Contact her right away. I'll be leaving in a few days. Clayton, here, will be at the house …tending to some loose ends for me. You'll see him in and out a lot. Don't be alarmed, I trust him with my business."

Rick nodded again. "I'll call Izabella and discuss the purchase with her. I do need to know what your asking price is."

"Of course." Lee stopped pacing. "I am asking for $110,000.00 in cash and that is a bargain."

Rick whistled. "I think you may have a deal…"

Chapter Twenty-Four

Izabella plopped the pillow over her head and tried to ignore the ringing phone. It rang persistently, on and on and on.

Finally stopping, relief surged through her being. She sank into the bed and the polyester, quilted cover caressed her lightly while she molded her body around the fabric. A cool breeze swept over her face as the ceiling fan ran on medium speed. Her arms and legs were tingly with sleep, and the annoying phone began to ring again.

She sat up in the bed, and in one swift motion, jerked the cellphone off the end table and answered it angrily. "What?"

"Izabella? It's Rick, and Susan is here with me. This is important. I'm sorry to bother you, but..."

"Okay, okay. I'm listening. Go ahead." She sputtered.

"I know it's late, but this is a great opportunity. Lee Miller, the owner of the house Susan lives in, is selling out. You could afford to buy it and move in...rent the side that Susan lives in. I would consider it myself if we weren't already building our own home. Izabella, this would be a great investment for your future. He wants an answer by tomorrow as he is leaving town, soon."

"How much?"

"He is asking $110,000.00 and I'm just saying...as a realtor...that's way below what it's worth. It is a steal at that price."

Izabella struggled to wake up. Words would not cooperate in spilling out of her mouth correctly. "Um...Rick...my house is appraised...it's appraised at $285,000.00. Rick, I could put it on the market." She rubbed her eyes and felt more alert. "If I bought Lee's house, I'd have an income for life with the rent, and a nice nest egg in the bank when I sold my house...and it's paid for. Hey, tell him I am interested."

"Will do. I'll get back with you in the morning."

Izabella mumbled something and pitched the cellphone toward the table, sinking back into the memory foam mattress.

◆

Did the phone ring all night?

Izabella glanced at the alarm clock; it was 7:30 A.M. She departed the bed, reluctantly, and searched for the ringing phone. It was lying on the floor.

Oh, yeah...Rick called last night...I remember...

"Hello? You want me to meet you at Susan's? Okay, Rick, I can be there in thirty minutes."

A frantic dash to the closet, and she jerked a grey and white pants suit off its hanger. Clutching the clothes in one hand, she rushed into the bathroom, grabbing make-up and toothpaste with the other. Within fifteen minutes Izabella left the house, fully dressed and groomed. Slipping into the front seat of her car, she paused to look at her watch.

Hmm, I can be at Susan's in ten minutes...

Driving through the deserted streets reminded her of the evacuation from the wildfires in 2011.

I don't know what was worse for so many people...having to leave or having to face what they returned to...it seems so long ago, but our town and our people have a strong resilience...look at all the progress that's been made already...

She squinted against the sun, entered Susan's driveway, and parked her car. Rick's truck was nearby. Walking to the porch, it suddenly occurred to her that this was about to be *her* home.

Definitely inspection time...

Rick held the front door open for Susan, and she stepped onto the porch carrying a tray loaded with finger food and drinks.

"Breakfast is ready," Susan announced merrily. "Compliments of the Handy-Dandy Donut Shop."

Izabella skipped up the steps and glanced at the variety on the tray. "Pigs in a blanket, fresh fruit, bagels and crème cheese, how nice!"

"We missed dinner last night." Rick chuckled. "I was starving this morning and stopped in at Handy-Dandy on my way here."

"*You* missed a meal?" Izabella teased.

Susan laughed. "We fell asleep in the porch swing."

"A likely story."

Rick handed Izabella and Susan each a bottle of orange juice. "Hope you like pulp in your juice."

"That's the only kind I buy. Thanks." Izabella twisted the lid off.

"Tell her how we woke up." Susan nodded at Rick, spread crème cheese on her bagel, and sank her teeth into it.

"Lee Miller and his buddy, Clayton Vaughn, were standing right here." Rick laughed. "Talk about feeling foolish...it is funny though, now. I can't believe we dozed off like that."

"You were both tired, but I'm glad you managed to think of me to purchase this house."

"We'll check the house for any possible needed repairs, and I've walked the property. Original survey iron rods are still in the ground at each corner. As a realtor, I've sold houses from this neighborhood before, and each plat is one square acre. If the house is sound, you have a great deal."

He sipped his orange juice, and piled his paper plate high with food. Izabella sampled a pig in the blanket and returned to the tray for more.

"Get a plate." Susan urged.

"I will. This is so good."

Breakfast ended with nothing left over. Plates and bottles were loaded on the tray. Susan grabbed it and turned to Izabella. "Ready for the grand tour?"

"Sure, lead the way."

Susan and Rick entered the house. Izabella followed, stopping to examine the wainscoting in the hall. She ran her fingers lightly across the wood while her friends waited for her.

"Beautiful." She nodded.

They walked on down the hall.

"The first door on the right is to my apartment. Lee Miller's apartment door is on the left, almost at the end of the hall." Susan opened her apartment door and ushered Izabella inside.

Rick took the tray from Susan. "You go ahead and show her the rooms, and I'll drop the tray off in the kitchen."

"Thanks."

He could hear the women talking in the distance as he made his way to the kitchen. He placed the tray on the counter and noticed extra bottles of juice. Sprawling in a chair, he unscrewed the top from another small bottle of orange juice and gulped it down.

"Hey, anybody home?" Lee called out.

"Come on in, Lee. I'm in the kitchen."

Rick stood as Lee entered, and they hardily shook hands.

"Care for some juice?"

"No, thanks, I'm good." Lee rubbed his hands together. "Hey, I noticed Izabella is here. I'd love to show her my apartment. If she really is sold on the house, I can make a few calls and schedule an appointment with the title company this evening."

Rick raised an eyebrow. "Nowhere else except in River Town can you close that fast. I've done it before."

"Yep, that's the perks of a small town and having everything right here. In a city, you could wait weeks on surveys, appraisals, paperwork to be typed; you know the drill." Lee nodded.

"I've certainly enjoyed doing business with Mr. Raymond Eisenberg. He prides himself on clear titles and has excellent employees." Rick paused as the women's voices grew louder. "We are in the kitchen, Lee is here," he shouted.

Susan and Izabella sailed in, both had a lighthearted manner about them, and Izabella walked straight to Lee.

"I am impressed. Show me more!" She prompted.

Lee grinned. "Well, at least my apartment is clean." He quickly glanced at Susan. "Oh, I don't mean to imply yours isn't, Mrs. Susan... it's a bachelor thing. I even vacuumed. Come on."

They explored his part of the house, and Lee pulled a chain to open the attic entrance. A built-in ladder extended out and they all climbed, one at a time.

"It is dusty up here, be careful. I have some belongings I'll have Clayton send to me, like the rugs, for instance. I have a cabin in the mountains, and the full size room rugs will be great for the winters. A lot of this stuff I will leave. Do you mind, Mrs. Izabella? That is, if you decide to buy it."

"Oh no. I see some quilts, and look...a full size wooden, baby cradle. Boxes, crates...what an assortment to delve into."

Lee coughed and choked, losing his breath. They all rushed to him, and he waved his hand, motioning for them stop. He was finally able to regain a steady breath and sputtered, "It's this dust, I've always had trouble with it."

Turning to face Izabella, he appeared lost in thought for a moment. "Um, don't get too attached to anything up here, until Clayton is finished moving out what I want."

"Oh, I would never get in the way. Tell him to let me know when he is finished."

"Will do."

Rick turned towards Lee and Izabella. "Do you two realize it sounds like a done deal? Are we even going to look at the garage?" He gave a half-smile.

Susan noticed Lee's eyes watering. "Come on; let's get you out of here. That dust is starting to get to all of us." She gave Lee a friendly pat on his arm, and they slowly departed the attic.

"I do want this house. I fell in love with it before I ever walked inside." Izabella glanced at Rick when they stood back in Lee's apartment. Lee shoved the ladder back into the ceiling and sneezed.

"It appears solid to me." Rick replied.

Susan nodded. "Everything works. I haven't had one problem, here."

"Did I mention a new garage door opener...installed last year? Also a new hot water heater for both apartments."

"I'm sold." Izabella made rapid strides towards Lee, and extended her hand.

Lee flashed a smile at her and vigorously shook her hand. "I'll call Mr. Raymond for an appointment at the title company. I'm positive we can have the closing today. You will need to bring a cashier's check for $110,000.00 made out to the Eisenberg Title Company. I will pay filing fees and any other additional costs they encounter."

Rick chimed in, "After Mr. Raymond deposits, he will then issue Lee a check for the sale of the house. That is his procedure, and that is the only way he will do it."

"I'll go to the bank, now." Izabella stated and looked at Lee. "When a time is scheduled, let Susan and Rick know. I can call them when I finish at the bank."

"Sounds good." Lee nodded.

Rick winked at Susan. "Ready?"

"Let's go." Susan and Izabella hurried out into the hall with Rick bringing up the rear. The instant he shut Lee's door, both women squealed and raised their arms up in a happy dance. Stomping their feet in unison, they were completely exhilarated. Exhaling deeply, they marched arm in arm down the hall and toward the front porch.

"May I open your front door, Mrs. Contrell?" Susan deepened her voice.

"Only if you let me touch it." Izabella laughed at Susan.

Rick shook his head. "Ladies, have a nice day. I'm going to work." He bent and kissed Susan quickly, then turned to Izabella. "You are making a wise decision. Congratulations."

"Thanks, Rick, and Lee doesn't know it, but the house I am in now is completely paid for. The Lord has certainly blessed me."

Izabella glanced at Susan. "Remember me telling you the story of my school teacher in Biloxi, Missippi?"

Susan frowned. "Vaguely. Didn't she write a best seller manuscript, but left it laying on a shelf for years while she went to college?"

"Yes. She was my inspiration."

"Was?"

"She passed away last year, and had no family left. In her will, she left me her entire estate; property, money, book, royalties, everything. That is how I am able to buy this property, and I'm so thankful. I consider this another blessing."

"Oh, it is. You so deserve it, Izabella."

"What a happy day!" She skipped down the steps and hurried to her car. "I'll call you later, Susan," Izabella yelled and drove off.

"Can I help you with anything before I go?" Rick glanced at Susan.

"No. Dixie should be released from the hospital this evening. I'll be cleaning and getting things in order here."

"Looks like today is spinning by fast." He waved as he crossed the lawn, and Susan returned the gesture. She stood on the porch and watched him drive away.

◆

"Mrs. Contrell, I'm Raymond Eisenberg. Have a seat, please." He motioned to a massive mahogany table with twelve, leather, swivel chairs on each side.

"Thank you." Izabella sat near the end.

"Mr. Miller will arrive soon, and we will begin the paperwork. Have you considered what you'd like to do with the new property?"

"Well, I thought about having a children's day care center."

"Years ago it would have been a productive venture. Now, however the laws would restrict your income tremendously. Liability insurance, property insurance, employee insurance...not to mention your own health and life insurance, your car insurance, and home owner's insurance; not much left for profit. Don't forget all the red tape and all the inspections by local and state authorities." He sighed. "Business is not the same as it was twenty years ago."

"I do love children that's why I thought about owning a day-care center."

"May I suggest the C.A.S.A. program we have here in Texas? C.A.S.A. stands for Court Appointed Special Advocates for children. These volunteers have the best interests at heart of abused and neglected foster children. They stay with a case until the child has a permanent home. Contact our county judge and join a training session. You are present at their court hearings, and other settings. Children have a better chance of not 'falling through the cracks' of our legal system, when a judge assigns an adult to be their advocate."

"I would *love* to be an advocate! Thank you for the suggestion, Mr. Eisenberg."

"You are very welcome."

The secretary entered the room and took her place at the end of the table. Lee Miller arrived and shook Mr. Eisenberg's hand.

"Have a seat, Mr. Miller, we may begin."

A stack of pages lay at the end of the table in front of the secretary. As Mr. Eisenberg explained each step, she handed a page to both parties to sign. The process was long and monotonous. Izabella and Lee sat straight in their chairs, and each held a pen in their hand.

The receptionist entered the room and whispered something to Mr. Eisenberg.

"Excuse me; I have to take this call. We can take a short break." He nodded to the secretary, and they both left with the receptionist.

An older woman quietly walked into the room and served Lee and Izabella a cold, bottled water. She handed them each a package of cookies and turned to leave when she glanced back at Lee.

"Well, hello! I thought I recognized you. How is Mrs. Miller?'

"She is visiting a cousin in Iowa. How have you been?" Lee inquired, politely.

"Too busy, but I can't complain. Thankful to have a job." She nodded and left.

Izabella studied the contented look on Lee's face. "Excuse me, but did she say Mrs. Miller?"

Lee laughed out loud. "It's hard to explain a wayward life to small town elders. A girlfriend moved in with me earlier this year, and it didn't last long. This lady thought I had married and still asks about 'Mrs. Miller.' I just tell her anything. The poor dear can't remember much, but for some reason my ex-girlfriend sticks in her mind."

"Oh, that is so considerate of you to pacify her." Izabella blurted.

Raymond Eisenberg and his secretary returned to their chairs. He glanced at Izabella. "We are nearly done, Mrs. Contrell."

The last page was soon signed, and the last copy handed to both buyer and seller. Izabella gave the certified check to the secretary, and Mr. Eisenberg stood and shook hands with Izabella and Lee.

"I'll file this at the courthouse, and your deed will be mailed to your current address." He smiled at her and raised his eyebrows at Lee. "And you, young man, I can remember when your mother gave you her Power Of Attorney. How many years ago was that?" He chuckled. "You have done well, Lee, I commend you."

"Thank you, sir."

Raymond Eisenberg turned to face Izabella. "Congratulations, Mrs. Contrell, and don't forget to check out the C.A.S.A. program."

"Thank you, I will."

The secretary handed her a yellow legal size envelope with her copies tucked inside and gave one to Lee as well.

Izabella shook hands with all of them and felt like she was walking on air as she left the office. Her heart raced with each step she took.

I did it...I did it!

Chapter Twenty-Five

"Mom? How do you like Skype? Hey, adjust your webcam, raise it up a bit." Scott's image stared at her.

"Oh, I love Skype." She changed the direction of the webcam on top of her computer. "How's that?" Susan yelled.

"Much better, I see your face. Don't yell, I can hear you." He quickly smiled, and the excitement of the moment overwhelmed Susan. "I'll never forget this, Scott. You are still in Afghanistan and brightening the entire room here with your smile."

"Aww, that is so sweet, Mom, but my news isn't." He lowered his voice, and Susan had to strain to hear him. "My intuition was right on target. The paternity test proved I am not the father of Dixie's baby." He drew his mouth into a tight line, paused, and continued in a firm, somber tone. "Dixie's behavior is erratic, and her actions are unpredictable. Do you think she will stay in River Town? Does she like it there?"

"I'm sorry about the results, but everything happens for a reason." Susan wrinkled her forehead immediately. "I'm not sure what she will do. I bring her home from the hospital later this morning. The baby is being monitored, has oxygen and I.V. tubes, and must remain at the hospital. Dixie seems to enjoy the company of our former landlord, but he is leaving...says she smothers him. I will tell her about him today." Susan's voice reached a high pitch tone. "And I'll tell her you are not the baby's father. She will be most upset."

"She brought it on herself, Mom. I regret putting you in the middle of this mess."

"Scott, you had no other choice, don't worry about it. On a lighter note, this is a special time for me. My wedding is this Sunday. I'm marrying a wonderful man. You will really like Rick Yeager. We pray and help each other deal with issues."

"I love you, Mom. Wish I could be there for the wedding. I'm glad you have Rick, and I hope to meet him someday."

"You will. We are building a house and have included two brothers into our family. Everyone here calls them M & M. Their names are Matt and Mead McKinley, and they want to legally change their last names to Yeager. Rick and I met them during the wildfires of 2011. They also work for Rick, such exceptional young men."

"I am impressed with them already. What an honor, wanting to change their last name to Yeager. Our family *is* growing. What do my sisters think about it?"

"I don't know. I haven't heard from Karen or Molly in months, but I am going to call them. It's only a few days left until the wedding. You never know, they might be able to attend."

"I hope so, and I do feel sorry for Dixie's little baby girl. Let's all pray for her."

"We are. I am anxious to get this over with. After Dixie explodes into a temper tantrum, I hope she sets a steady course toward a more progressive future....for her sake as well as the baby's."

"So do I, Mom. The divorce will be finalized next week. It's time she made a new life for herself. Write me, and let me know what she does."

"Oh, I will."

"I'll look forward to your letters. I have to go, now. I love you, Mom. See you in a few months."

"I love you, too, son. I pray for your safety."

"Thanks, bye, Mom."

"Bye, Scott."

◆

Susan left her computer, sunk into the couch in the living room, and closed her eyes.

Lord, I pray for Scott's protection, I pray for guidance with Dixie, and I pray for that poor, innocent baby. May she be loved and have good health…

Going through the motions of a daily routine, Susan first enjoyed her quiet devotional time. She dressed for the day, had breakfast, and crammed a load of clothes in the washing machine, when Rick abruptly crossed her mind. Quickly, suspending any further household activity, she sprawled in the recliner and called Rick on her cellphone.

How unusual, his answering machine came on…wonder where he is…

"Rick, it's me, Susan. Call me when you get this message. It's important. Love you, bye." She ended the call and walked to the broom closet. Opening the door she stared at the Swiffer Sweeper and considered freshening the floors before bringing Dixie home.

"Utter nonsense, it's clean enough. I'm done with this apartment," Susan mumbled to herself. Restless, she left at 10:30 A.M., and drove straight to the hospital. She hurried to room 480 and a wave of energy quickened the pace of her steps. Shoulders straight and arms swinging, she entered with a determination to remain friendly.

"Ready to leave, young lady? Has the doctor written your release orders?"

Dixie squirmed on the bed and pointed to her packed suitcase. "Yes. Is Lee at home?" Her voice was flat with no emotion.

"I don't think so." Susan located the combination T.V. remote control with an emergency call button. She depressed the button.

A nurse responded loudly on the intercom. "Did you intend to buzz the nurse's station, or was that an accident?"

"No accident. I'm here to take Dixie home."

"I'll send someone with a wheel chair, and we'll wheel her outside to your car." She bellowed.

"Thank you." Susan glanced at Dixie.

No sign of feisty traits. She appears meek—defeated...not herself.

"Do you want to see the baby before we go?"

Dixie shrugged. "Not now. She is okay. Let's leave."

"Okay." Susan, intent on being kind and patient, turned and patted Dixie on her shoulder. "I'll meet you by the hospital's main entrance in the circle drive. Want me to carry your suitcase?"

"Not necessary." A nurse answered as she pushed the wheel chair into the room. "We will lay it across her lap."

Susan nodded and took off.

I guess she is acting strange because of Lee. Surely her feelings can't be that strong for him...she hardly knows anything about him...they don't even have anything in common. Is she mistaking an attraction for serious bonding?

Slipping her car in the line to pick up and deliver patients, Susan dismissed Dixie's reasoning and considered where to take her out to eat for lunch. The nurse arrived, pushing Dixie toward the car, and Susan hopped out as the nurse set the suitcase on the concrete walkway.

"Here, let me give you a hand." She opened the passenger's front door and helped Dixie into the seat. Glancing sideways, she smiled at the nurse. "I'll put the suitcase in the back." Susan rushed to retrieve it while the nurse opened the door. Setting it upright on the floorboard, she turned and waved to the nurse. "Thanks."

Dixie stared out through the front window displaying no emotion.

Driving out of the hospital parking lot, Susan decided to give Dixie some space and listen to whatever she wanted to talk about.

"I imagine you are tired of hospital food. Any favorite place you want to eat at? I'm starving." Susan eased the car out into the street and blended in with the traffic.

Dixie leaned back into the seat. Her face slowly displayed a half-smile, and she raised her voice. "Are you kidding?"

Dixie is finally speaking with spunk...

"Ci Ci's Pizza will lose money on the buffet if I eat there today."

"I enjoy their buffet, too. Ci Ci's it is." Susan swung the car around and headed in the opposite direction. She glanced at Dixie. "You have lost weight. Pizza will build up your strength and pile on the calories."

"Exactly what I need and don't say I'm eating for two now. It's just me."

"Eat as much as you can. The baby will be home soon."

"Well, I'm not sure about the baby. My family never was one to *be* a family if you know what I mean. All my life it was everyone for their own selves." She fidgeted with the control lever for the side window on the car. Dixie would lower the window a few inches, and then quickly raise it, completely lost in thought. "Sometimes it is scary to think I have a baby to take care of."

"We will help you, Dixie. All new mothers are overwhelmed at times."

Dixie turned and glared at Susan. "Except you... I bet you have never been overwhelmed or afraid of anything."

"No, that's not true, Dixie. I pray a lot for strength, guidance, and forgiveness. I couldn't make it without Jesus in my life. That's what helps me."

Dixie stared out the front window, and Susan refrained from starting another conversation. She zipped into the restaurant's parking lot and smiled at Dixie. "Here we are."

After a hearty meal, Dixie relaxed and began to talk again. Anxious to return to the apartment, Susan backed the car from its parking slot, and they took off.

Might as well get this over with...I'll try to break the news to her as easy as possible...

"We have had some changes since you have been in the hospital." Susan casually mentioned without looking at Dixie. Watching the road ahead of her, she continued driving. "Lee is preparing to move."

"Move?" Dixie twisted in the seat and frowned at Susan. "Lee is moving? What happened?"

"He sold the house to a friend of mine. Izabella will move into his apartment when he leaves."

"What?" Dixie demanded shrilly.

Susan stole a glance at her and saw the crushed look on Dixie's face.

There is no easy way to do this...and how do I approach the subject of the paternity test? Lord help me...I don't want to hurt her... she's already so hurt...

Dixie turned away and yelled, "Don't feel sorry for me. You know I liked him." Her posture slumped slightly, and she folded her arms over her stomach. Absentmindedly, she started rubbing her hands across her arms, and she moaned. Barely audible, she moaned again.

"Dixie, he is not worth your pain. Don't do this to yourself. Don't let him stress you."

"Don't tell me what to do." She tried to stifle a sob, and her shoulders shook.

"I have your best interests at heart, Dixie. Please, believe me." Susan spoke in a soothing voice. Reaching across the front seat, she quickly patted Dixie on her knee.

Dixie sat up straight. "You said 'some changes'...there is more isn't it? What else?"

Susan took a deep breath and nodded. She steered into the driveway at the apartment and parked. Both sat in silence and remained seated.

"I'm waiting. Tell me." Dixie stared out the side window and tapped her fingernails on the door release handle.

Susan's heart raced and pounded so loud inside her ears, she felt the sensitive beginnings of a migraine headache. The daylight began to hurt her eyes. She blinked in pain, and opened her mouth to breathe.

Ever so slowly, Susan moved to face Dixie. "Results from the paternity test show my son Scott is not the father of your baby."

Dixie's nostrils flared and sarcasm spat from her mouth. "*My* baby? So now it's *my* baby?" She shook her head, exited the car, and ran to sit on the front porch.

Strange…Dixie sounds strange…

Susan climbed the steps leading to the porch, paused at the swing Dixie was on, and managed to speak. "Dixie, I'll help you with whatever you need. Please think it over. I'm going to lie down for about thirty minutes."

Dixie would not acknowledge Susan's presence and refused to talk. Susan noticed Dixie had an unfocused gaze out toward the street. Frowning, Susan entered the apartment and made her way to the bedroom. Now quietly crying as the headache pounded louder than a jackhammer, she darkened the room by pulling the draperies. Completely vulnerable, she sank into the bed and instantly said a silent prayer.

◆

I won't rot on this porch. I'm too young to sit here…

Dixie walked down the steps and meandered across the front lawn. The peaceful melodies of birds singing, and their distinctive calls to each other was disturbed by the unmistakable grinding sound of a motorcycle engine. Dixie stared down the street and saw the tiny dot grow in size, and grow louder as it approached. Amused, she danced toward the curb, determined to meet this obvious menace to the quiet neighborhood.

A biker…

Dixie waved her arms high into the air and flagged him down. He stopped with caution and scanned the area. He didn't wear a shirt, and she admired the red, white, and blue tattoo of an eagle across his entire back.

He raised his head and regarded Dixie. He observed her long hair. She was thin and excited.

Dixie studied him. It occurred to her that he was available…a possible boyfriend. She grinned.

"You got a name?" He remained focused on her, and his chest rose while he slowly breathed in.

"Dixie."

"Want a ride, Dixie?"

In a daze, she walked closer and ran her fingers across the back seat.

At the same moment, Lee Miller walked out of the garage and saw Dixie flirting with the biker.

"Who is that?" The guy motioned to Lee.

"He's nothing to me."

Nodding, he raced the engine of the Harley. "I'll be back." He gave a sly smile. "Later. We'll ride." He left in an annoying noise that seemed to exhilarate Dixie.

Lee went back into the garage, and Dixie glared at Susan's apartment.

Mrs. Perfect…I don't have to listen to you…and I don't need your help…

Dixie hurried up the porch steps to the front door of the house and entered the long hallway inside. Stopping at the entrance door of Susan's apartment, she marched about searching for her mother-in-law. The soft snoring from Susan guided Dixie to the bedroom, and Dixie walked in defiantly. A light sleeper, Susan was alarmed by Dixie's intrusion and sat up in bed frowning.

"Come with me." Dixie instructed, and Susan tried to clear her aching head. Unable to reason with Dixie, Susan merely gave into her request, following Dixie into the living room.

"I hope you aren't angry." Susan sighed.

"Angry? Oh no, I'm not angry."

Without warning, Dixie suddenly jerked the door open to the broom closet, grabbed at Susan and deliberately shoved her inside. Susan struggled to escape, kicking at Dixie and pushing at the door before Dixie slammed it shut.

"Let me out," Susan shouted and beat on the door with her fists. A sharp point of something metal jabbed at her side. Changing position, she leaned against the door, and the metal object crashed to the floor. Susan stood in total darkness as her fear of Dixie intensified.

"How does it feel?" Dixie taunted her. "How do you like being alone like I am?"

"You can be happy alone, Dixie. You don't need someone to take care of you. You can take care of yourself. We will help you. Your baby needs you..."

Susan heard the muffled sound of Dixie's shoes on the hardwood floor as she left, and the closet seemed to crowd into her body.

Sweat popped up on Susan's clammy skin and a wave of claustrophobia engulfed her.

"Help! Someone help me! Help!" Her voice cracked. She felt nearby objects and recognized the Swiffer Sweeper. Using as much force as she could manage, Susan knocked it repeatedly against the door handle, until it slipped, and her knuckles slammed into the handle. She yelped, dropped the sweeper, and rubbed her throbbing hands.

Hearing someone run down the hall, she took a deep breath, and yelled louder than she ever had. "Help! I'm locked in here!"

"I'm coming. Hang on."

Lee Miller unlocked the door, and Susan fell out of the closet, crying with relief.

He reached for her arm and gently helped her stand. "How in the world did you end up in the closet?"

"Dixie…it was Dixie." Susan shook, sobbing.

"I thought something wasn't right. She rushed out of the house minutes ago, and I watched her run down the road. I figured you two had an argument about that biker."

"What biker?" Susan immediately felt like she'd been drenched in cold water as her intuition kicked in.

"I was sorting through boxes in the garage earlier and heard a loud rumbling sound. I came outside and noticed her flirting with a biker. He had parked at the curb and was racing his motor."

Alarmed, Susan involuntarily shivered. "Can you describe him?"

"Sure. Typical shaggy beard, skull-cap rag tied on his head, and a huge tattoo on his back."

"What did the tattoo look like?"

"A red, white, and blue eagle."

Susan sucked her breath in sharply. "It *is* him. It's Mack Reynolds. I have to call the Sheriff's Department. He is wanted in connection with a bank robbery." She glanced at Lee and observed his face turning pale.

"Hey, I don't want any part of this. Leave me out of it." He stumbled backwards out of the room. "I'll be out back grilling a burger." He frowned and disappeared down the hallway.

Susan winced and made the call. "Hello, I'm Susan Penleigh, and I have to report that Mack Reynolds could be in my neighborhood. He is riding a motorcycle. I know you have a warrant out for his arrest in a bank robbery because my finance's daughter, Tessa Yeager, allegedly robbed the same bank."

She listened as the dispatcher took the information and assured her someone would check it out.

Susan ended the call, hit the speaker phone option, and frantically dialed Rick. He answered on the first ring.

"Hello?'

"Rick! Where have you been? I tried calling you earlier." Overcome with emotion, words tumbled from Susan as a cascade of tears fell down her face.

"I drove to Trico Lumber Company in Hughes Springs, Texas and picked up a load of Hardy Board."

"Hardy Board... what's that?"

"Concrete panels for the outside of our home. Remember, I showed you samples?"

"Yes, I do now...a wise choice. I'm glad our house is coming along, but we need to talk." Susan's voice sounded strained, and she choked on a sob.

"Susan, what is wrong?"

"It's Dixie. She locked me in the closet. Lee heard me yelling and got me out. He saw Dixie earlier with a biker. Lee described him as Mack Reynolds and didn't even know it." She caught her breath and rushed on. "Lee said Dixie was running down the road the last time he saw her."

"I'll be right there. Lock the door."

◆

Dropping the trailer from his truck, Rick shouted orders at M & M.

"Guys, unload the material. I'll be back as soon as I check on Susan. She could be in danger."

Matt and Mead sprinted to the truck. "Scoot over, we're coming with you."

"No, I'll call you if I need you. Work on our home. That's what we all need right now." Rick climbed in the truck and drove off.

He accelerated and zoomed down the highway. Traffic was light. In the rear view mirror, he caught a glimpse of an approaching motorcycle.

Mack Reynolds, and he has a girl holding onto him...

Rick watched in amazement as they passed his truck and raced down the highway. The girl's hair blew in the wind, sailing out behind her.

Shaking his head, Rick gasped as he recognized the girl.

"It's Dixie. How did they get together?" He muttered out loud.

The motorcycle headed north, going out of town. He noticed another car advance behind him...with lights flashing and sirens blaring. Rick quickly exited onto the shoulder of the road, and the sheriff's patrol car sped past him.

Caught up in the moment, Rick jumped out of the truck and stared as the patrol car raced down the highway.

"I hope you catch him, buddy...but with his Harley reaching speeds up to a hundred miles an hour or better...I don't know..."

Chapter Twenty-Six

Thoughts of the manager's actions gnawed at Izabella's conscience, and she experienced an uncomfortable sensation of dread. Forcing herself to enter the grocery store, she hoped to not encounter Mr. Shafer today and clocked in for her early shift at work.

I won't let him rob me of my joy and by working early, I'll have time this evening to run by the courthouse and sign up for the next C.A.S.A. training session...

Forming the image of her new property and considering its potential, she smiled as she approached the service desk.

"Aren't you in a good mood, I wish all my employees came to work with a smile."

Izabella's heart skipped a beat, and she stared at Mr. Shafer in disbelief. Nodding her head, she slowly looked around and saw no other employees.

"Where is everyone?"

He handed her a till. "You are it until Iris gets here in an hour. Open lane four. The night shift is clocking out now. I have to go upstairs. If you get busy, call me and I'll help." He left her standing at the service desk and hurried to the back of the store.

Izabella, still dazed, stood holding her till and watched him walk further down the aisle.

Of all things...and of all people to be stuck with at work...

She heard someone clear their throat and noticed a customer standing nearby holding a box of granola bars in one hand and a gallon of milk in the other. She appeared weary, but thankfully, polite.

Izabella felt her face flush. "I'll be at lane four, ma'am."

They both darted to the closed lane. Izabella stuck her till into the register, leaned over the counter, and unhooked the chain.

"Sorry you had to wait." She glanced at the woman who put the box and milk on the conveyer belt. Izabella scanned both items and sacked them before the woman had a chance to open her purse. She dug into it, retrieved her billfold, and finally paid for her purchases. Izabella handed her change, and a receipt as the customer brought her car keys out of her purse.

"Now that's what I call fast." The woman laughed and took off to the exit door.

No one else approached, and Izabella strolled to the magazine racks. Straightening them, she recalled the proper term used by the grocery industry; conditioning. She chuckled out loud.

I am conditioning the magazines...

Izabella glanced at the food items at the end of nearby aisles to discover what was displayed. She was told while in training that the store hired physiologists to pick items for those specific areas. Those areas were called end-caps. The items were displayed to appeal to impulse buying customers, and for that reason alone, Izabella refused to buy anything on an end-cap.

Stick to your list...that is my motto...

Two older women and a younger, very pregnant woman strolled toward Izabella from the back of the store. All were extremely quiet, and all wore store employee uniforms.

Must be the night shift leaving...

"Hi, I'm Izabella."

"I'm Charlene, that's Melanie, and the expectant mother is Debra." The oldest woman pointed to each as she spoke. "You must be new."

"Yes, I am, and I'm learning more than I want to know about a grocery store every day." Izabella sighed deeply.

"Well, you are about to learn more." Charlene laughed. Melanie and Debra quietly exchanged knowing looks at each other.

"Don't ever refuse any job here." Charlene continued. "You do whatever they tell you to do."

"Why? What happened?" Izabella walked closer to the trio, and observed no one else was in the store.

Charlene lowered her voice. "It's about Mr. Shafer. Debra is our Union Steward. She is also eight months pregnant. Last week, Mr. Shafer made her sweep the front entrance of the store—as hot as it is outside. She contacted the Union Representative and was informed that as long as Mr. Shafer pays her the same high, hourly wage she makes as a cashier, she has to complete any work he instructs her to do. Even if that includes sweeping the parking lot. This week, Mr. Shafer has Debra working the night shift from 11pm until 7am. scrubbing the public restrooms on her hands and knees. He inspects each commode and stall before she can leave the next morning."

"But she is huge! She is eight months pregnant!" Izeballa's voice rang out with indignation.

Debra, exhausted, leaned against a crate of nicely stacked produce. "He is trying to get me to quit. I speak up too much about the things he does here. So far, he always has an excuse or lies out of it. I'm not leaving, though. My baby is due in a few days, and then I will get six weeks maternity leave. After that, I will be back." She raised an eyebrow and smiled.

Melanie glanced around. "We need to go. Nice meeting you."

Charlene and Debra nodded.

"Nice meeting you, also." Izabella watched them walk out, and once again, stood still; stunned at what had transpired.

The automatic door opener noisily parted and Izabella whirled to look at who had entered.

"Pastor Williford! You just made my day. It's so nice to see you." Izabella rushed to his side.

"Nice to see you, too. How do you like your new job?"

Frowning, Izabella lowered her voice. "Please put this store on our prayer list. Someone is doing a lot of evil here. I don't use that word often, but that's the only way to describe it, evil." She fell silent and shivered.

He placed his hand on her arm, and softly patted her. "I only came in to check on you, now I know why. I will pray immediately and put this store on the prayer list as soon as I get back to the parsonage. I'll call the prayer partners, and we will all start praying against this evil." He turned and left, muttering a prayer under his breath.

Customers started sailing in. Iris arrived and opened another lane. Business was steady, and Izabella remained busy until her shift was over.

Within fifteen minutes Izabella arrived at the courthouse and made her way to the Judge's office. His secretary stopped typing, glancing up at her as she opened the heavy, oak etched glass door and entered.

"May I help you?"

"Yes, ma'am. I am interested in the C.A.S.A. program and was told to come here."

"You are at the right place." The secretary stood and extended her hand. Izabella leaned forward and shook it.

"Please, have a seat."

"When does the next session begin?"

The secretary laughed. "Not so fast. You need an application, it will be reviewed, and if you pass the requirements; you are admitted to your first training session of the course."

Exhilarated, Izabella beamed. "I can hardly wait."

"Here you go." She handed Izabella a stack of stapled pages, a pen, and continued typing.

Minutes later, Izabella returned the completed application, her driver's license, and insurance card to the secretary.

"I'll scan your cards and make a copy." She hurried with the process and returned them to Izabella. "Thank you for your interest. I will give your information to the Judge, and contact you for a scheduled appointment if you pass."

"Great, I'm happy to get this started." Izabella left the office and breathed a deep sigh of relief.

Lord, if it's Your will, please open this door for me and for a child that needs me as much as I need the child...

◆

Izabella beamed all the way home. She parked her car in the garage and sprinted behind the house to the patio. Dragonflies zipped by as she wandered past the flowering bushes and walked across the wooden deck to a lounge chair. Stretching out in it, she considered adopting a child...any child. Overwhelmed with tenderness, Izabella knew she could offer a child what it needed most...a loving family...even a family of one.

The child's well-balanced life as a Christian will be an obtainable goal...and God willing, I will be blessed with a child...to mother...

She scanned the outside of the house and thought of Rick. Sitting up straight, she grabbed her cellphone and called him.

No answer.

She waited for the answering machine to turn on and left her message. "Rick, it's me, Izabella. I want to list my house with you. Not the house I recently bought, I'm talking about the one I am living in now. Maybe we can get together soon. I do want to sell it, and you are the best realtor I know."

Ending the call, she left the patio and walked to the side door of the house. Upon entering, she looked at the contents as if seeing everything for the first time. Not with nostalgia, but with a seller's market in mind. In constant motion, she went from room to room, deciding on what to keep, and what to sell.

I don't need all of this...mementoes, yes...pictures, yes...the best mattress I have ever slept on, yes...

Izabella grinned.

Old people deserve some form of comfort...and I am getting there...

Moving past a full size mirror, Izabella saw her reflection and pondered on the work uniform she was still wearing.

"What a job..." She mumbled out loud. "Who'd ever think it would end up being a learning experience in human treatment? Or an example on greed?"

Izabella remembered her morning devotional journal. At the end of each daily page, after the scripture and accompanying story, a space was provided for whatever you wanted to enter. She located a pen and quickly wrote her thoughts for the day.

You know, as a Christian, I won't support this grocery store with my money. I have seen enough, and I don't want my friends to think I approve of the actions taken by management. I do not want to work there any longer...

Chapter Twenty-Seven

Nervous tension strained Susan's body. The tightness— like a rubber-band stretched as far as it could be pulled, slowly diminished as Rick's embrace brought immediate comfort. She trembled in his arms while they stood on the porch. Sighing, she eased away from him.

"It's too much…way too much stress. If I ever see Dixie again, I'll call 9-1-1 and keep her at arm's length. I can never trust her."

"You need to press charges. Her locking you in the closet needs to be documented. She had every intention of hurting you. I won't allow another crisis with Dixie. It *could* end in tragedy. She has to be apprehended."

"You are right, and if she doesn't get her way, she'll lash out at anyone. She needs help, maybe medication, who knows?"

"Well, we have a wedding to prepare for, and I'll be glad when I'm living here with you, especially with Dixie running loose like a crazed animal. Oh, that reminds me. On my way over here, I saw her with Mack on his Harley roaring out of town. Talk about excessive speed." Rick paused and shook his head. "They zoomed by so close when they passed me; I actually saw her long hair blowing in the wind. Wasn't even tangled, just sailing out behind her. They were soon far ahead of me and looked like a tiny dot. That's when a sheriff's patrol car raced by me, and I hope he was chasing them. There *is* a warrant out for Mack's arrest."

"It *was* Dixie with Mack?"

"Oh, yes. No doubt. I can't figure out why he was still in this area, and how he got together with Dixie."

"Lee saw them, and I reported Mack's presence in the neighborhood to the Sheriff's Department. Lee can tell you what he described to me. Here he comes."

They watched as Lee backed a U-Haul trailer into the driveway and stopped near the garage. He hurried to the porch and ran up the steps.

"Rick, you missed it. Dixie made a real spectacle of herself, earlier today."

"That's what I've been hearing. What did you see happen?"

"I saw Dixie at the curb, flirting with a biker. He left, and she went inside the house. I was sorting through boxes in the garage. I don't think she saw me. Anyway, she ran out of the house, and down the road. That's when I heard Mrs. Penleigh hollering. I found her locked inside the closet. You know the rest."

"I sure do. Thanks for your help."

Susan opened the screen door and turned to face Rick and Lee. "I'm going in to report Dixie." Displaying a brief smile, Susan spoke softly. "So much has happened; I have no idea where I put my cellphone."

Quickly disappearing down the hall, she caught bits of conversation between the two men.

"Need a hand loading the trailer?" Rick's voice trailed behind her.

"Sure."

Two sets of boots pounded down the steps from the porch as Susan entered her apartment. A sense of normalcy returned. Strolling into the kitchen, she poured herself a large glass of iced-tea, and scanned the room, spotting the mail she'd tossed in a pile on the counter.

She lowered herself onto a stool, took a sip of tea, and relaxed.

...ahhh...feels great to get back in a routine...I meant to sort through this yesterday...

Grabbing a fistful of letters, the corner of the cellphone peeped out from under the pile, and she quickly retrieved it, dropping the neglected mail. With the flick of a finger, she selected speaker phone and called the Sheriff's Office.

The automated recording came on. "You have reached the Sheriff's Department if this is an emergency, please hang up and dial 9-1-1. If you know your party's extension, you may enter it at any time, followed by the pound sign. If you do not know your party's extension, press 1 for the directory. If you wish to speak to a detective, press 2. If you have a friend or family member incarcerated and wish to speak to the jailer, press 3. For all other inquires, press 4, or stay on the line for the operator."

Susan pressed 2, waiting patiently while soothing music played in the background. It ended abruptly as someone answered.

"Jack Delmar. How may I help you?"

"I want to report something. I had called earlier today."

"Excuse me, ma'am. I need your name."

"I'm sorry. I realize you get many calls each day. I'm Susan Penleigh, and Mack Reynolds was in my neighborhood earlier. You have a warrant for his arrest."

"Yes, ma'am."

"Well, my daughter-in-law, Dixie Penleigh, is with him. She locked me in a closet and later was seen leaving town with him. I want to press charges against her."

"I'll need a statement. I can't leave right now, but I can be there this evening. What is your location?"

"Oh, you don't have to come here. I don't know if I'll be home later. Can I drive to your office and get this over with?"

"If that's what you prefer. Ask for me when you arrive."

"Thank you, Detective Delmar."

"Thank you for calling, Mrs. Penleigh."

Relieved, Susan absentmindedly glanced through the mail.

...water bill, advertisement to lower car insurance, advertisement for custom windows, phone bill, postcard from dentist... appointment reminder, mail order catalog, advertisement to buy vinyl siding, another mail order catalog, letter from Karen...

"Karen?" Susan stood, knocking the stool over. "My Karen?" She ripped the envelope open, and its contents spilled onto the counter. Holding up a colorful circular, Susan read about the latest fundraiser in Seattle, Washington. Karen and Molly were both involved in the annual event, and all proceeds would go directly to charity.

Reaching for the enclosed, hand-written letter, Susan felt a sweet, peacefulness spread over her body as she thought about both of her daughters. She quickly read the letter. It was full of energized details, and Susan blinked when she noticed the date of the fundraiser. For a split second, her breathing was suspended. Slowly, she set the pages on the counter.

Sunday...their event is the same day as my wedding...

Sighing deeply, Susan hit the speakerphone, and called Karen.

After the third ring, Karen answered. "And who do I know calling me from Texas?" She laughed light-heartedly.

"Karen it's me, your mom. How did caller I.D. list me, anyway?"

"R.T., Texas. I saw that, and thought...oh, it *has* to be River Town, Texas. I'm so glad you called."

"I had to, you won't believe what all has happened. I'm sure you know Scott and Dixie are divorced, your brother has told you, hasn't he?"

"Yes. She should have been an actress. Dixie stepped into whatever role suited her at the time, and used people to her own advantage. The innocent, wide-eyed, bubbling girl she pretended to be was most appalling."

"Well, that innocent, bubbling girl locked me in a closet. She was last seen leaving town with a biker who allegedly robbed a bank. Both have warrants for their arrest. Karen, she abandoned her baby! It's still in the hospital. Scott paid for a paternity test, and he is not the father. I feel so sorry for that poor baby..."

"Mom," Karen sputtered, "How horrible. I can remember how she always blamed others whenever something went wrong, and she constantly went to everyone else wanting sympathy for herself." Karen sighed.

"Well, she'll have to be responsible for her own actions, now."

"It's about time. What will become of the baby?"

"Oh, I'm certain it will be adopted. We visit the hospital nursery and check on the baby's progress. They are monitoring her heart. It is a she, and her name is Vinita Irene Penleigh."

"Now, that's the mother, I know. You genuinely care."

"How kind...thanks, Karen."

"Mother, did you get my letter?"

"Yes, I am looking it over now. You and Molly have done an excellent job of organizing the event. Listen, I have something else to tell you." She paused. "I'm getting married. Rick Yeager is a wonderful man."

"What? You are? When?" Karen voice lifted excitedly.

"The same day as your fundraiser," Susan announced.

"You are kidding!"

"No, I'm not. Things like that happen... sometime. We have no control on other schedules."

"Oh, I wish we could come, but we can't. I'm so sorry, and I know Molly will be also. She is at work. I have today off. I'll see her at the meeting this evening. We have last minute issues to resolve. I'll tell her then. Oh, Mom, I hope you understand."

"I do. I remember life going by so fast each day; I hardly had time to wash my face, much less make plans with my parents. I had work, kids, and cooking, cleaning, running errands—not enough hours in the day, believe me, I do understand."

"Someday we will have kids, but our days are still busy. I have to pick up some clothes at the cleaners, now. Love you, Mom. We'll talk later, and congratulations!"

"Thanks, love you, too. Bye."

"Bye, Mom."

Susan sighed and picked up the stool. She hurried outside and found Rick and Lee loading bedroom furniture into the U-Haul trailer.

"I'm going to give a statement to a detective about Dixie. I won't be gone long."

Rick nodded.

Lee frowned. "Tell them if they want a statement from me, they need to let me know. I won't be living here much longer."

"Will do," Susan yelled, clutching her purse and keys. She dashed to her car and quickly took off.

...So much for routine...

Chapter Twenty-Eight

Izabella watched as Rick hammered the 'For Sale' sign in her front lawn. Sporting his realtor logo and phone number, it drew immediate attention. Strangers slowed their cars while driving by. One neighbor went outside to pick up her newspaper and ambled over to Izabella.

"After all these years, are you really moving?"

"I sure am, Sue. Hard to believe, isn't it? I decided to downsize and bought a smaller home. It even has an apartment I can rent."

"Sounds like a good deal. We'll miss you, though."

"Oh, I'm not leaving River Town. I'll still be here. The new house is only a ten minute drive away." Izabella had a bright-eyed look. "Today, I'm getting ready to have a garage sale. Got my paper tape and permanent markers. What a busy Saturday this turned out to be! I will drag stuff out of the house all day."

"Busy lady! So, you are having it outside?"

"Yes. My ad comes out in the Sunday newspaper, tomorrow, and I'll be posting signs around town Sunday night. The sale is on Monday."

"Well, I might have to come and see if I can find a bargain."

"You are more than welcome." Izabella smiled as the neighbor sauntered back to her home.

Rick finished hammering and strode towards his new client. "Sure glad you left a message on my answering machine. I knew we'd agree on the contract. Thanks for signing with me."

"Thanks for coming early and placing the sign." Izabella sighed. "Tell Susan I'm working here all day, but I will be at the wedding tomorrow with bells on!"

"It's almost happening." Rick paused. "Susan and I don't want anything upsetting our wedding, so we haven't talked to you about Dixie. I will tell you this, she is gone, and we three will discuss this later."

Izabella frowned. "You are so right. This is not the time to discuss Dixie."

"Got to run." Rick nodded.

Izabella couldn't help wondering about Dixie. Still frowning, she waved to Rick as he took off in his truck.

Pulling a chair from the garage, she placed it amidst several boxes scattered about the driveway, sat down, and started marking prices on items to sell. Time marched on, and she soon finished her task. Next, she located a dolly and wheeled furniture out of the house and into the garage. Ripping off a section of tape, she quickly wrote a price on it and stuck it on the mirror of a dresser.

A car slowed and the female driver stopped. Lowering her car window, she hollered," Are you having a garage sale?"

Izabella stood and approached the woman. "Yes, on Monday. It will all be marked and out here then."

"Thanks, I'll be back." The car sped off and Izabella continued.

Boxes from the kitchen and bedroom were next. She had filled them earlier, stacked the boxes on top of each other, and left them in the hall. Rubbing the back of her neck, Izabella realized how tired she was. Shoving the boxes onto the dolly, she hurried and dropped them off in the garage. Her phone rang while she brought everything from the driveway into the garage. Weary, she let it ring. Finally all items were inside the garage and she locked the door. The phone rang again. Izabella followed the sound and snatched the cellphone off a flower stand. She pressed the speaker option and leaned against the side of the house.

"Hello?"

"Mrs.Contrell? This is Shirley Fisher with Judge Reagan's office. You have been accepted into the C.A.S.A. training program. We meet from 4 -5 p.m. Sunday, that's tomorrow evening in the law office of Calloway & Nesbitt on Whetstone Street. It's on the south side of the courthouse square. Congratulations!"

"Oh, thank you so much! I will be there." Izabella answered. Her mind whirled at the thought of being a foster parent, and an over-scheduled weekend.

Chapter Twenty-Nine

My wedding day...is getting close!

Happy to get her wedding flowers, Susan stepped inside the busy florist shop, took a deep breath, and let the heavy aroma overpower her senses. Easing past customers who browsed displayed arrangements, she smiled; cheerfully making her way to the crowded counter, and waited her turn...and waited...and waited. She shifted her weight to her right leg and flinched as someone accidentally pushed into her side. More customers entered the store, and Susan scooted to the end of the counter. Standing near a miniature gardenia plant loaded with blossoms, she bent to enjoy their fragrance and felt lightheaded.

...waves of claustrophobia...not again...

Susan rubbed the back of her neck and considered this was more Saturday business than she wanted to be included in. Chatter grew louder. Suddenly four women paid and left with one enormous purchase.

The owner focused on Susan and seemed pleasant. "May I help you?"

"Yes, I'm here to pick up the Penleigh order."

"I think you will be pleased. It is a beautiful combination of lilies. I'll get the boxes for you." She walked to the cooler and returned with eight boxes of flower arrangements. Upon opening the boxes, she seemed as delighted as Susan at the beauty of each one.

"I am impressed at the talent shown in this work," Susan exclaimed.

"Let me help you carry these to your car." She glanced at the other customers. "She's getting married tomorrow. These are the flowers for the wedding."

"Oh, congratulations," the customers all spoke at the same time and moved to open a path for her and the owner to walk out the exit door.

After placing the boxes in her car, Susan glanced at the owner. "Thank you so much."

"Be blessed." She hurried back inside her shop, and Susan drove the flowers to the church. A lump formed in her throat as she veered her car into the church's parking lot. She stepped out of the vehicle and glanced over the top of the open driver's door.

...the church...it's like I'm seeing it for the first time...a whole new life is about to begin...thank You, Lord...

"I stop sometimes and look at it too. I think about what it represents. I still get an incredible feeling, after all these years."

"Pastor Williford," Susan called out, and shut the car door, hurrying to meet him on the sidewalk. "I remember what you said last week, 'church is for sinners and what better place to grow in His Word.' It *is* a new beginning. I guess I'm getting nostalgic, what with the wedding, tomorrow." She beamed.

"You are marrying a good man, and he knows he is marrying a good woman. You will grow together." He paused. "Did you bring the flowers for the wedding?"

"Yes, and thanks for meeting me here. They need to be refrigerated."

He raised his head toward the sky and squinted. "Sun's already blazing, come on. I'll help you bring them inside."

"Great." Susan blurted and rushed back to the car. He followed standing patiently while she stacked several boxes in his arms. She gathered the rest, and they took off to the church. Pastor Williford unlocked the side door. They entered into the fellowship hall and hurried to the kitchen. After positioning the boxes in the nearly empty refrigerator, he turned, smiling. "Most women prefer to decorate, but I'd be glad to help."

"Appreciate the offer, but I'm really not decorating. I'll arrive early, set the flowers out, and that's it." A warm smile spread across her face, and he nodded.

"Thanks, Pastor Williford, for everything." They walked to the door, and he quickly held it open for her.

"You are welcome." He gave her a thumbs up sign. "See you tomorrow."

"Yes sir, tomorrow." She sighed, and rushed to her car. Rick crossed her mind, and she considered calling him but decided not to.

...Rick may have tons of things to do before the wedding...and so do I...

Arriving home, Susan gasped at the sight of Lee and his packed belongings. He had parked his truck on the street with the U-Haul trailer still attached. More boxes and furniture were crammed together and piled high in the bed of the truck. Held together with green, yellow, blue and orange bungee cords strapped across the top, they crisscrossed each other colorfully but secure.

She drove up the driveway and parked near the garage. The door was open, and the garage was empty. It had always been so full, reminded her of a rented storage unit. No one could have parked a vehicle there.

She strolled to the curb and experienced an uneasy feeling of something not being quite right.

...stop it...the guy is moving...he's been packing for days...

"I'm nearly done," Lee blurted and unfolded a new, blue tarp.

"You certainly have been busy." Susan walked closer. "Need some help spreading the tarp?"

"Sure. Thanks. Hold this corner." He handed her a riveted edge and tossed the tarp over the gigantic mound.

Hurrying to the other side, he tugged at each corner, until all four corners were perfectly balanced—only two feet of boxes could be seen all the way around under the tarp. He strapped it down, using more cords.

"It's safe now." He leaned against the truck. "Come on, look inside my apartment. It is definitely vacant. Izabella Contrell will be happy."

"It's empty?" Astonished, Susan stumbled back a step.

"I guess you didn't realize I'd leave so soon."

"Uh, no, I didn't. I'm sure Izabella will be glad. We will miss you."

"Thanks, Mrs. Penleigh, Rick said you two are getting married tomorrow, congratulations!"

"Well, thank you. Rick will be moving in here with me. Our house isn't complete yet. Can't complain about the builders though." Susan laughed. "Rick is in charge."

Lee joined her infectious laughter. "Hey, I like Rick, and when he gets through building the home, I assure you, it will be solid."

"I agree, and he *does* have high standards."

Lee raised his arm, motioning towards the house. "Shall we?"

Susan gave a half smile. They slowly inched across the lawn and silently climbed the steps onto the porch. He led her through the front door and down the long hall.

"I'm not accustomed to walking past my apartment door and going to yours." She blurted and paused at her door. "This feels weird."

"Weird won't last long when your friend Izabella moves in." He continued down the long hall and approached his apartment door. Swinging it open, he stood aside while Susan entered, utterly speechless. She scanned the bare walls and the immense open space of the room.

"Wow. I had no idea this apartment was so much larger than mine."

"It needs cleaning and some fresh paint."

"Well, Izabella can handle that." Susan turned and walked out to the hall. "I'll tell her she can get started right away."

Lee stepped into the hall and eased the door shut. "Oh, wait before saying anything to her. Clayton isn't finished with the attic. He will come tomorrow and remove a few more things." Lee shrugged. "I can't take anything else on this trip. I have a full load."

"You sure do."

They ambled back to the front of the house and stepped out on the porch.

"Well, Mrs. Penleigh. I'm on my way. If you need to get in touch with me, call my buddy, Clayton Vaughn. His phone number is in the book. He and I go back a long way. He's going to join me at the mountain cabin later."

"I pray all goes well for you. Be safe."

"Thank you, ma'am, goodbye."

"Bye."

She watched him saunter to the curb. He rechecked the load on the truck and entered the vehicle. As he drove away, Susan thought she saw him wipe his eyes.

...must be my imagination...

Her cellphone suddenly rang and Susan grabbed it from her pants pocket. Holding it in front of her face, she smiled at the name displayed on the caller I.D., Rick Yeager. She pressed the speaker phone button and slipped into the wooden porch swing.

"Hellooo..." She sang out.

"Well, hello, soon to be Mrs. Yeager." His voice lightened at the sound of hers. "What are you doing?"

"I'm sitting in the swing and enjoying talking to you."

"Glad I called."

"How has your day been?" Susan released an appreciative sigh.

"Number one, I thought of you all day. Number two, I attempted to work. Number three, I can't wait for tomorrow...I keep picturing you walking down the aisle...then I picture you staring at me through a veil...will you be wearing a veil?"

"Yes, a small one barely covering my face."

"Perfect, and I have surprise plans for after the wedding. I think you will enjoy them."

"Rick, I love surprises."

"I know you do, and how was your day?"

"Great. I picked up the flower order from the florist and took eight boxes to the church. All I do early tomorrow is remove them from the refrigerator, and set them out.

"Sounds like you are enjoying your Saturday."

"Yes, it's been a little nostalgic, but you know how I am."

"I wouldn't change anything about you."

"How sweet, you are so thoughtful, Rick." She pointed out. "Oh, I almost forgot. Lee is gone. He left just now."

"So fast?"

"Yes, I wasn't expecting him to leave so suddenly either. I returned home from taking the flowers to the church, and he was all loaded up, ready to go."

"Well, we will have the place to ourselves after the wedding."

"Maybe that is why he left so soon. He seemed considerate."

"Yes, he did, and it *is* our wedding day, tomorrow. I want us to spend some time alone; no Lee, no Izabella, no one."

"So do I."

"Okay, I will get off the phone. We will not see each other tonight but know that I love you, and I'll see you for the rest of my life."

"I love you, too, Rick. I'm so thankful we have a life together."

"Goodnight, Susan."

"Goodnight."

◆

The side door was unlocked, and Susan entered the fellowship hall. Veering to the kitchen, she grabbed the arrangement for the refreshment table and hurried to place it. Swallowing hard, she scanned the table. It was full. Everything was already laid out. The only item missing was her flower arrangement.

...how nice of the congregation to supply the paper plates, napkins, utensils, and the cake ...and the punch...

She sighed.

...my church family...

"Susan? Where are you?" Izabella called out from the sanctuary.

"I'm here in the fellowship hall." Susan glanced up from the main table, and Izabella rushed into the room.

"Look at you, Susan...absolutely beautiful! Glowing with happiness!" Izabella hugged her and caught a glimpse of the wedding dress. "Your dress, light blue...how pretty with your blond hair! Form-fitting, and knee length. You can wear it later. Smart girl. What is that material?" Izabella gushed and ran her hand over Susan's short sleeve.

"Polished cotton... has a nice sheen, and it feels cool." Susan inhaled quickly. "Well, we need to set the boutonnieres out for the wedding, get your corsage, and my bouquet." She hastened to the refrigerator, yanked the door open, and handed all eight boxes to Izabella.

Carefully setting them on a table, she oohed and aahed as Susan opened and found the box for Izabella.

Quickly attaching the corsage to the lapel on Izabella's jacket, Susan smiled at her brunette friend. "You look great yourself. Pastel green dress with matching jacket...very becoming. Oh...I forgot the arrangement for the refreshment table." Lifting the lid on another box, Susan placed the lily arrangement directly in the middle, then slightly rotated it. Retrieving her wedding bouquet from the largest box, she nodded as Izabella quickly drew in a deep breath.

"Susan, it is splendid!" Izabella ran her fingers over the trailing ribbons.

A few people entered the church, and their voices rose as more of the congregation arrived. Susan suddenly heard Rick, Matt and Mead talking as they approached the fellowship hall.

"It's them." She whispered to Izabella and cast a frantic look at her friend.

"Hurry, hide in the women's restroom."

The men entered, all smiling. Rick glanced around the room. "I wanted a peek at Susan."

"Not going to happen. Here, let me attach these to your lapels" Izabella pinned each boutonniere in place as the organist began playing a few notes of the wedding march. She pushed Rick and Matt out of the room. "Hurry, Rick, you need to be standing in front of the church."

Rick turned to Izabella and grinned. "I feel so exuberant I could stand on my head."

"Go on!" Izabella laughed as he quickly left.

Susan emerged from the restroom and stood next to Mead.

"Ready, guys?"

Everyone nodded.

"Follow me," Susan whispered. They hurried outside and ran the length of the church, stopping at the closed, double-doors in the front entrance. Music began. Matt opened the doors and escorted Izabella down the aisle leaving her on the left side, and took his place on the right standing near Rick.

Abruptly, the wedding march sounded, and Mead threw the doors open walking down the aisle beside a beaming Susan. They stood in front of Pastor Williford. He led a prayer. Rick and Susan 's glowing faces held a long look at each other, emitting love for all to behold. Mead gave Susan in marriage. As the Pastor spoke one at a time to each Rick and Susan, they both stumbled on their vows while placing a golden wedding ring on the second finger of each other's left hand. All too quickly, the ceremony was over.

With a wide smile, Pastor Williford faced the couple. "I now pronounce you husband and wife." He glanced at Rick. "You may kiss your bride."

Pulling her into his arms, they hugged tightly and kissed.

"Ladies and gentlemen, I present Mr. and Mrs. Rick Yeager." The pastor nodded. Rick and Susan walked down the aisle together as the congregation stood and cheered.

"Refreshments are in Fellowship Hall. Everyone is invited." Pastor Williford's voice rang out.

Rick stopped mid-aisle and drew Susan to his side, kissing her again. "We are married, we are finally married." A wide smile grew on his face matching the one on Susan's.

Chapter Thirty

Izabella, happy the wedding and garage sale were over, kept thinking about her first training session with C.A.S.A.

...Terrific people...I've already learned so much...but such major events in three days—no wonder I feel so zapped...

Setting a cup of coffee on the side table, Izabella sprawled into her overstuffed recliner, content to rest. Between sips, she turned the television on and watched the local morning news. Security cameras from a service station had captured a crook on their video. It showed a clear picture of someone pumping gas into the tank of a truck and driving off without paying for it. Alarmed, Izabella suddenly squinted and leaned forward. She sucked in a small breath of air as the video played.

...Ben...its Ben Wakefield...

Her hand fumbled across the seat of the recliner searching for the cellphone. She grabbed it the same instant the doorbell rang. Quickly, she pulled the handle on the side of the recliner, and her feet hit the floor with a thud.

"I'm coming," Izabella hollered, and ran to the front door. Not peeping through the windows to see who was outside, Izabella jerked the door open and almost fell into Rick and Susan. Breathing hard, she faced them wide-eyed.

"Izabella! Are you okay?" Susan demanded.

"I'm sorry. I was watching the news and saw Ben on television. I am in total shock." She caught her breath and appeared pale. Glancing at the worried expressions on their faces, she waved her arm and motioned them inside. "I'll explain. It happened so fast. I was about to call and report him."

Rick and Susan flopped onto the couch and frowned.

"What did he do this time?"

"He stole gas for his truck. He was caught on a surveillance camera. I watched it on the news. The authorities wanted any information about his identity or his whereabouts."

"Turn the channel. The news is still on, could be the other channel will run a copy of the same security tape." Rick stood and paced as Izabella changed channels.

"There it is," she yelled.

Susan jumped up and all three stared at the television as the video played. Ben's face was in full view of the camera. Later, the phone number of the sheriff's office flashed across the screen. The announcer urged the public to please call if they have any information or know the identity of the man.

"Yes, it's him." Rick signed and glanced at Izabella. "You want to call, or do you want me to?"

"I will call."

"Hit speaker phone." Rick instructed.

"I know." Izabella nodded, pressed the speaker button and entered the sheriff's department phone number for non-emergency calls.

Listening to the menu for a few minutes, she waited on the line for the operator and didn't select any option.

"Hello?"

"I'm Izabella Contrell, and I can identify the crook on the video who stole a tankful of gas today. He is Ben Wakefield, and he is on probation."

"Thank you for your help, ma'am."

"You are welcome. I hope you catch him." Izabella ended the call and breathed deeply.

"What a morning," she exclaimed.

Susan hurried to Izabella and hugged her. "He is history. I don't think we'll be seeing Ben around our town anymore."

"Or in any town." Rick added.

"I agree. Now, enough about Ben, it's great to see you two." Izabella stated.

"We had to stop by and tell you Lee has moved out. You can start the cleaning and painting anytime. The apartment is empty." Rick announced.

"So is the garage. " Susan added. "It's empty too. His friend, Clayton Vaughn, hasn't come to remove Lee's belongings from the attic yet. You can't put anything in the attic until Clayton is finished. Lee told me Clayton is going to join him at the cabin in the mountains."

Rick turned to look at Susan. "Did he ever say which mountains?"

"No. I guess I was too excited to question it. I knew Izabella would be glad he was gone."

"Well, I sure am glad he's gone. I will start cleaning soon. I'd like to walk through the apartment and decide on what color paint I'll need to purchase. No cleaning today, though, but the walk-through, yes, it's a great day for that."

"Take your time," Susan suggested.

Izabella nodded.

Rick poked Susan lightly in her side. "Come on, lady, we need to go."

She turned to face Izabella. "Rick is completely moving in today."

"Yes! No more living out of bags and suitcases." He walked towards the door, and Susan paused. She chuckled at Izabella. "If you will *hurry*, we can enjoy being neighbors."

"If *I* hurry?" Izabella smirked and shook her head. "I'll see you two later today. Thanks for stopping by and bringing the good news."

The couple left, and Izabella locked the door. She hurried with breakfast and took off to the apartment. Rick and Susan were not there when she arrived. Savoring the peace and quiet, Izabella strolled to the porch swing, eased in the seat, and swayed it into motion. She stayed in the swing for nearly fifteen minutes and yawned. She heard the sudden blast of a horn coming from a nearby truck, and it startled her. Raising her head she watched Rick and Susan pull into the driveway. They exited the truck and sprinted to the porch.

"Hey...you aren't getting any work done there." Rick teased.

"Hush, Rick" Susan glanced at Izabella. "Scoot over, girlfriend."

"I'm outnumbered." He plopped down in a chair and leaned his head back. "Careful, you can doze off in that swing."

"I can't imagine that happening to anyone *I* know." Izabella laughed.

"Sometimes *neighbors* do." Rick held his hands up in the air as Susan smiled at him. "I'm just saying..." He repositioned himself and purposely dodged further looks from Susan. "Now, you can't see me, my dear." He crossed his hands behind his head and yawned loudly.

"I see you relaxing." Susan carefully left the swing. "I'll get us all some iced tea."

"Wait. I want to help my bride." Rick stood and stretched, raising his arms into the air. "We have been hard at work, and we will return." He followed Susan into the house, and Izabella chuckled at their antics.

Susan not only brought out a tray of iced tea, but she had iced tea in cold, frosted mugs. Passing out the mugs and napkins, she uncovered a stack of tea cakes on the tray.

"Tea cakes?" Izabella grabbed one off the tray.

"Homemade." Susan smiled, and Izabella snatched another one.

"You know... when you first told me how you two dozed off in the swing, I mentioned how tired you were." Izabella gave a sly smile at her friends. "No offense but it's a wonder it hasn't happened again or happened to me."

"We've all been going non-stop for days." Susan sighed, and glanced at Rick as he snatched another tea cake.

Izabella took another bite and moaned. "Oh, this is so good, Susan. Thank you."

"You are welcome." She stifled a smile.

Rick consumed three tea cakes while Susan and Izabella chatted. Susan quit looking at him and bit her bottom lip trying to act nonchalant as Rick slowly chewed his tea cake.

He finally took a long swallow of tea and had a serious expression on his face. "This is as good a time as any to discuss Dixie." He drew his mouth into a tight line and nodded toward Susan.

"Yes, it is." Susan frowned at Izabella. "We don't know what is going on with her. She left without talking to us, and we don't know when, or if she is ever coming back."

Izabella wrinkled her nose. "How can she leave the baby?"

"We don't know. What we *do* know is Lee saw her flirting with a biker, right here. He had parked by the curb. Lee described the biker, and it *is* Mack Reynolds...the one who robbed a bank with Rick's daughter Tessa. Oh, that robbery is on a surveillance camera, too." Susan vented.

Izabella noticed the heavy rise and fall of Susan's chest and immediately observed a nerve in Rick's neck twitch.

He jumped into the conversation. "Anyway, long story short; Lee didn't know it but after the biker left, Dixie locked Susan in the broom closet. Lee was outside and saw Dixie run from the house. He said she kept running on down the road. Then he heard Susan yelling for help and found her locked in the closet. He let her out, and Susan reported Mack to the Sheriff's Office."

Susan interrupted. "I told them he had been spotted in our neighborhood. He allegedly robbed a bank with Rick's daughter, Tessa, and there was a warrant out for his arrest."

Rick continued. "Susan called me, and I hurried to the apartment. I had been in Hughes Springs, Texas buying material for our house, and I actually *saw* Mack and Dixie leaving town on his Harley. Later, a patrol car chased after them. Haven't seen or heard anything about them since." Rick stood still as he looked at Susan. "If we don't hear from Dixie, we will have to report this to the Child Protective Services. The baby can't stay at the hospital much longer."

Susan glanced at Izabella. "I called the nurses' station the day before the wedding. They told me the baby was recovering from surgery. Apparently, Dixie signed papers earlier, stating they could operate."

Izabella gasped. "What was wrong? Why did the baby need surgery?"

"They bypassed a blocked artery. She is doing great. No infection, she is gaining weight, couldn't be better."

Izabella spoke in a low voice. "I know one thing for sure... most people won't adopt a child with health issues."

"She is doing better, though," Susan blurted.

"The fact that she has had surgery is enough to scare people from considering her. Poor baby." Izabella raised her wrist up and studied her watch. "Visitation time is over for the nursery. Let's go see her tomorrow."

Rick and Susan both nodded solemnly. "You better believe we will."

Izabella whistled and shook her head. "She needs our prayers. Okay, we meet at 10:00 in the morning at the hospital." She walked slowly and opened the screen door. I'll hurry through the apartment now and check it out."

Susan hastened to Rick. "Let's unload the truck."

Rick reached for her hand and squeezed it. "Deal"

Chapter Thirty-One

Susan stood in front of the hospital nursery gazing straight at Dixie's baby. In all outward appearances...totally mesmerized by her. Rick leaned in and stared through the window with Susan crowding him on the left and Izabella scooting closer on his right. Izabella broke the silence.

"I wish she would wake up and let's quit calling her 'the baby'...Vinita is such a beautiful name."

"Hello, Venita." Rick cooed and tapped on the glass.

A nurse entered the nursery, and all three of Vinita's visitors waved at her. The nurse pointed to Vinita, and they nodded. Carefully, she gathered the baby in a blanket and holding her snuggly carried her close to the window.

Adult arms and hands immediately sailed across the glass as they pointed and talked as fast as possible. The nurse patted the babies arm, and Vinita awoke.

"Her eyes are blue." Izabella muttered.

"No, I think it's the way the light is reflecting. They are brown." Rick spoke with authority. Susan and Izabella exchanged knowing glances and both smiled at Rick.

Vinita tightened her hand into a fist and quickly opened it while moving her arm across her chest.

"Active, isn't she?" Susan stood on tiptoes to look over Rick's shoulder.

"She's doing great." Izabella whispered.

The nurse waved as the curtain was closed by another employee. Susan moved back from the window, and the group left, walking quietly. Susan felt Rick grasp her hand with his, and they ambled down the hall with Izabella behind them.

Susan's pace sped up. Worried, she wore a determined look on her face. "I'm going to the nurses' station; it's time for some answers."

Rick kept in step with her, and Izabella hurried. No one spoke as they rounded a corner, and approached their destination.

Susan raced to the nurses' station and folded her arms on the counter. Rick and Izabella were behind her. A nurse briefly left a monitor and glanced up at Susan.

"Yes? Can I help you?"

"I hope so. I'm Susan Pen..uh..Susan Yeager." She shook her head and smiled. "I've recently married, and I'm getting used to my new last name."

"Well, congratulations."

"Thank you." She hesitated. "We came here to see the Penleigh baby. How is she doing?"

"Let me check. My computer is up so it won't take long." She sat at the side desk and typed instantly. Susan could see a screen appear with Vinita's name and complete chart. The nurse studied it a moment and talked under her breath. "Uh-huh." Going to another screen, she repeated the same process.

A smile flashed on her face, and she pivoted from the computer. "Vital signs are good, no infection, gaining weight, and no longer on oxygen. Looks like a little girl will be going home soon." She assured.

Susan sucked in her breath and realized what they were all facing...custody. She flinched. It occurred to her in that moment...baby Vinita would be raised by all three of them. She didn't know how, but she knew as well as she knew her name, it would happen.

Susan pressed a hand against her chest with fingers splayed out. "We are so ready to hear that." She gave a half-smile. "Oh, I was wondering, has little Vinita had any other visitors?"

"Not to my knowledge, at least not on my shift."

"Well, thank you for the great news. We'll be going, now, but we'll keep in touch." Susan's voice rose happily.

Smiling wide, the nurse nodded. "I'm sure you will."

The trio returned the gesture and left the hospital. A slight breeze sailed through the parking lot, and a few chirps from birds passing overhead felt promising to Susan.

"Seems like a regular day, doesn't it? No crime, no crooks, no one to report..." Her voice trailed off.

"It's the wicked world we live in. The choices some people make, and the lies they try to broadcast as truth...for their benefit." Rick sighed. "How can Dixie take off without the baby? Self-centered? Scared? I don't know, I don't dare try to judge. Everything happens for a reason."

"Yes, it does." Izabella added. "I read the Bible, and we win. Lots of turmoil, but we Christians win."

"Amen, sister." Susan quickly slapped Izabella's hand high in the air, giving her the high-five sign. She turned to face both Izabella and Rick. "We have a long road ahead, but not only do we have Vinita's best interests at heart... we have a child of God to raise." Melancholy tugged at Susan's heart as the baby's birth mother crossed her mind, and she dismissed the emotion welling up inside her. "Isn't Vinita beautiful?"

"Always." Izabella gave a quick, warm smile to her friend.

Rick pulled at Susan's hair, and stepped back, playfully. "Coming?"

"Yes, I know. We all have work to do." She laughed, and waved to Izabella. "See you later."

"You can count on it." Izabella chuckled and ambled to her parked car.

Susan strolled side by side with her husband, and neither spoke.

...I feel strong...like I'm covered with God's full armor... thank you Lord ...

Rick helped Susan into the truck, and they drove off in peaceful silence. After traveling several miles, he started humming a tune. They glanced at each other, quickly, and he winked at her. She looked him straight in the face and tried to wink back. A half-smile crossed his face, and he looked straight ahead. Silence prevailed as they drove towards town, and Rick suddenly cleared his throat.

"We need to discuss Mack and Dixie. They still haven't been found."

"We can only hope someone will report seeing them, somewhere. Personally, I do not expect Dixie to return."

"Neither do I." He drew his mouth into a tight line and fell silent.

Susan noticed his tenseness and tilted her head towards him. "What are you thinking about?"

"Oh, I still wonder what Mack was doing at the courthouse the day we saw him."

"Maybe he was about to rob someone. Who knows?" Susan ran her hand through her hair and looked out the passenger's side window.

"We may never know until they catch him. Even then, he might not say what his plans were. Some things in life remain a mystery."

"True."

Rick hurried into the driveway of his and Susan's apartment and parked the truck. His cellphone rang as he turned off the ignition. "Would you answer it for me?"

She retrieved it from the truck console. "Hello?"

"Wait, please. I'll get him." She frowned and held the phone towards Rick. "It's the District Attorney in Tyler, Texas."

"Hello?" Rick fumbled and activated the speaker phone.

"Mr. Yeager, we have had a new development with your daughter, Tessa's case. At a preliminary hearing she plead guilty, and agreed to a plea bargain. She has a twenty-year sentence and an extensive drug rehabilitation program. No chance of parole. She has back slid too many times. We want to detox her, and we want her drug free."

"I will pray this helps her... nothing else has." Rick wiped his brow in a nervous gesture and sighed. "What about Mack Reynolds?"

"Tessa gave us all the evidence we need to convict him, and we *will* find him. It's just a matter of time."

"I saw him heading out of town on his motorcycle with my wife's ex-daughter-in-law, Dixie Penleigh.

Please notify us if and when you locate them. It appears Dixie has abandoned her baby."

"I was not aware of that. Where is the baby?"

"It is a newborn baby. Recently had surgery and isn't ready to leave the hospital, yet. Who knows? Dixie may return when the baby is healthy enough to leave."

"If she doesn't return, Child Protective Services will be notified by my office."

"If she doesn't return, we will notify C.P.S. ourselves."

"We'll keep in contact, Mr. Yeager."

"Yes sir. Thank you for calling."

Rick ended the call and took a deep breath. "Susan, Dixie is your ex daughter-in-law, isn't she? The divorce is final with her and Scott?"

"He didn't say, but time wise, it had to be over weeks ago. Scott would have been most upset if it didn't go through."

"Well, that is not the issue anyway. Find the number for the Child Protective Services and tell them what is going on. They need to know, now, and they need to hear it from you."

"I'll also have to tell them Scott is not the father." Susan bit her lip.

"Then do it. We have to get this over with."

Nodding, she grabbed her cellphone, and her hand trembled.

Chapter Thirty-Two

The painters left, and Izabella inspected each room of her apartment with a satisfied nod. *...job well done...completely ready for the movers...my furniture will arrive any minute...*

Marveling at the recent turn of events, she thanked God for the opportunity to purchase this home remodeled into two apartments. Bursting with enthusiasm, Izabella ran outside at the hammering sound of the diesel truck backing into her driveway.

Watching the men open the back of the truck, and begin to work quickly; reminded Izabella of the work yet to complete...on her part.

...the cleaning I did is nothing compared to unpacking, lifting, bending, sorting...

Sighing deeply, she vowed to finish this exhausting process of moving by the end of the week.

Organized, the workers removed blankets covering five rooms of her belongings, untangling what stood intertwined together, tight as pieces completing a puzzle. Awed, and suddenly tense, Izabella decided not to watch as they pulled the legs of a table away from other furniture.

She hurried to the front door on the porch and stood, eager to give directions. One man guided the others as furniture was hauled on heavy-duty dollies across the lawn and up the steps of the porch.

"Follow me down the hall. This goes in the apartment at the first door to the left."

They expertly positioned each piece to her specifications, and upon leaving, had the living room, dining room, kitchen, laundry room, and one bedroom functional.

She thanked the workers and plopped into the swing on the porch.

I still have to bring more boxes of my belongings, and all of my pot plants... that is just for downstairs. The movers will help with that tomorrow. Why isn't Clayton Vaughn removing Lee's belongings from upstairs?...I need that space for storage...

Impatient, Izabella's interest with the apartment faded. Try as she may, regardless of being super busy, thoughts of baby Venita returned.

...it's like a favorite movie playing again...and you snuggle on the couch with a bowl of popcorn...in anticipation.

Izabella sighed.

The image of a baby all alone...in a hospital nursery...with a missing mother...consumed her. Longing to hold and comfort the baby, she couldn't shake off the image. Dusk settled and Izabella forced herself from the swing. Tired, she entered the apartment and spent the first night at her new home.

◆

Unable to remain in bed with so much work facing her, Izabella had a breakfast bar and a glass of milk as daylight filtered through the windows. Unpacking boxes was her number one priority, and she was making progress. Cleaning supplies, groceries, dishes, pots and pans, glasses, eating and cooking utensils were finally in place. Izabella ran her hand through her hair and pulled a chair out from the table. She rested for a few minutes and glanced at the wall clock—9 a.m.

Satisfied with the results of her work, she took a deep breath, and got to her feet.

...no longer chaotic, my kitchen is done...now to unpack the bathroom boxes...

She ripped the tape off of one large box crammed full with towels and sheets when someone pounded on her apartment door.

"Coming, "Izabella called out, and took off, dodging scattered boxes. A fast look at the peephole on the door revealed Susan and Rick talking quietly to each other.

She flung the door open and saw Susan's upturned face smile at Rick while he winked at her.

"Well, hello, happy neighbors!" Izabella beamed.

"Happy for you." Susan teased.

"Is that a hint? Do I detect something going on?"

"Yes ma'am." Rick extended his right hand towards her and shook her hand as he spoke rapidly. "Let me say it has been a pleasure doing business with you, and congratulations are certainty in order. What a fine way to start the day." A smile appeared on his face and he reeled back glancing at the sky.

His voice rose in merriment. "Yes, ma'am. A fine day indeed."

"What are you talking about?" Amazed, Izabella stared openly at him.

Susan lunged forward and briefly hugged Izabella. "Oh, it is great news. A buyer phoned Rick less than five minutes ago. He wants to buy your house today. It's a cash deal. No inspection."

"What?" Izabella leaned against the door frame. "I'm still moving out..."

"It's okay." Rick pointed out. "You won't be rushed to vacate. He wants to buy it before someone else does.

He is getting married next month. He and his fiancé drove by and fell in love with it. They looked in all the windows, and it's exactly what they want."

"Who is it, someone from around here?"

Rick shook his head at Izabella. "No, he is a doctor, internal medicine, I think."

"This is incredible, what a blessing." Izabella said half-aloud. "Thank You, Lord Jesus."

"Amen." Susan and Rick added.

"You need to call him back and agree on a time." Susan spoke to Rick.

Nodding, he retrieved the cellphone from his pocket and ducked out into the hall. Izabella and Susan overheard him scheduling the business appointment with the buyer and also discuss a time with the title company.

Rick returned and glanced at his watch. "Izabella, we need to leave."

"I know you're busy, Izabella. What can I do while you're gone?"

"Oh, Susan, I appreciate your help. The movers are bringing the rest of my belongings for downstairs after lunch."

"I'll be here. You two go on. I've got this covered." Susan waved them off. "Scram." She smiled.

Izabella grabbed her purse and keys. "Thanks, Susan," she yelled and followed Rick out of the house.

◆

...the house has sold...closing was unusually quick...

Izabella scooted back into the seat in Rick's truck. He whistled while he drove. Izabella considered a pressing problem and cleared her throat. She drummed her fingers on the side of her purse while making her decision.

"Rick? There is some more business I need to take care of today. Would you mind taking me to Corner Grocery?"

"No ma'am. It's right on the way."

He soon veered into the parking lot and waited while she darted inside. Making a bee line straight to the service desk, Izabella smiled at the few employees working at the registers. Mrs. Duvall stood at the service desk and hung up the phone as Izabella approached.

"Hi, Mrs. Duvall. How is Debra doing? Has she had her baby, yet?"

"Why yes, she had a boy. Debra is on maternity leave." Audrey Duvall paused. "I didn't know she was a friend of yours."

"Yes ma'am, she is...and a real hard worker, too. I'm sure you will find plenty for her to do when she returns. Oh, another friend of mine, Judge Reagan, will like her also."

Audrey cringed.

"I'll tell him all about her. He'll want to start shopping here and look her up sometime. I won't be around, but you never know when *he* will be." Izabella turned to leave and gave one last parting glance to Mrs. Duvall.

"By the way, I quit." Izabella walked out with a pleasant smile on her face.

Chapter Thirty-Three

"You quit your job?" Susan sputtered.

"I sure did, right after I deposited the check for selling my house. Rick got his check the same time I received mine." Izabella chatted. "Tomorrow, I'll return to the bank and put the majority of that in a C.D., add to my I.R.A., and invest in some gold and silver coins. A safe deposit box at the bank is where I'll keep them."

"Well, I'm proud you're not going to rush out and spend it. Seems to me this is a blessing for your future."

"I agree, and I praise God for it." Izabella walked across the porch and veered towards the front door. "Thanks for waiting here for the movers. Are they finished?"

"The garage is full, but they did leave a space where you can park your car. Pot plants are on the back porch. I had them leave a dolly there so you can move them where you want them. Boxes are stacked next to walls of the rooms they belong in. Some antiques are still at your old home but have to wait until the attic here is emptied. Lee's friend still hasn't returned to start moving his things out. Don't know what the holdup is. Maybe he is sick?" Susan shrugged.

"Maybe. Anyway, I have another C.A.S.A. meeting this evening. I'll unpack some boxes before I go. Thanks again," she sang out, opened the screen door, and rushed to her apartment.

Susan waited as Rick locked his truck, and carried his briefcase with him to the porch.

"Izabella couldn't wait to get out of the truck." He laughed. "She saw you on the swing and took off running. She is one happy lady."

"I'm happy for her." They entered the house and headed down the hall to their apartment.

"Clayton is really dragging his feet on removing what Lee wanted from upstairs. Hope it doesn't put her in a bind—she needs that storage space." Susan gave Rick a curt nod as they stepped inside the apartment.

"Well, maybe we can help." Rick glanced at Susan. "Something sure smells good."

"Pizza...your favorite." A sly smile crossed her face, and Rick stopped in his tracks.

"Taco pizza?" His voice echoed down the hall. "Cooked with refried beans, and melted cheese?" He drew his hands to his heart. "For me?"

Susan shook her head and laughed. "For you."

"Wait. I'm drooling." Izabella hollered from the hallway. She stumbled in the doorway out of breath. "I overheard Rick and rushed over. The aroma is tantalizing. May I have a piece?" She sputtered.

"Of course, come on in." Susan stifled a smile. "By the way, I add taco seasoning over it, before baking. It's almost ready."

They followed Susan into the kitchen. She removed the pizza from the oven and sprinkled sliced, black olives, tomato pieces, and bits of lettuce across the top. After cutting it into eight pieces, she set the pan on the table and handed out cold, bottled water, and paper towels. All three sat down immediately.

"There it is; taco flavor without the grease."

Rick took a bite and winked. "Thanks."

"Oh, this is *so good.*" Izabella moaned with her first bite.

Susan bit into hers and savored the taste.

"Izabella, do you care if we poke around upstairs? Clayton is falling down on the job. Maybe Rick and I could restack Lee's stuff and put it against one wall. You could finish moving, and have the rest of the attic available for your antiques."

"That would be a big help. I'd be done with moving in no time at all, then." Her slice was nearly devoured.

Susan whirled about to face Rick. "What do you think?"

"I don't see how it can hurt anything. We can start tonight." Rick took another slice.

"Great!" Izabella sang out. "Thanks for everything." She peeked at her watch and suddenly rose from her chair. "Got to run, can't miss the meeting." She hurried out of the kitchen and they heard her shoes pound the floor as she left their apartment.

Rick focused on his wife. "She'll be fine."

"I know."

"Have a paper towel." He shoved one at Susan.

She took it, and picked at her food. "Rick…"

"What's wrong?"

"I haven't talked to the Child Protective Service since I called them about Vinita. I'm positive they are checking out my story. I wish I knew what their procedure is in a case like this."

"I'm certain the case is presented to a judge. I have no idea how long it would take, though." Rick frowned.

"It's possible Izabella can discuss Vinita's case with the judge that approved her for C.A.S.A. Maybe she hasn't left, yet. I'll hurry and try to stop her." Susan sprang from the chair, raced from the apartment, and collided with Izabella in the hallway.

"Oh!" Izabella rubbed her shoulder.

"Sorry, I didn't know you were coming down the hall. Are you okay?"

"Yes. What's going on?"

"I was hoping to catch you..."

"Well, you did." Izabella burst out laughing, and quickly stopped when she noticed Susan was serious.

Throwing her hand up in the air, Izabella shook her head. "I couldn't resist. Please continue, I'm listening."

Calm and sincere, Susan spoke in a steady low-pitched voice. "I've prayed for God's will, and I hope you understand. I had to contact the Child Protective Service about Vinita's situation. They needed to know Scott is not the father, and Dixie still hasn't returned."

Izabella frowned.

"I'd like for you to discuss Vinita with the judge that approved you for C.A.S.A. training."

Izabella's frown disappeared. "I will. As a matter of fact, this is perfect timing. He is going to visit us at our meeting, tonight." Excited, she spoke in a loud tone and took off down the hall, slamming the front door as she left the house.

Susan made her way back to her own apartment. Rick sat in a recliner in the living room staring at the evening news on television. He quickly turned the sound down when she entered, giving her his complete attention.

"How'd it go?"

Susan stood in the middle of the room. "She seemed determined. The judge will attend the C.A.S.A.

meeting tonight. Izabella is fortunate for the opportunity to talk to him about Vinita."

"Yes, she is, and Venita is fortunate to have you in her life. As a matter of fact, the same principle applies to Izabella. She is also fortunate to have you in *her* life." Rick got to his feet, approached Susan, and kissed her. He stepped back and looked straight at her. "And that goes for me, too. I thank God you are in *my* life. It was difficult for you to call the C.P.S. but you choose the correct, legal course of action, and I'm proud of you."

Susan's face lit up with a warm smile. She whispered, "God brought us together. It was His will, and I thank Him daily for you." She hugged Rick and taking him by the arm, they walked to the other side of the living room. Rick grabbed the T.V. remote from the recliner, and they sat together on the couch. He raised the volume, and they studied the long range weather forecast. During the next commercial, Rick glanced at Susan. "Do you realize if you hadn't taken Dixie into your home, none of us would even know Vinita existed?"

"I've never thought of it like that." Susan, with a sidelong glance, smiled. "Enough about me. God has a purpose and plan for all of us...and right now, our purpose is to go upstairs and help put Izabella's attic in order."

"Point taken." Rick groaned as he got off the couch. "Ready?"

"Ready. Lead the way."

They made rapid strides down the hall and stopped at her door. Rick fished in his pocket for the key, and unlocked the apartment. "Funny. The only entrance to the attic is from her apartment. Good thing she gave us a key."

"Well, Lee was renting out the other apartment. I'm sure he didn't want strangers rummaging through his belongings in the attic."

"True." Entering Izabella's apartment, Rick led Susan to the collapsible stairs in the hall ceiling near a bedroom. He yanked a chain, and the stairs descended. Susan flipped the light switch on, and the attic was instantly flooded with light.

"Here, let me help." Rick guided her to the first step. It was two feet off the floor. "You go first, and I'll be right behind you." Susan nodded and slowly climbed to the top.

She stood in the attic, looked down at Rick, and sneezed. "I forgot how dusty it is. Ugh, stale and musty. Probably hasn't been fresh air in here in ages."

"Probably…" Rick muttered as he made the climb. He stood next to Susan and put his hands on his hips. Glancing about, he pointed to the north wall.

"Let's start there. Looks like mostly trunks and boxes scattered about. Should be easy to stack."

They walked to the area and shoved boxes together. Occasionally, either one would stop when something caught their eye, and they'd wander around exploring old items used at the turn of the century.

"Izabella will love all of this." Susan remarked and sneezed again.

"Want to come back another time? We are stirring up the dust, girl."

"No, I've adjusted to the stale air and the dust. Let's try to empty half a wall and call it quits tonight."

"That's my girl." He saluted her, and she threw an antique sun-bonnet at him. He batted it with his hand, and it sailed across the room, landing on a pile of quilts. Susan's adrenalin raced at the unexpected sight of homemade quilts.

"Quilts! I have to check this out." She sidestepped more boxes, walked around a baby's wooden crib, and moved a stack of pictures out of her way.

"Oh, Rick...these are gorgeous..." She held one up, and the entire pile fell onto the floor.

"I hear something humming...Rick..." Susan turned to look at Rick, still across the room positioning another box carefully on top of two others.

He eased it down, and wiped the sweat off his brow. Raising his head, he spotted Susan and made his way to her.

"What?"

"You tell me. It is definitely not an antique, whatever it is."

Frowning, Rick stood beside Susan and listened. "Sounds like a motor. So much stuff is piled on and around it, there is no telling what it is."

"Well?" Susan leaned across a dresser drawers and pushed more quilts to the side.

Rick was astonished. "A freezer, it's a chest type freezer. Who would have guessed?"

"That's the humming sound! Can you believe anyone would leave it turned on? Can you imagine the effort in coming up here to get something from the freezer?" Her voice rose in an emotion-choked voice.

Rick took a deep breath. "I don't want to alarm you, but are you thinking what I'm thinking?"

"...Wha...what?" Susan stuttered.

"Someone went to great lengths to hide something in there..." Rick hesitated. "I'm going to open it." He stepped closer and reached for the handle.

"No! Don't do it!" Susan, engulfed in fear, pleaded with Rick. "I don't want to know. It's none of my business. I'm scared, Rick. Something isn't right, here."

"Susan, we can't walk away and leave this freezer plugged in."

"I know. Maybe I'm over reacting...go on...open it." She turned her back to the freezer. Rick raised the handle and jerked the top of the freezer open. Wide-eyed, he slammed it shut and gagged. "Out... we have to get out."

Terrified, Susan trembled. "I don't want to know, not now...don't tell me now..."

He nodded, and they stumbled to the stairs with Rick clutching his heaving stomach.

Susan shook so much she thought it would be impossible to walk down the stairs. Holding onto the hand rail, her knuckles turned white, and her posture was rigid. "Rick, I can't bend my knees." She felt waves of claustrophobia surround her on the narrow stairs.

"I'm right behind you. I'll hold onto you. Go ahead now."

She said a prayer for strength and carefully placed each foot on the solid steps. Finally, she stood on the floor of Izabella's apartment. Drenched in sweat, she smiled as Rick made it down the stairs and joined her.

"Leave the lights on." Rick grimaced. Putting his arm around her, he led Susan to their apartment.

"I want you to rest. Sit here, and I'll get you a glass of iced tea."

"I'm okay, Rick. I had to get away from the attic. What about you, are you better?"

"I will be after I make a phone call." He hurried to the kitchen and returned with a glass of iced tea. "Here, drink this; it will settle your nerves."

She took a sip. "Thanks."

He grabbed his cellphone. "I'll be out on the front porch. I have to call 9-1-1."

She nodded, and he rushed outside activating the speaker phone. He slumped into a wicker chair and pressed 9-1-1.

"9-1-1, what is your emergency?"

"I just found a body in a freezer."

"Sir, what is your location?"

Rick sighed and tried to get the mental picture of the body out of his mind. He quickly gave the dispatcher the address and his name. He glanced around and saw Susan. She leaned against the door frame and shook her head at him in disbelief. He continued.

"I rent an apartment here. The owner lives in the other apartment. She isn't here and doesn't know what has happened."

"I have a unit on the way, sir. Please don't touch anything."

"I'm sitting outside on the front porch." He ended the call, looked at the starry sky, and rubbed a shaky hand across his damp forehead.

Rick heard the approaching sirens and felt a heavy burden ease from his body. Susan walked to where he sat. She gently massaged his shoulders and neck as the deputy drove into the driveway. Another patrol car parked at the curb, and Rick stood to greet them.

"I'm Rick Yeager, this is my wife, Susan. If you'll follow me, I'll show you what I found."

Susan went to the swing, and the deputies followed Rick into the house. He talked non-stop while taking them to the attic, giving names and background information on anyone associated with the house. Pictures were taken. The justice of the peace was notified, and the coroner. The attic was taped off, and Rick was advised it was now a crime scene. Officials trampled in and out for hours, and the body was finally removed.

Rick returned to the front porch out of everyone's way. He sat next to Susan on the wooden swing. A detective opened the screen door and left the house, glancing at Rick. He walked across the porch, frowned, and drew his mouth in a tight line.

"Mr. Yeager? We checked out Clayton Vaughn. His house is empty. It appears he didn't want to move Lee Miller's belongings out of the attic. Must have known about the freezer. Do you have any idea where Lee Miller is?"

Rick shrugged his shoulders. "I can't help you. I don't know."

Susan raised her head and made eye contact with the detective. "He told me he had a cabin in the mountains, and his friend Clayton would bring the rest of his belongings to him. Lee moved out, and that was the last we saw of either one of them."

"The coroner and the justice of the peace both identified the body. It was Mrs. Miller, Lee's mother. No puncture wounds, no bruising, no indication of foul play. We have to wait on an autopsy report, but it looks like she died of natural causes. We have reason to believe the son kept depositing her social security checks, and no one knew she had passed. Clayton was probably in on the money, also. This will be an ongoing investigation, and facts will surface."

Headlights blinded them as another car zipped into the driveway. Izabella looked at the nearby sheriff's deputy patrol cars, exited her vehicle, and raced to the front porch.

"Susan…Rick…" She glanced at both of them, and her voice rose shrilly. "What? What is wrong?"

Susan rushed to her friend and put her arm around Izabella's shoulders. "It's all over now. Come inside, and we'll talk." She ushered Izabella into the house and took a deep breath.

Chapter Thirty-Four

Izabella, with a slow, disbelieving head shake, let out a whimper. "That poor woman. No one knew she died."

"Lee and Clayton knew. I wouldn't have suspected either one of them. Scary, isn't it?" Susan saw the color drain from her friend's face and quickly changed the subject.

"I feel led to do something, anything, to prevent this from happening to other seniors. I want to start a community outreach center, manned by volunteers to call the elderly each day. Sign-up sheets could be passed out at local churches, and doctors' offices. Rick encouraged me. He even said I could use the empty room in his realtor office. It wouldn't take much to get it ready."

"What a kind heart you have." Isabella spoke in a quiet voice. "I think it's an excellent idea."

"I can't wait to start." Susan replied. "So tell me, did you get a chance to talk with the judge at the meeting?"

"Yes, I told him I want to petition the court for custody...I want to legally adopt Vinita."

Susan gasped. "Izabella, this is wonderful! You have already been investigated and cleared with the C.A.S.A. program. That means you may have a greater chance for the adoption to be approved!"

"Oh, Susan. Vinita would be such a blessing..." Izabella smiled. "The hearing is tomorrow at 10:00 in the morning. Could you go with me?"

"Of course, I will."

"Thank you. I'll try to get some sleep, and not think about Mrs. Miller. I will pray for her."

"Why don't you stay in my spare bedroom tonight? The authorities may not have completed everything they need to do in the attic and might be in and out of your apartment for hours."

"I didn't think about that."

Susan grimaced. "Rick is outside talking with a detective. Come on." They left the living room and veered to the bedroom. "You look like you are about to drop."

Izabella nodded and yawned.

◆

The stately courthouse, three stories tall and sprawling across a square city block, was over a hundred years old. Izabella gazed upward as they neared the building and a light breeze tugged at their hair. It was forecast to be a bright, sunshiny day. White clouds billowed like tufts of cotton against a brilliant blue sky. Izabella pivoted to face Susan. With a radiant glow on her face, her voice rose in light-hearted merriment.

"I can't contain my excitement. I feel energized like a kid bouncing up and down, ready to take off running!" She waved her arms into the air in a grand, wide gesture. "Justice is about to *prevail!*"

Susan gave her a good-natured shove. "Come on," she chuckled, and with a fast paced walk, they arrived at the entrance early. The double doors automatically opened, and they placed their purses at the deputies desk for inspection. Each walked through the metal detector, and their purses were returned to them with instructions to cut off their cell phones.

Susan said a silent prayer concerning God's will about the hearing and felt washed in happiness as her determined friend made rapid strides down the hall. Izabella stopped at the courtroom door and waited for Susan.

"*This is Vinita's day,*" Izabella whispered. Pushing the door open, they were greeted by a court clerk.

"Name, please."

"Izabella Contrell, and this is my friend, Susan Yeager."

Thumbing through pages on a clipboard, she stopped. "You are here for the Penleigh baby hearing?" She raised her eyebrows at Izabella.

"Yes, ma'am."

"We begin in a few minutes. Please be seated." The clerk advised.

They glanced at the seating area where two, long, rows of benches, similar to church pews, were scattered with people. Izabella and Susan quickly sat on a nearby bench in the quiet, carpeted room. Four other people rushed in and scanned the seating area. Izabella and Susan scooted over, clearing a place for them to sit. They nodded and hastened to the vacant spot.

The bailiff walked to the front of the room and cleared his throat.

"All rise for the Honorable Judge Reagan."

Benches, laden with the weight of many, creaked as all stood from their seats. The judge entered. The bottom of his long robe made a swishing sound as he hurried to his position behind a massive wooden desk. He quickly sat in a brown, leather chair and glanced at his constituents.

"You may be seated."

He turned to address the bailiff. "We may begin the first case."

"State versus Penleigh. All parties approach the Judge's bench."

Izabella and Susan stood and made their way past the seated strangers, who being cordial, slid their feet to the side unblocking the path.

Both stationed themselves in front of the seated judge standing stiff and erect. His head was bowed while he flipped through pages on his clipboard.

Izabella, sensing the seriousness of the hearing, suddenly had a mood change as the fluttery feeling of butterflies in her stomach unnerved her from head to toe.

Two men wearing C.A.S.A. name badges, whom she did not recognize, quickly advanced to the front, and stood opposite her and Susan. A woman hurried to join them without a C.A.S.A. badge. They nodded at the judge and each gripped a briefcase.

Izabella's heart pounded loudly in her ears, and she took a deep breath, finally making eye contact with Judge Reagan. He acknowledged her with a brief smile.

"Mrs. Contrell, you may speak to the court."

"Your Honor, I am here to petition for full custody with the legal adoption of Vinita Irene Penleigh, a baby abandoned by her mother, Dixie Penleigh."

He addressed Susan. "And you are?"

"I am Susan Penleigh. Dixie was my daughter-in-law. She and my son, Scott, are divorced. Scott is serving in Afghanistan, and has DNA proof that he is not the father."

He examined another page on his clipboard. "Let's see, ah...here it is. A Dr. Adahy included that information in his report."

The judge paused, glancing at the woman with the C.A.S.A. officials. "You represent the Child Protective Services. I've met you before. Your office obtained these medical records from the hospital, correct?"

"Yes, Your Honor."

"It states here that the baby has recovered from surgery. I know from past experience it is difficult to place babies for adoption with any history of disabilities."

The judge turned to face Susan.

"Any comments about the adoption request?"

"I know Izabella Contrell, personally, and highly recommend her. She has the baby's best interest at heart and will provide a warm, loving, home for her."

"Ma'am, any final thoughts, or concerns?"

"Upon investigating, the C.P.S. is in agreement."

"Gentlemen?"

"We also recommend Mrs. Contrell's petition to the court."

Judge Reagan slammed his gavel down. "Motion granted. Congratulations, Mrs. Contrell."

Overwhelmed with emotion, Izabella tried to speak and couldn't at first. She sucked her breath in, and her hand flew to her mouth. "Oh, thank you," she gushed, and with adrenaline spikes, turned to face the three officials.

"Thank you, too."

Izabella blinked rapidly as tears welled up.

Susan understood the tears beginning and briefly hugged her. "I'm so proud for you. Just think, it's over."

Izabella nodded and the teary moment passed.

"Our office will contact her this evening." The woman from C.P.S. announced to the Judge.

Izabella flashed a wide, joyful smile at Judge Reagan. He appeared as delighted as Izabella, and suddenly standing, bent forward and shook her hand.

The bailiff called for the next case, and the clerk ushered the group toward the door.

"Hurry," Susan exclaimed. "I want to get outside and call Rick."

They darted to the elevator, and within minutes, exited on the ground floor.

"What is that scripture? Where two or more are gathered?"

"And...remember the one about ...shout to the heavens?"

Izabella pivoted to face Susan, and her eyes twinkled. She grabbed Susan's hand. "Ready to give Him thanks?"

"Yes Ma'am. Let's do it." Susan sang out. Not caring what others thought, they took a deep gulp of air and shouted together. "Thank You, Lord Jesus!"

People on the sidewalk stopped momentarily from hurrying into the courthouse, and smiled.

"Oh, that feels great!" Susan retrieved her cellphone, automatically pressing speaker phone, and Rick's number.

He answered immediately.

"Susan? Is it over? What happened?" Rick's anxious voice rang out across the courthouse lawn.

"Izabella's adoption is approved!"

"Praise God!" Rick yelled. "I'll phone M & M and get them to come over. This calls for a celebration. We men are cooking today," he exclaimed.

"Wonderful, I'll tell Izabella."

"Oh, that reminds me. Tell her the detective left about thirty minutes ago. He said they are finished with the upstairs. Izabella can move the rest of her belongings into the attic now. Warrants are issued for both Lee Miller *and* Clayton Vaughn. They will keep us informed about the case." He paused. "Oh, and tell her I reviewed the contract. He listed a specific date for the remainder of his belongings to be removed from the attic. Anything remaining after that date is Izabella's. The date was yesterday, so Izabella can legally claim the property in the attic."

"More good news...wow." Susan declared. "We'll be home soon."

She ended the call and glanced at Izabella. "You heard?"

"I did." Excitement mounted in her voice, and they sprinted across the street to the parking lot.

Izabella paused to glance at the sky, again. "What a glorious day."

◆

Susan and Izabella chatted non-stop on the way home, both making plans for Vinita. Susan summed up the discussion as she turned and headed the car up the driveway. "I'll baby-sit anytime you need to run errands. I'm glad you decided not to take her out in the public for a while."

"She's been through so much. I'd rather not push her immune system to the limits."

"Wise decision." They exited the vehicle and neither noticed M & M sitting on the porch.

"Congratulations!" The boys called out. Running across the porch they motioned to Izabella and Susan. "Come on, Rick is grilling out back."

Matt held the door open, and they all marched down the hall straight to the back porch. Rick met them as they left the house.

"Congratulations! Ladies, it's been a long time since I held a baby, but I know she'll smile for me." He spread his hands open in the air. "Fair warning, just saying, don't be surprised." He teased.

"Mrs. Contrell, we consider you, and the baby as part of our new family. Our house is nearly built so when you need a babysitter, let me know." Mead solemnly announced.

"That goes for me, also." Matt agreed.

"Thanks, all of you. I certainly won't have a shortage of sitters." Izabella turned to face Rick. "I'm sure you will have other houses for them to build, but none as special as the Yeager home."

"So true. It will be a new beginning for all of us." He put his arm around Susan, and winked at her. "Did you tell them about your new goal?"

"I told Izabella, but haven't had time to tell M & M." She paused and addressed the boys. "I am going to open a community outreach center to have volunteers phone the elderly, daily. They need someone to check on them, find out their needs, and simply have someone they can talk to each day."

"Oh, there is definitely a need for that service. I think it will be well received." Matt stated.

"And it's kind of you to offer to serve." Mead added.

"Guys, I thought so, too. That's why I'm asking her to quit her job..."

"What?" Susan interrupted Rick.

"...so she can give 100 % to the call center, because I know that's where her heart is..."

Susan didn't hesitate. "Yes it is. I'll phone the store today and tell them I won't be returning to work. Oh, Rick, thank you so much." She whirled about and hugged him. "It will also help the remaining employees have increased weekly hours on their schedule."

Puzzled, M & M fell silent and frowned.

She raised an eyebrow. "It's a story I'll explain later, but believe me, they need help at that store."

"Sounds interesting." Mead speculated.

"Hey, don't leave me out, when the time comes, I mean."

"I won't, Matt." Susan assured him.

"Hello? Is anyone home?" Someone called out.

Glances were exchanged by those outside as muffled voices from the house grew louder.

"Guys, will you see who it is? I have to turn the meat." Rick retrieved his tongs hanging from the side of the barbecue pit.

M & M left as Susan and Izabella hastened to the grill. Rick held up juicy T-Bone steaks, and both women took a deep breath.

"Oh, I can't wait, nothing can beat that delicious aroma. What a treat." Izabella drew her mouth together, and Susan laughed. "Girl, that's what I call anticipation."

Instantly, the screen door opened, and all three turned at the creaking sound. M & M entered the back porch followed by a woman carrying a baby, wrapped snuggly in a light blanket.

Izabella stared in shock and cried out, "Oohhh, is it...? Can it be...?" She stood as still as a statue. The woman smiled and nodded her head. She walked to Izabella and carefully placed Vinita in her arms.

"I...I don't want to startle her." Izabella peeped at the sleeping baby and was overcome with a peaceful sensation. She gently hugged baby Vinita, and lightly kissed her cheek.

"Here are her things." The woman held up a large diaper bag. "I set her carrier on the front porch."

Matt quickly took the bag.

"I have scheduled follow up visits with her pediatrician. The appointment cards are in the side zipper pocket with his address and phone number. Instructions for her daily routine are included. It's all in her bag. Formula, and enough diapers for a few days."

She patted Vinita's tiny arm. "We're going to miss you, little one." Extending the same gesture to Izabella, she turned and hesitated. "You are very fortunate. This adoption wouldn't have happened so fast without orders from the Judge. Congratulations."

"Thank you." Izabella beamed.

"I'll take you through the house and get the carrier." Mead offered, and they left.

"Oh, come look at her." Izabella invited the others. Susan, Rick, and Matt rushed to her side in awe of the baby's presence. Susan shared a warm smile with Izabella.

"Our first time to see her out of the hospital. I am overwhelmed." Rick admitted.

Their pleasure was suddenly interrupted by the jingling of a cellphone. Surprised, Susan snatched her phone from her purse.

"Hello"

"Mom?"

"Scott, how nice to hear your voice. Where are you?"

"I'm still in Afghanistan. How are things going?"

"So much has happened since I last talked to you. We have a new addition to our family. My friend, Izabella, is standing here with her new baby. Scott, she can't have children. She adopted Dixie's baby. Vinita is adorable."

Scott gasped. "I wasn't expecting that, but ...well, Mom, everything happens for a reason. Be careful, though. I hope Dixie doesn't come back, and I doubt if the birth father even knows he has a baby. But... what if the birth father learns of the baby, and wants his child?"

Before Susan could reply, Mead charged out of the house and playfully argued with Matt.

"I'm here to tell you *I* will hold her first. You don't have a clue on how to hold a baby."

"Oh, yeah? Well, let me tell you something. Vinita will feel how much *I* care for her, and won't be the least bit upset when *I* hold her."

"Hey, don't be so loud, besides, she already asked for *me* to hold her." Rick stepped sideways and dodged as M & M approached with a sly smile.

"So she *asked*, huh?" Laughter exploded as they chased Rick around the side of the house.

Scott could hear the background commotion, and addressed Susan. "Sounds like a lot is going on. I'll call you later, Mom. Love you."

"I love you, too, son." Susan heard the click when the dial tone ended and stood silent treasuring the entire day. She held onto the phone, and nervously bit her bottom lip.

"It's been an emotional day for all of us." Izabella speculated, not knowing what Scott said.

Rick and M & M returned, breathing hard. Rick sprinted to the grill. "Steaks are ready, let's go inside to eat." He grabbed a platter and removed the meat with long-handled tongs.

Matt grabbed the baby carrier. They piled into the house and made their way to Rick and Susan's apartment. Entering the kitchen, Susan's mouth fell open, and she stopped mid-stride. "Look at this… what a surprise…the table is already set."

She scanned the place settings…each held a baked potato with a small salad nearby. A tray of grilled corn-on-the-cob sat in the middle. Salad dressing, butter, and salt and pepper were within everyone's reach.

Hands were cleaned, and Mead retrieved iced tea glasses from the freezer, frosted and full of ice. Matt poured the tea and set the glasses on the table as Rick placed the sizzling platter of steaks near the corn.

Izabella gently sat Vinita in the carrier.

Susan's attention was automatically drawn to the baby. The thought crossed her mind of Scott's concern about Dixie and the birth father, and she quickly dismissed it as everyone pulled out chairs, taking their seats at the circular table.

Izabella shook her head. "How impressive, thanks. You three have certainly been busy."

"Yes, and how special for us to celebrate our first meal together." Susan sighed.

"In more ways than one." Rick slowly looked at each face at the table. "We have all overcome awful experiences. We have learned and grown from them. I thank God for this happy day and look forward to our new life together. Let's pray."

Silently, they held hands, and bowed their heads as Rick gave the blessing.

"Dear Lord, we are gathered here today to give thanks for the blessing of a precious baby in our life, and good food, good family, and good friends. Bless the meal set before us, and we pray for forgiveness where we have failed you. We praise Your name, and pray for guidance. In Jesus holy name, Amen."

A chorus of "Amen" followed as hands gripped together in loving fellowship.

The End

www.ingramcontent.com/pod-product-compliance
Lightning Source LLC
Chambersburg PA
CBHW071110250626
47159CB00002B/682